Affection for Crime

T. M. Smith

Affection For Crime
First edition, published 2017

By T. M. Smith
Cover design: Kitsap Publishing

Copyright © 2017, T. M. Smith

ISBN-13: 978-1-942661-40-5

Published by Kitsap Publishing
P.O. Box 572
Poulsbo, WA 98370
www.KitsapPublishing.com

Printed in the United States of America

TD 2017

50-10 9 8 7 6 5 4 3 2 1

Dedication &
Acknowledgements

Affection for Crime is for my parents, Bob and Irene Rosendale. In a time when young girls were not always encouraged to achieve, my parents taught me that all things are possible and that dreams may come true.

Thanks to Kelleen Pellegrino, Mike Edwards, and Penny Porter for reading the early drafts of my novel and laughing occasionally, often at the right times. Thanks to Lou Aronica, a well-respected author and editor, who edited what I thought was my final draft. Little did I know that I had much work ahead of me. The novel is better because of Lou's comments.

Chapter 1

I tried to slam the door coming out of the newsroom. It had one of those thingamabobs on it, though, that made it close slowly. I think the thingamabob was installed recently because the last time I was this mad the door slammed shut just fine.

Re-opening the door, I yelled in to anyone in the newsroom who would listen, "Who does he think he is? Whatever happened to freedom of the press?" Then, for effect, in case the staff didn't already know that I was upset, I crumpled up the section of the paper where my column should have been and threw it on the floor. No one was looking or listening, though. I think I'm beginning to lose my edge around here.

Just as I was getting off the elevator, still in an ineffectual huff, I saw Richard Steele, Rick for short, through the front glass doors. He was about to enter the building. I barely had time to dart into the women's bathroom around the corner from the elevators. Rick is a real investigative reporter, not a columnist like me. He was recently hired by the *Gazette* and is the kind of man that makes you drool all over yourself. Usually my heart beats fast when I see him, and I throw myself in his path. My heart was beating fast now, but Rick was not the cause. I, at least, had the foresight to run into the bathroom, realizing that I looked a mess having left the house in a hurry this morning. If he saw me looking like this, I knew he would never ask me out. Oh sure, I could still get him to go to bed with me because, let's face it, he's a man. Anyway, I waited until I thought he caught the elevator and, then, ran out of the bathroom and through the front doors.

My car was parked nearby in a metered spot. Oh, and lucky day, there sat my '97 Mom-hand-me-down BMW with a parking ticket on the windshield. I ripped the ticket off, thought about tearing it up, and then threw it into the glove compartment with my growing collection of parking tickets. Note to self: "Call my buddy down at the court house and take care of these pesky little tickets." I pulled my car from the curb, tires squealing, and headed to Uncle Dutch's house.

My name is Maggie Hall. Maggie is short for Magdalene, actually Marie Magdalene. I'm pretty sure Mom and Dad had one too many martinis when they named me. And, it was a cruel trick to play on a girl. Name her Marie Magdalene and send her to a Catholic elementary school. She's bound to have childhood scars. And, I do

I'm a columnist for the *Las Vegas Gazette,* the second most popular local morning newspaper, the first being the *Las Vegas Review-Journal.* My column *Crime After Crime* appears three times weekly--Sunday, Tuesday, and Friday. I report on crime in Las Vegas, everything from charging too much for drinks, and believe me, that's become a crime wave, to bribing politicians. Which, by the way, was my latest column. The FBI is investigating Georgy Garbarino, owner of two local strip joints and a female impersonator club, for bribing county commissioners.

How did I get such a choice job at the *Gazette*? Simple! I slept my way to the top. Wait a minute. I'm not on top; I'm just a columnist. I must have gotten my job another way. That's right, I got my job the next best way. The managing editor-owner is my uncle—Dutch Hall.

I dropped out of high school near the end of my senior year when I had Kitty. After Kitty was born, Mom babysat her while I finished high school at an alternative school. During the next decade, I worked a variety of odd jobs—some were odder than others. I even did a stint as a showgirl. Uncle Gus got me that job. It only lasted one night, though. It seems that tripping over the stage lights is not part of the routine for a Las Vegas showgirl. It wasn't my fault, though. Those feathers streaming down the headdresses are heavier than they look. I was told to come back if they ever decided to do a comedy review. I didn't mind losing that job because I was cold with no top on. When I was 30, I decided to go to college. I had worked enough odd jobs. Did I mention 7-Eleven clerk? That's when Kitty and I moved in with Mom, again. I went to UNLV and majored in English and political science. With those majors it was a good thing I had an uncle in the newspaper business.

——

Driving faster than I should have been, I barely made the turn into

Uncle Dutch's driveway where I slammed on my brakes inches away from his garage door. Uncle Dutch is my dad's brother, one of many. Dad's side of the family originally came from Holland. The family name was something like *Halstjzer,* but like many foreign-sounding names it was changed to *Hall.* Uncle Dutch, though, is not called "Dutch" because our family is from Holland. You've heard of "Dutch treat?" That's Uncle Dutch, cheap to the bone.

I didn't see his car but suspected he might be hiding from me. I can be pretty scary. Even when I'm better dressed. I got out of my car, charged up to the front door, and rang the doorbell. Aunt Ann, Uncle Dutch's wife, answered the door.

"Where is he?" I screamed, gently pushing past her. "Where is the sorry, sneaking, snake-in-the-grass, sanctimonious son-of-a-bitch?" Okay, I didn't say 'son-of-a-bitch' because I wanted to keep my job, but Aunt Ann was smart. She knew what I meant. She could read the snarl in my expression, see the glare in my eyes, and taste the spit coming out of my mouth. I was mad.

Ann and Dutch have been married for, at least, 25 years. No one can understand why. She is petite, pretty, reserved, well educated, and composed at all times. Even now. Dutch is big, loud, overbearing, ugly, and illiterate, even for an editor. Mind you, I didn't let my current state of mind color my opinion of him.

"He's in his study," Aunt Ann said. "I think he's been expecting you because he's been cleaning his Glock all morning." She was grinning and looking pretty excited to see some action; apparently, life with Uncle Dutch is normally quite boring.

"He doesn't own a Glock or any other gun," I shouted over my shoulder, while heading for the study on the first floor. "He's pro-gun control."

I opened the door cautiously and stepped to the side—just in case my aunt was right. You never know. Despite his long-held pro-gun control stance, Uncle Dutch might have gone out and bought a gun after he deleted my column.

But no, there he sat. Hands empty and above the desk.

"Maggie, how nice to see you." Uncle Dutch rose and pushed his chair back. He smiled as if he meant it. "I see you were in a hurry. I like the new hairstyle."

Okay, I had rushed out of the house in torn, baggy shorts, a cut-off shirt, and worn tennis shoes. My hair was uncombed—which means it was down, long, and curls-turning-to-snarls messy. My face was unwashed and my teeth unbrushed. I'm surprised Aunt Ann didn't say anything. She usually has such good taste. I suppose she didn't want to unnecessarily upset me.

"You have a lot of explaining to do. How dare you omit my column without consulting me." It's hard to be indignant when you look so bad, but I gave it my best shot. I needed a newspaper in my hand to shake at Uncle Dutch, but I had rashly thrown it away in the office earlier.

Uncle Dutch began to explain his action, a gesture that goes against his personality. "I called you several times. You didn't answer the phone at home; so, I left a message. Then, I called your cell phone. You didn't answer there either; so, I left another message. I would have sent a carrier pigeon, but I didn't want you to shoot the messenger."

"Oh! I didn't check my messages at home, and I have a little cell phone problem right now," I explained with a grimace and dismissive wave of my left hand.

"What's wrong with your cell phone this time? Did you run over it with your car again?"

"No!" I gave him my insulted sneer. "The phone might have gotten wet."

"What do you mean 'might have'?" Uncle Dutch asked. He apparently thought he had a right to know since he paid for the phones used by the *Gazette* staff. And, it's not as if this was the first cell phone I ruined.

"Okay, not 'might have.' It went through the washing machine in my jeans, and it's waterlogged. It doesn't even gurgle."

"How do you do it, Maggie? I've had the same phone for years."

"I don't know. It's an art. And don't try to change the subject. We're talking about my column."

"Get a new cell phone. Again." He shook his head and returned to his justification for omitting my column. "Anyway, legal said the column couldn't run as it was. As editor—which you recall I still am--I decided it was in the best interest of the paper not to run the column."

He paused to look at me closely and give me a superior-than-thou grin for effect. "Answer your home phone next time or try to keep a cell phone operable. Then, you'll know what's going on, honey. You'll be able to yell at me before I take your column out of the paper instead of afterwards." By this time, he had slunk back into his desk chair. He looked tired. I wondered if he was getting enough rest.

Choosing the hard, upright chair near his desk rather than the over-stuffed comfortable one, I sat down. I didn't want to appear relaxed. "Why did legal think it shouldn't run?"

"You need a corroborating source," replied Uncle Dutch. "Writing 'a source close to the investigation,' who we both know is Rita Ortiz, your friend, isn't enough. You know that, honey. What were you thinking?"

At least, Uncle Dutch was giving me credit for thinking, and he was still calling me "honey."

He was right about the story coming from Rita. Yesterday afternoon I met my longtime girlfriend at the Drop Bar in Green Valley Ranch Resort for a drink. The bar décor there is modern with a lot of purple and black neon. The waitresses wear close to nothing, which means Rita and I can have a conversation without guys hitting on us. They're too busy leering at the waitresses. In between talking about dates we didn't have, she mentioned that something big was going on at La Tigra. Rita is a stripper at La Tigra and overhears tidbits that I use in my column.

She and I have been friends since elementary school. On my first day at St. Anne's Rita was assigned to me as the official student tour guide. I remember that she was wearing a short red frilly skirt and shiny black shoes when she first bounced into the headmistress' office to meet me. She gave me a girlish grin and a big hug. In addition to showing me the lunch room, the classrooms, and the playground, Rita made sure I knew that Sister Agnes, the headmistress, could be a push-over if she liked you and that my teacher Sister Anne preferred choc-olates over apples. This valuable information gave me an advantage at St. Anne's, and I always took advantage of a good advantage.

Later, at Las Vegas High School, we shared a locker and heartbreak over one boy or another. Oh, and once we shared Tom Nichols, captain of the basketball team. That tested our friendship; so, we both dumped Tom in favor of each other. Later, Amy Hinds and Lois Avernil, other friends, deserted me when they found out I was pregnant, but Rita stuck by me. Instead of shopping for nose rings and black Goth clothes, as was the fashion, Rita went with me to shop for maternity clothes.

Anyway, she heard Georgy Garbarino, La Tigra owner, talking on the phone to his lawyer. Georgy went to Las Vegas High School with Rita and me. For open house night our junior year, Rita and I brought our parents; Georgy brought his lawyer. What's that tell you? He never knew when he might need one. Georgy was always cutting school and peeking into the girls' locker room.

Petey Goldberg is Georgy's lawyer. Petey went to Las Vegas High also but before the three of us. He graduated from some law school in California that nobody ever heard of, but Georgy likes him. Personally, I think he's sly, sleazy, and crooked. In short, the perfect lawyer. Anyway, Rita heard Georgy talking to Petey about being investigated by the FBI for bribing certain county commissioners: namely, Bruce Pritchard, Joann Kirkoff, Ernest Ortega, and Raymond Angelo. Their end of the deal was to get the zoning laws changed to help Georgy. Pritchard and Angelo lost their seats in the last election, though, but not before the zoning was changed.

I thought it was common knowledge that Ray Angelo worked for Georgy. Ray and Georgy went way back. Ray attended Las Vegas High School with us, too. We were all Wildcats. In fact, Ray was Georgy's Peeping Tom partner. They were also busted all the time for smoking in the guys' bathroom.

While I wasn't surprised to hear about Ray taking bribes, I was surprised when he was elected to public office. The other commissioners' dirty dealings were news to me, however.

I was eager to break this story; so, I used what Rita gave me to write my column for Sunday's paper. Imagine my surprise when it wasn't there. Instead of finding my column in all its pithy glory, all I found in today's paper was a notice under my column logo stating that I was on vacation. If I was on vacation, I think I'd know about it. I also think I'd be on the beach in Hawaii wearing a skimpy bathing suit with sand stuck to my tanning oil, getting too much sun, and holding a Mai Tai.

My omitted column led me to my uncle, the editor, and to this moment of thoughtful reflection.

I offered Uncle Dutch my explanation for hurrying to print with the story of political bribery. "I was thinking I had to make the deadline and that it was a great story. Besides, Rita's a very credible source. She practically had her ear on the door while Georgy was talking," I explained.

With that, Uncle Dutch rose from his chair and pointed toward the door. "Get out of here. Let me enjoy my Sunday without having to explain myself to your mother and Ann. Go find another source. Talk to people, involved people. Then, we'll run the column. It's a great story. Take Steele with you. If you get a second source, he can write the front-page story. Get the information before anyone else gets it. And, get that new phone today."

Oh! I hate it when he's right. And when he talks in short, clipped sentences. I backed out of the room, still glaring at him. I didn't want him to think I was a pushover. After all, I might need to intimidate him at a later date.

Aunt Ann was waiting eagerly in the hallway. I think she had been pacing outside the study door. "You look okay. Is my husband still alive or did you make me a rich widow?"

"He's alive and still sitting in there, pretending to be a good editor. He's right this time, but don't tell him I said so, Aunt Ann." I thought she looked a little disappointed that no one was shot.

"Maggie, dear, I never tell him he's right. That would upset the balance of power around here. By the way, I think you need to do something about the ensemble, hair, and makeup."

There it was. She just restored my faith in her taste. "I was in a hurry. Someone pissed me off."

"Anyone I know?" She smiled, winked, and hugged me, saying, "Goodbye and tell your mom 'hello' for me."

"Sure thing. Bye, Aunt Ann."

I headed back home to change the way I looked. As I was driving, I made a mental list of what I had to do today. I needed to go to Verizon for a new phone and to the office to reread my notes, find Steele, and call Rita.

Chapter 2

I pulled through the guard gate at Anthem Country Club in the Green Valley area of Henderson, waving to the armed security guards. I try to stay friendly with them. That way, they won't shoot me if I'm driving too fast through the country club or if I wear denim into the restaurant. They take the rules here very seriously.

I'm 39 years old and my daughter, Caitlyn, is 21, soon to be 22. She begins teaching second grade this next school year. You're probably saying, "Wow! How can she have a daughter that old?" Well, you are right, but I didn't know anything at age 16 when I met the biggest loser of my life. Caitlyn's dad was captain of the football team, had an active social life, and was a real sweet talker. I was gullible, shy, and stupid. He wooed me at age 16, I got pregnant, he disappeared, I had Kitty at 17, and he's still out of the picture. By the way, she's the best thing that's happened to me. We call her Kitty because when she began to talk she could not pronounce *Caitlyn*. She said *Kitten*; so, Caitlyn became Kitty.

Kitty and I live with Mom. We moved back in when I started college (like I said, that was when I was 30), and I haven't moved out yet—just lazy I guess. We're trying to be on our own, but that would mean that one of us would have to search for a place to live. Oh, and did I mention that Mom is a great cook? Did I mention she has money? She and Dad were in the real estate business in Vegas when everyone began moving here. That was about one million people ago and years before the housing bust. He died 10 years back, and she ran the business for years until she retired not long ago. She still works part time for her friend Suzie's company. Mom says the real estate business is a great way to meet men who have money to spend. She lives in a 10,000-square-foot custom home in Anthem Country Club with a great view of the city. So, if Kitty and I moved out, one of us would have to learn to cook, and we'd both have to appreciate a small apartment with no view. That's probably not going to happen any time soon.

Several months ago Kitty broke up with the love of her young life, better known to me as Rod the Bum. "Rod," that's Rodney Witcowski, ex-boyfriend and fellow student teacher, left to go to graduate school somewhere on the east coast. He called Kitty on the phone to tell her he was leaving. Can you imagine? Mom even used the phrase, "No balls." And, that's quite harsh coming from her mouth.

Anyway, Rod called Kitty after he had already arranged everything for the move. He was packed, had given his notice at the apartment, and had taken back his application with the school district. Apparently, he had been planning the move for a long time. And, he made it clear that he didn't want Kitty to come along.

I mention all this because I am trying to be very sensitive of Kitty's feelings while she is going through her first rejection. And this certainly wouldn't be the right time to make a move and uproot her. So, we'll continue to live with Mom for the time being. What a thoughtful mother I am.

I parked in the driveway and sneaked inside, not wanting to answer questions about today's missing column. After brushing my teeth, washing my face, and showering, I changed into a pair of jeans, a white shirt, my favorite Ralph Lauren blazer, and Manolo Blahnik heels. Then, I combed my hair and artfully applied makeup. Okay, I put on blush and mascara. Quietly, I crept back down the stairs and out to my car unseen and unquestioned.

₧⁖

Better dressed and on my way back to the *Gazette,* I popped into the new Verizon store down the hill from Anthem. I didn't recognize the kid at the counter. He looked about 20 or 21, had on a wrinkled shirt with a small unrecognizable stain on the front, wore glasses, and needed acne medicine and a referral to a good barber.

"Hi, I'm Maggie Hall and I work for the *Las Vegas Gazette.* I need to get a new cell phone on their account." I gave him my best business-like smile and showed him my credentials.

"Sure," he said. He took a few minutes to call up the *Gazette* account on his computer. His eyes lit up. I imagine he was thinking that I would want a phone with the works since it was on the company.

"I have some great Smartphones. I can set you up with the latest iPhone. Retina HD display with wide color and 3D Touch, A-10 Fusion chip, 256 gigabytes…"

"Don't bother to go all high techy on me. You're wasting my time and yours. What's the bottom line cost?"

"I can get you into one for just under a grand."

"Yikes. I don't want to buy stock in the company. Just a plain phone will do. I read that an exploding cell phone killed a South Korean man. I don't want a complicated phone that is likely to explode. And, if it could explode, believe me, mine would."

"The newer phone will probably sync with your car. Hands-free is good for your job."

"Ha! Then, I'll be free to put on my mascara. Look, guy, my car's old. Nothing will sync. Just get me a cheaper phone. I'm not here to break the newspaper. Haven't you heard? We're a dying breed as it is."

"I can get you an older model iPhone, but I think you'd like the newer one with more gigs better. You might be out on assignment and need to submit a story while you're at the scene. This phone has a lot more capacity, and I can guarantee that not one of our phones has exploded."

"Terrific, I'm sure, but I'm not that kind of reporter. I can do without phoning a story in at the scene."

"But the new phone is cool."

"I don't need "cool." I need indestructible. Do you have one of those?"

He was clearly disappointed but he went to the backroom and brought out an older iPhone.

"Is it durable?" I asked.

"It is if you get that case over there." He pointed to a gadget on the wall.

"Great. I'll take one of those, too. Can you transfer all my phone numbers over?"

"Sure, do you have your old cell phone to turn in?"

"Yes, I do." I took it out of my purse and handed it to him.

He took the new phone and my ruined phone into the back of the store where he was going to perform technical magic. He returned shortly.

"I can't transfer your numbers," he explained. "This phone doesn't work." He then gave me the kind of smirk reserved for those cell phone users who are technologically challenged.

"You can't transfer numbers if the phone doesn't work?" I asked.

"Duh!"

"That is so passé," I said.

"What's passé?"

"Duh!"

"Huh?"

"Never mind." I sighed. "My phone got wet."

"You dropped it in the water?"

"No." I was clearly tired of his attitude. "It was dirty so I washed it in the dishwasher to get it clean."

"Really?"

"No! Not really. It was an accident! Could I just have my phone without the third degree?"

"You don't have to get snippy. I was just making conversation. Are all reporters so cranky?"

"No, they aren't. And, neither am I. It's been a bad day. Sorry, but I would like my phone today." The kid might have a technological IQ of 140, but his social IQ was closer to 85.

"I'm getting it. I'm getting it. Jeez. But, I won't be able to get the old numbers transferred." With that he returned to the magic back room.

In about fifteen minutes and after signing a stack of papers, I had my new cell phone and all the accessories. When I said, "Goodbye," I gave him my pleasant customer smile.

"Goodbye," he replied. "It was so nice helping you. Please come back with any problem."

I turned to look at him and frowned since I was pretty sure he was being sarcastic.

Chapter 3

Proudly carrying my new cell phone, I walked through the door of the *Gazette* a little more calmly than I had the last time. As I walked in, the office was noisy. Suddenly it became quiet. I think the reporters were waiting for me to entertain them again.

Finally, I heard, "Nice to see you back from vacation, Hall. You look a little tanner."

"Bite me, Monroe!" I snarled.

"I dream of it every night," he said.

Eek! What a thought! Monroe and me together, even in a dream. I think everyone in the newsroom shuddered at the thought. Monroe was about 50, smelled of old smoke, and had a beer belly that protruded over his sagging pants. Every shirt he owned seemed to have a button missing so that his hairy stomach peeked out. His hair hadn't been cut or washed in a long time. Nobody knows his first name. He's just Monroe.

I sauntered over to Rick at his desk. Unlike mine, his desk was uncluttered and clean. No dirty coffee cups or food wrappers were in sight. He had his feet up on his desk and was leaning back in his chair. His hands were locked behind his head, and a great smile was on his face. I could see his muscles rippling even though they were hidden behind a striped shirt with rolled up sleeves. Rippling requires a lot of working out, and I was impressed. Rick's face is rugged, and his eyes are dreamy. His hair is sandy-colored with lighter streaks of blond in it. I hope he doesn't get his hair done at a salon. I could never have a meaningful relationship with a guy who gets his hair frosted. If he does, I'll just have to settle for casual sex.

With all the cool I could muster, I moved a neat stack of papers aside and sat on the edge of his desk, crossing my legs. Drats! I have on pants, I thought. This pose would look better if I was wearing a short skirt.

"Hi, I talked to Dutch today. He said to involve you in this column I'm working on. If you have the time, I can call my friend Rita who works at La Tigra, and we could go see her about the bribery scandal I'm looking into. If this works out, Dutch wants you to do the hard news story on page one."

Rick took his feet off the desk and sat upright. He looked interested. I wasn't sure if he was interested in the story or in me. I'm thinking it was the story.

"Sure, what's going on?" he asked. That clinched it; it was the story.

"The gist is Georgy Garbarino, who owns the strip club where Rita dances, has been bribing some county commissioners, and the FBI is on to him. I'll fill you in on the way to see Rita. First, let me call her to find out when and where she can meet us."

"I'll be waiting." He smiled, sat down, leaned back, and crossed his arms behind his head again.

I stared breathlessly for a moment, gave him a squirrelly smile, and turned to walk to my desk.

The newsroom is large and subdivided by various portable walls. These walls create cubicles, and each cubicle has a desk, chair, file cabinet, computer, printer, and assorted supplies and equipment. About ten to fifteen reporters are in the newsroom at any given time. Other floors and offices in the building house different departments necessary to operate the *Gazette*.

I went to my cubicle, which is on the other side of the room. Given the nature of my column, I am more comfortable with a desk where my back is against a wall far from the entrance. I didn't want any surprises. Covering crime puts me in contact with some unsavory characters.

For instance, I once did a story on *The Ice Pick Don Gets Iced*; it was about Las Vegas mobster Donnie Delvecchio's body being found in Red Rock Canyon. Some people didn't like my looking into "who done it." It was a good thing I had gone to school with some "connected" guys, if you know what I mean. It just shows that I was right to help them with their homework in school. Las Vegas is really a small town, and those of us who have been around for a long time are close-knit; we have a certain camaraderie that many people can't understand. And, you never know when you might need a friend to make sure nobody puts a hit out on you.

I have a couple of things going for me as a crime columnist, other than being able to construct a perfectly acceptable sentence at the eighth-grade level. First, I was born and raised in Las Vegas. That means I run into people I know all the time. Second, people talk freely to me. They always have. In high school I was the unofficial counselor, the go-to-girl for jilted hearts. Put the two together and it means I find many friends who are willing to talk to me about what's going on behind the scenes in Las Vegas. With my listening skills, if I hadn't become a journalist, I would have been a hooker; and, since I don't like to work at night, journalism seemed the better choice.

I phoned Rita and arranged to meet her for coffee at Panera's in The District this evening. The District at Green Valley is an urban, mixed-use community, one of many springing up in Las Vegas. Here shops, restaurants, and condos reside in the same area. It's next to Green Valley Ranch Resort and is a favorite meeting place for Rita and me. The District is laid out like a small village where people can walk along the street. In the evenings, bands, wandering minstrels, and other entertainers showcase their talents; and the restaurants and walkways are pretty crowded.

We left the *Gazette* a half hour before our meeting with Rita. Rick and I debated his car or mine. We decided on his. It's a new Mercedes sports convertible. I wondered if he makes more money than I do. Note to self: "Ask Uncle Dutch if I'm being paid enough."

₧₧

We arrived and found Rita sitting at a table outside even though it was a little warm. It could be worse this late in June, though. When I saw Rita, it occurred to me that it probably wasn't a good idea to bring Rick to meet her. Rita is a knockout. She is 5 feet 9 inches tall and weighs about 130 pounds, most of it in her boobs. She has long dark hair and deep, brown eyes. Her "Hello" is more flirtatious than my "Hey, do you want to go to bed." She was wearing a knee-length, red-flowered Mexican cantina dancing skirt by Oscar de la Renta and a tight red t-shirt. Big red earrings dangled from her ear lobes, and a matching bracelet made soft, tinkling noises. She made bohemian look chic. I looked at Rick, he looked at her, and nobody looked at me.

"Rita this is Rick; Rick, Rita. What are you drinking?" I asked her.

"Just an iced tea."

"What do you want?" asked Rick turning to me but still mesmerized by Rita. "I'll get it."

"I'll have a blended café mocha." If I can't have the man, at least, I can have the calories.

As I sat down and took off my blazer, Rick went to get the drinks.

By the time Rick returned, I had told Rita that Dutch wasn't about to let me print my column without more information and a backup source. I asked her to repeat what she had told me for Rick.

Rita turned to Rick, crossed her legs seductively, gave him a suggestive smile, leaned forward on an elbow, and rested her chin in her hand. Her eyes were on Rick. When her body language was just right, she proceeded to tell her story. "I was in the hallway outside Georgy's office at the club. Georgy, that's George Garbarino, owner of La Tigra where I work. I was about to go in when I heard him on the phone. He sounded pretty serious."

She paused and turned to me. "I knew he was talking to Petey because he called him by name." Turning back to Rick, she explained, "Petey Goldberg is his lawyer. He's this tubby, balding, little guy with a perpetual grin. You know, like the Cheshire Cat's in *Alice and Wonderland*." Rita looked at me as if for confirmation.

When I nodded, she began again. "He's always trying to pat my ass, but I'm too fast for him. Georgy tells him he should watch it unless he wants to lose a hand. I know self-defense. I'm taking a class called Kickass at the gym. I figured in my business it's a good skill to know."

By the way, that's why Rita and I are friends. She can't tell a story without digressing either. Rita also talks fast; so, I noticed that Rick was trying to hang onto every word during all the twists and turns.

After pausing momentarily to remember where she was, Rita continued, "Anyway, he's asking Petey if he really thinks cooperating with the FBI is the best thing to do." She paused to take a breath. "Oh, I also heard him say that the FBI has tapes of Bruce Pritchard, Joann Kirkoff, and Ernest Ortega on the phone with Ray Angelo. Ray's phone must be tapped. Apparently, they were blabbing about bribes in exchange for a favorable vote on zoning. You probably know that Pritchard, Kirkoff, and Ortega are county commissioners. At least, Pritchard was before he lost the last election. Kirkoff and Ortega are still on the commission. I don't know how we keep electing these people to office. Do you? You'd think we'd learn. I took this political science course once…"

Rita looked at me and I was shaking my head. She got the message. "Anyway, I hear Georgy say the FBI knows that Angelo was his go-between all these years. Angelo was a county commissioner, too; but he also lost his seat in the last election. That's all I know. Jaime Rodriquez, La Tigra's assistant manager, came down the hall and I had to stop eavesdropping."

Rita looked at me and smiled. "Georgy's gotten himself into a mess this time. He never was very smart. Remember that time in world history when Mr. McCormick asked who knew about Karl Marx, and Georgy raised his hand and said Karl was the Marx Brother who beeped a horn all the time because he couldn't talk? Mr. McCormick was at a rare loss for words."

I know Rick was a little surprised that Rita could string a coherent sentence together in between her digressions, but Rita is smart. She has a biology degree from UNLV. After college she did some outdoor environmental work. Then, she just got too hot and too dirty after countless years of chasing down endangered tortoises in the desert outside Vegas; so, she took up stripping full time. Also, stripping is more lucrative than nosing around desert tortoise habitats. Rita is very particular about where she works and whom she works for, though. She strips at Georgy's club because she says he has good security, the place is clean, and Georgy can be trusted as long as you know his limitations.

I asked Rita, "What do you think about our talking to Georgy? If he's cooperating with the FBI, he might talk to us. We need another source."

"Like I said, Georgy's not too smart. Go by the club tonight. He's there every night. He'll probably tell all. I have to go," said Rita, glancing at her watch. "Bye, Rick. Nice to meet you." She shook Rick's hand and held it a long time while gazing into his eyes. When she looked at me and saw my expression, she said, "Maggie, walk me to my car."

"Okay." Obviously she saw I wasn't happy with her and wanted to talk to me in private. "What's up?" I asked when we were away from the table.

Rita gets right to the point. "Rick's a hunk. Do you have dibs on him? Because if you don't, I think I might have to marry him."

"Keep your 'I do's' to yourself," I said. "I haven't decided yet whether I want to seduce him, but I'll get back to you as soon as I know." I felt a little guilty keeping Rick to myself, given that Rita is my best friend.

"Fair enough," she said. See? This is why Rita's a great friend.

"Okay, see ya." I waved. "I'll call."

When I got back to the table, I examined Rick. Boy, he looked good. I am having a boyfriend blight and haven't had sex for a long time. I was struggling to keep my mind on work. "So, what do you think?" I asked, pushing sex from my mind.

"I think we should go see Garbarino tonight. How about dinner first? The Presidio or Lucille's?"

Dinner? Oh, was this an opportunity for romance? I asked without thinking, "Are you inviting me on a date?"

"No," he said. "I'm asking if you want dinner before we go to interview a source. I'm hungry." For a moment, I thought he looked at me as if I had a parrot on my head. But, I swiped my hand over my head to check. No--no parrot there. Then, Rick just grinned.

I should have been embarrassed, but this sort of thing happens to me way too often to put a damper on my mood. "The Presidio," I responded. It's quieter and more romantic. It never hurts to be prepared, in case there is an opportunity.

Chapter 4

The Presidio is a leather and chrome trendy restaurant in The District. A black granite bar is in the middle of the room with tables on each side of the restaurant. Red brick lines the walls and accent columns in the restaurant. One of the decorative highlights of the Presidio is the floating glass panel display over the bar. The clear panels are dotted with red splotches. I can never decide if the splotches look like rose petals or blood. I used to make a trip to the women's room when the Presidio was Kennedy's because while washing your hands at the sink you could look out into the dining area through a large fish tank. Of course, the diners could see into the women's lounge also; so, you had to be careful that you didn't lift your skirt to adjust your slip or do any unsightly grooming while at the lavatory. The Presidio changed all that though; now you can't see out or in. Takes all the fun out of using the ladies' room.

I wanted the fondue as an appetizer, but we decided it might be a little heavy with work ahead of us. For the entree, I couldn't decide between the sea bass and the surf and turf. The waiter suggested the surf and turf. Rick ordered the ribeye. Funny, I figured him for a fish kind of guy. My drink of choice was a glass of pinot blanc, and Rick ordered a California merlot.

The *Gazette* is fortunate to have Rick as a reporter. He showed up several months ago asking Uncle Dutch for a job. He had been a foreign correspondent with the Associated Press for years. He covered Bosnia and the Gulf War. According to Uncle Dutch, Rick went to Iraq at the beginning of the war for the 'Hearts and Minds' of the Iraqi people but soon tired of the guts and glory. He said it was one war too many. Uncle Dutch thinks something happened that Rick's not talking about. Rick published two books on wars he covered as a correspondent. They were both commercially successful. Uncle Dutch told me that Rick is occasionally called to Washington as an adviser on the Middle East. I don't think he has to work, and the job with the *Gazette* is the next best thing to retirement after what he's seen.

During dinner I gave Rick my best Scarlett O'Hara smile and batted my eye lashes in between bites. If only I had a fan and could talk Southern. I emphasized points in my frivolous conversation by reaching over to touch him on his arm. I laughed even when what he said wasn't all that funny. In short, I thought I was a great coquette.

Finally, Rick leaned in towards me. I leaned in towards him. He was close enough for me to smell his aftershave. It was a manly scent with a dash of lime. As I inhaled, I knew our relationship would be more than colleagues. Then, dashing my hopes, he said, "We aren't going to go out so stop flirting with me."

"Who's flirting with you and who says I want to go out with you?" I responded peevishly. Reluctantly, I had to reassess where our relationship was headed.

"Oh, you want to go out." He smiled his irritating smile. "But we're not going to."

"Not that I would go out with you even if you asked, but why aren't we?"

"For many reasons. For one thing, your uncle owns the newspaper. For another, I think you're probably a lot of trouble. And, finally, we work together. It's never a good idea to mix business and pleasure."

"What? Do you think you'd break my heart?"

"Hell, no. I think you'd break mine. Then, I'd have to leave, and I kind of like it here. I like to keep my life simple, and you're not simple. You're easy --but not simple."

"You're...you're...What's the word?"

"Insufferable?" he provided.

"That's it! You're insufferable. And what do you mean 'I'm not simple'?"

"Well... to put it into terms that we who deal with words can appreciate...in this world, people read magazines or books. When you buy a magazine you browse through it, you read all of an article or only a little, you look at the pictures, and you move on. When you're through, you probably throw it away. If you buy a book, you have to be loyal, loyal to the written word. You make a commitment to finish the book, and you have to pay it some serious attention. You probably don't throw it away after you read it, especially if it's a good one. You're a book, Maggie, a good one. You expect loyalty, commitment, and serious attention."

"What's wrong with that?" I asked, still more peeved.

"Nothing, but I'm not that man. I'm a magazine kind of guy right now."

"You're being insufferable again."

"This requires a great deal of strength and control on my part. I hope you appreciate the sacrifice I'm making. Come on, let's head to La Tigra."

"Just because you want to make a sacrifice, doesn't mean I have to. I can be simple and easy both. I can do magazines and books."

"No, you can't. Come on. Let's go."

We paid our separate checks and headed for Rick's car. He walked to the passenger side door and opened it for me. Then, he leaned in and whispered, "Maybe we'll do this again?"

"I thought you said we could never go out?"

"I did. I just might end up being weak willed, though."

"Oh sure," I said casually, closing the door. Is 39 too young for a hot flash?

℅℆

During the ride to La Tigra, Rick asked how long I had worked on the paper. "I started in my early 30's while still in college. Then, after college I began to write my column. So, about seven years." Oops, I had just about given away my age.

Rick's a good investigative reporter because he read my expression. "That long." He was using his charming smile. He added, "You have a good reputation around the newsroom. Contrary to your intentionally trying to make other people underestimate you, no one at the *Gazette* takes your skills for granted."

I smiled at the unsolicited compliment. We had the top down on the car, my hair was blowing wildly, and a classical number was playing on the radio, a waltz by one of the Strauss's, I think. Too bad that we were on the way to a strip club for a story and that I'm always professional.

Before arriving, we made our plans for tomorrow. I would do research for my column and then write it up for Tuesday's paper. I needed background on the commissioners involved and the zoning laws. Rick said he wanted to look into some other angles. If he found anything helpful for me, he would let me know. We decided that his story and my column would come out on the same day, though. At least, we agreed on that.

It was about 8:15 when we got to La Tigra, and the lot was nearly full. We parked and went inside. Looking around, I decided La Tigra was a pretty classy place for a strip joint, not that I had any point of reference. But I was expecting the smell of smoke and stale booze surrounding a lot of sleazy men who were sitting around doing obscene things with their hands. I could smell the smoke, but the main room was large, though dark, with tables covered with cloths, candles, and flowers. Some men were in suits, and some were with women. I couldn't see anyone using his hands inappropriately. A woman was dancing on stage in front, but I was too chicken to look. I didn't recognize the song, but it sounded as if a woman could peel her clothes off slowly and provocatively while still keeping time to the beat.

I was glad Rita didn't work today. I didn't want anything to interfere with our friendship; watching my best friend strip down to her pasties and a G-string in front of a bunch of people would definitely stand between us—the elephant in the room, if you will. Besides, I didn't want to think she might be the reason Rick was starting to pant.

I gave Rick the wait-a-minute finger and walked over to the bartender. When I got his attention, I said, "Hi. I'm Maggie Hall, an old school buddy of Georgy's. Where is he tonight? I'd like to talk to him."

"Georgy, who?"

I could tell he was going to be tough; so, I leaned far over the bar, gave him my sexy smile, and let him look down the front of my shirt. The bartender picked up the phone, made a call, and then pointed us toward a back door.

Rick looked at me and grinned knowingly. "Good job," he said. "Those tricks don't have the same effect when I do them."

I don't know. I wouldn't mind looking down his shirt.

On our way to the back I heard a familiar voice squeal, "Baby Doll."

I turned and saw Gary, a friend of Rita and mine.

He ran up to me throwing his arms around me and giving me two of those Hollywood air kisses. Gary is a female impersonator at Queens, Georgy's specialty club.

"Gary, you look stunning tonight," I said, eying his clothes. He was dressed in a gold lame Thirties-style evening gown. He had no hips and great fake boobs. The dress had slim straps, a fitted bodice, and a slit up to his thigh. He was wearing gold platform shoes, which made him tower over me. Making him look even taller was his red hair, which was piled on top of his head in some kind of a French twist. All in all, as I looked at him, I realized that he was a much better looking woman than I was. But, then again, he was a woman by profession. With me, it was an accident.

I was always happy to see Gary. Sometimes he went out with Rita and me and provided the comic relief for the evening. He had something viciously funny to say about everyone.

"What are you doing here?" I asked.

"I'm just here with some of the guys from the hood," he said, pointing to a table in the middle of the room and waving. Four glamorous girl-guys waved back. One looked remarkably like Marilyn Monroe. As if he were sharing a confidence, Gary said in a low voice, "Those guys really are queens. Me, I feel ridiculous out in public in this getup. But, it's a great dress; so, what the hell. And, I don't want them to feel out-of-place. Anyway, we're here to watch how the 'real' ladies do their stuff. You know getting pointers from the pros."

"Like you need pointers. Oh, Gary, I'd like you to meet Rick. Rick is a reporter at the *Gazette*." I could tell Rick was a little confused. He probably thought Gary was a knockout until I called him by name. "Rick, Gary works at Queens as a female impersonator."

"Oh, he is cute," Gary said to me. "Hi," he teased, turning to Rick and putting one hand on his hip and the other in the air.

Rick was clearly embarrassed to be admired but started to shake Gary's hand. Instead, Gary just grabbed him and hugged him. Rick stood in shock, not quite knowing how to react. Gary loved it, though. He liked what he called "taking the piss out of people."

"Oh, I'm just funnin' you, Rick. You're not my type anyway," Gary said.

"What's wrong with him?" I was a little indignant. After all, I thought Rick was drop dead gorgeous. This could be an insult to my taste in men.

"Too hunky. I like my guys slimmer and softer."

"Really? You don't like his muscles?" I asked, touching Rick's arm. "How about his firm shoulders and abs." I was caressing parts of Rick's anatomy since it seemed appropriate to point out what I was specifically talking about.

"Nope, not interested."

"But other than that, you think he's handsome?" I continued.

"Oh, sure, if you like your men rugged."

Hum, I thought I probably did.

"If you two could stop sizing me up like a piece of meat, I would appreciate it. This is de-humanizing." Rick was clearly upset by our conversation.

We apologized.

"We're working, Gary. Rick and I came to see Georgy,"

"Ooh! Everyone around here seems a bit uptight. What's going on?" he asked.

"I can't say right now," I responded.

"Well, I've tried to stay away from whatever it is. Ta ta. So long, Rick. Maybe we'll meet again."

Rick, having regained his manly composure, said, "Yeah, I look forward to it."

We knocked on the door the bartender had directed us to, and Georgy opened it. The door opened onto a hallway where I could see several doors, probably leading to different offices. Georgy led us into one of the offices.

"Long time no see, Maggy." Georgy always had a way with words. He had changed a lot since high school. You could tell he had money by the way he dressed. Black collarless silk shirt, khaki pants, and black loafers. He had a bit of a paunch, though; had lost a significant amount of his dirty blond hair; and his skin was kind of sallow. Probably from too much time indoors drinking and pawing women. I hoped I was aging better. I knew Rita was.

"Yeah, Georgy. How's it hanging?" I didn't want to seem out of place at a stripper club.

"Not bad. How about you?" he responded as we walked to his office.

"Great. Well, not great, but okay." I started to tell him my life story after high school but thought better of it. "This is Rick Steele. Rick works at the *Las Vegas Gazette*, too."

"Nice to meet you, Rick." He took Rick's offered hand. Turning to me, Georgy reminisced, "How's your Uncle Dutch? I haven't thought about him for years. Remember when he used to come to the games wearing that crazy Wildcat hat on his head. He once ran down on the field and got into a fight with that referee, the one with the long nose."

"Oh, he's fine," I explained. "Actually, he's the reason I'm here." I paused. I wasn't sure how Georgy was going to take this. "Uncle Dutch got wind of an FBI investigation of certain county commissioners." I didn't want to mention Rita. "Rumor has it that you're cooperating with the FBI. True?" Sometimes the direct approach is best. Besides, like I said, people talk to me. I never understood it, but it sure helps me get information for my column.

Georgy motioned for us to sit, and he went behind his desk and sat down. I could hear music coming from the stage. His face was turning red and he tugged on his shirt collar as if it were too tight.

Georgy had a reputation for exhibiting a bi-polar style of management. He looked ready to explode, and I braced myself for one of his famous temper tantrums. Instead, he shrugged, pursed his lips, and lifted his palms upright. "What are ya gonna do? I guess it's going to get out anyway," he said after thinking about it for a minute. "I'd rather someone I liked got the story."

"You liked me, Georgy? I didn't know that."

"Well, sure, why do you think I used to put those little love notes in your locker?"

"They weren't love notes, Georgy. They were porno pictures of men and women in disgusting poses."

"They weren't that bad," he said. "I thought they might give you ideas, you know?"

They did give me ideas. They gave me the idea that Georgy was an annoying creep and a pervert. Of course, I didn't tell him that now. After all, I was trying to be nice so that he would spill his guts to us.

About this time, Rick spoke up. I don't think he wanted to hear any more high school stories at the moment. "What commissioners are involved?"

Rick and I both took out small notebooks and pens. His notebook was larger than mine, much neater, more expensive, and had a leather cover. Mine was very small, cheap, and looked as if I had run over it. It might have gone through the washing machine with my cell phone. I noticed he had an ornate black and silver pen while I had a Dollar Store find. It was clear to me that I was going to have to change some of my ways if I wanted to move up the newspaper ladder.

"Oh," said Georgy, brought back from his high school reveries, "Bruce Pritchard, Joann Kirkoff, Ernest Ortega, and Raymond Angelo. Ray and Pritchard aren't commissioners anymore, though. You remember Raymond, don't you Maggie?"

Before I could answer, Rick asked, "What are you telling the FBI about them?"

"Well, Ray has worked for me for years as sort of…uh… a consultant, even when he was a commissioner. I was paying him $6000 a month to…uh…smooth things over with people for me. Some of those people he was smoothing over were Pritchard, Kirkoff, and Ortega. That was when we were getting ready to build this place. We had a slight zoning problem that was eventually solved."

"Are you saying you bribed them to help with a zoning issue?" Rick clarified.

"Yes."

"Why are you talking to the FBI, Georgy?" I interrupted.

"The Feds have wiretaps on phones, at least, Raymond's; and they have videotapes of meetings. According to Petey, they've got me cold, and they're willing to deal in order to get the politicians. I guess they're bigger fish than I am. Also, if I talk, I stand a chance of keeping my clubs open here, and maybe they'll stay away from my club in Los Angeles."

"You might stay out of jail, too, Georgy," I offered.

"Sure, there's that."

"Why did the FBI suspect Raymond and tap his phones?" I asked.

"I don't know," Georgy shrugged. "Anyway, I guess Raymond made a lot of his offers over the phone, the idiot. He also talked to me on the phone quite a few times. They even have pictures of Pritchard, Ortega, Raymond, and I meeting here, some free lap dances, free drinks, and girls, that sort of thing. One time Raymond called Kirkoff on the phone to arrange a meeting, and the FBI got pictures of the two of them at dinner. Raymond handed an envelope to Joann during dinner. Not long after that the zoning was changed in my favor. The commissioners did some other things for me as the building was going up, too."

"How much did you pay?" Rick asked.

"I don't know the exact amounts right now, and I handed my records over to the FBI. I paid them monthly, maybe one or two thousand depending on what was going on."

"How did you make the payments?" Rick continued.

"When they were campaigning, I made campaign donations within the legal limits. Beyond that amount, Raymond collected campaign donations from various people and then reimbursed them with my money later. After they were in office, I made cash payments."

"Were those the only payoffs?" Rick asked.

I stretched over Rick's shoulder and noticed he was writing more in his notebook than I was. In order to look equally busy, I started to doodle in addition to taking notes. Rick gave me a puzzled look and a shake of his head. I guess I wasn't fooling him.

Georgy was still thinking. "I bought a car and a Rolex for Raymond."

"Anybody else involved?" I asked.

"The Feds also know that I was bribing a Metro detective, named Coop DeMarco. He's a real bad ass who comes around here now and then. I pay him off to warn me about vice raids. He's a scary guy, but he's proved useful."

We talked for a while longer, getting more details, until Rick said, "Anything you would like to add, Mr. Garbarino?"

"Just that pretty soon I think I'll be indicted. I probably won't be able to operate this place, the one on Fremont, or Queens for a while, maybe forever. It depends on what they get out of me and how useful they think it is. I'm hoping the Feds let the clubs stay open with someone else running them."

"One more thing, Georgy," I said. "Have you talked to anyone else about this investigation? Any reporters? Any other people not involved?"

"No, except Jamie Rodriquez, the assistant manager here, he knows about it. Jaime's new around here. You don't know him, Maggie."

"Thanks," said Rick, "and could I call if I have more questions?"

"Sure," responded Georgy. "Don't be such a stranger, Maggie." Wow! There was that clever verbiage again.

Georgy suddenly looked very sad. I guess an FBI investigation will do that to you.

Chapter 5

Walking out of Georgy's office, we ran into Gary again. Gary was a very sociable guy; he was walking around working the room, talking to everyone he knew. I grabbed his arm; he turned around and smiled when he saw I was the intruder. On a whim, I asked him if any politicians we might know were at the club tonight.

"Sure," he said. "Ernest Ortega's here. You know of him. He's a county commissioner. That assistant district attorney, something Barber, is with him."

"John Barber?" I asked.

"Yes, he's the one. They're over at that table beside us. See?" Gary pointed to a table where two men were sitting. It was pretty dark in the club, but I could make them out. A woman was at the table also. She had on a skimpy but colorful costume; so, I guessed she either worked at the club or had bad taste.

"Thanks, Gary." I patted his arm as he turned and walked to the next table where he knew someone. "What do you want to do?" I asked turning to Rick.

"No time like the present," he said. And, we headed to Ortega and Barber's table.

When we got there, John Barber stood up. "Maggie, I didn't expect to see you here." I could tell from the expression on his face he meant what he said.

"Hi, Johnny. I didn't expect to see you here, either. Conducting business?" I introduced Rick to the table, and John introduced Ortega and a girl named Rhonda to us. She excused herself and left, though. She said she had a number coming up. I was relieved that she was a stripper and not just a bad dresser.

Ortega held on a little too long as we shook hands. I finally pulled my hand from his grasp. I knew John Barber from a column I did once. John was the assistant district attorney handling a case I was reporting.

John is a dapper looking man, tall, and thin. He was casually dressed in black slacks and a red Polo shirt. He always wore tasseled loafers. In high school, we described guys like him as preppies.

"I don't come very often," John offered. "But, I was here to see George; and, then, I saw Ernest out here. So, I stopped to have a drink." He was kind of embarrassed. "Why are you here?"

"Oh, we're working," I explained.

Ortega laughed unpleasantly. "Oh, you work here. When do you come on?" He looked me over very carefully as if I had forgotten to put on all my clothes. "I'll hang around for your number."

Ernest Ortega was wearing lightweight tan summer slacks and a brown striped shirt. He had a mustache and ruddy complexion. His eyes were dark and small and sat below bushy eyebrows. Jowls that made him look slightly overweight accented his face.

John turned to Ortega and told him I was a columnist for the *Gazette*. I explained that Rick was a reporter at the *Gazette*, too.

When Ortega heard that, he just said, "Oh, great. I'd like it better if you were a stripper. At least, that's honest work." He turned away from us and went back to drinking.

I could tell we in for a pleasant interview.

John asked what we wanted to drink, but Rick said he would get our drinks. Rick bought a round of drinks for the table. He had beer, and I had a glass of wine. Ortega had already had a few drinks too many. He was loud and a little too boisterous.

Eventually, Ortega turned around to face me again. "Why would a great looking chick like you be a newspaper reporter? You're so hot you could be stripping here. In fact, I wouldn't mind seeing you with your clothes off." I expected him to start twirling the ends of his mustache while he watched me. I was beginning to feel like the canary to his cat.

"I can't dance," I said, ignoring that he called me "chick."

"Have you seen the broads here? They can't dance either." I thought that was rude because I knew Rita could dance. He was saying all this in a loud voice and splashing his drink as he talked. "Yeah, I'd really like to see you take your clothes off and get on stage. I'd really like to see that."

"Some other time," I said. I was starting to get steamed but needed to get his take on the bribery story.

"We have a few questions," Rick said diverting the attention from me. I was taking a few drinks of wine every time Ortega spoke.

"Yeah? What?" asked Ortega.

"We're about to break a story that says George Garbarino bribed certain county commissioners for their vote on zoning. What's your comment?" Rick asked with his notebook out again. I hastily grabbed mine, not wanting to be outdone.

"You break a story like that using my name and I'll have your job and enough of the *Gazette's* money to retire. Don't use John's name either. Right, John?" Ortega turned to Rick. "I'm not telling you anything." Then, he leaned over to me. "I might talk to you, baby, if you take your clothes off."

I looked at Rick. "Did he just call me 'baby'?" I took a few more drinks of my wine.

Rick just nodded his head, "Yes."

John said, "Leave me out of this, Ernest."

"Are you out of it, John?" Ortega asked.

"You're drunk. Shut up," John said to Ortega.

I mentally jotted down Ortega's inclusion of John and John's reaction. I'd look into that later.

We had been at the table for a while when another girl walked by whom Ortega apparently knew. He grabbed her by the arm and talked to her while his other hand was rubbing her waist and heading south. At least, she captured his attention for a while.

I was trying not to look on the stage, but I glanced at Rick to see if the show on stage was attracting him. Sure enough, I think he was catching a peek now and then. I took some more drinks of my wine.

"What's the girl on stage doing?" I asked Rick.

"Why don't you look for yourself?"

"I can't. Come on, tell me."

"Well, I think a man and a bird had sex, and the stripper is the off-spring."

"You mean like Zeus and Leda, the swan. Wow! How literary."

"Yeah, this is very literary."

Eventually, I couldn't avoid looking on stage; and when I did, I grabbed Rick's arm and exclaimed loudly, "Whoa! Look at her! She's huge. They can't be real. And I don't mean the feathers. What do you think, Rick?" She did have feathers everywhere. Smaller ones were lying all over the stage but now she was stripping huge ones off her boobs. They must have been ostrich feathers. I could use feathers from a wren.

"I think we're better off focusing on Ortega," he said. Hum…no wonder his name was Steele.

I kept starring, amazed by the thought that some women just had more ammunition. By this time, she had plucked herself clean and was hanging onto a pole. She slid down the pole with one leg wrapped around it. Not only was she well endowed but she was limber and acrobatic also.

Rick looked at me. "Be careful. Your mouth is open."

"I was just fascinated by her swan song?" I said, sipping more wine.

"I think you need to stop gawking at the strippers. People are going to wonder," he laughed.

As I was looking around the club and trying not to look on stage, I saw a man standing in the corner by the bar. It was hard to make him out because it was dark in here and his face was in the shadows. He was big and well built. I could tell that. He was leaning casually over the bar playing with his bottle of beer. He seemed to be paying attention to our table, though. Now and again his eyes would look in our direction.

I turned to John. "Who's that at the corner of the bar?"

"That's a Metro cop, Coop DeMarco."

"Does he hang around here a lot?" I asked. I remembered Georgy talking about Coop DeMarco.

"Oh, he's a frequent customer. He pretty much stays to himself, though. He's not what you would call friendly."

By this time, Ortega was laughing loudly and getting pretty touchy-feely with every girl who passed our table. I hoped they were getting big tips.

John was trying to get Ernest to quiet down a little bit, and he put his hand on Ernest's arm. Ernest brushed his hand away and slurred, "Let me alone. I can take care of myself. You better take care of yourself."

As Ortega got progressively louder and drunker, John finally said he was on his way out. He looked at us. "If you know what's best, you'll be leaving, too."

Ortega kept ordering more drinks. Finally, I turned to him again, pushing for a comment. "Did you accept bribes from Garbarino?"

"That's none of your business, baby." And he reached across the table and grabbed my hand. Since my notebook was in that hand, it was getting crumpled.

"What's your relationship with Raymond Angelo?" I asked, drinking more wine and pulling my hand and notebook away.

"Don't be a bitch," he said. "You're much prettier when you don't talk." With that, he leaned across the table and grabbed the sleeve of my jacket and yanked on it. "How about taking your clothes off instead? Start with this." He was tugging on my jacket, trying to take it off me.

I turned to Rick while trying to pull my jacket out of Ortega's grasp. "Did he call me a bitch this time?" Now, I was getting angry and ready for a good fight.

Rick shook his head "yes" in answer to my question.

"Don't call me a bitch and take your hands off me," I shouted above the music, pushing Ortega's hand away. I can be pretty intimidating when I want.

About this time, Gary walked up to the table. "Hi, again, Maggie?"

"Get out of here, you bum bucker," Ortega said.

"Bum Bucker?" Gary looked at me. "Is that really what he said?"

"Yep," I said, sipping my wine. "He's called me 'baby,' 'chick,' and 'bitch' so far." I held up three fingers and looked at them to make sure I was accurate. "That's three politically incorrect slurs."

Gary turned to Ortega. "You're not very politically correct for a politician."

"Oh, bugger off," Ortega said. Then, he turned to me again. "Where do you want me to put my hands, baby?" and he grabbed for me again.

I hit at his paws to keep them off me.

Rick said to Ortega, quietly, "Don't touch her. It's not a good idea."

"I'll do whatever I want." With that Ortega jumped up, knocked his chair over, and came towards me. When I saw him coming around the table, I stood up, reached over, and punched him in his jaw. It wasn't too difficult to do; he was drunk and kind of stumbling already. My punch just made him stumble a little more.

Rubbing his chin, Ortega shouted, "You bitch. Nobody hits me and gets away with it." He started coming towards me again.

I turned to Rick and Gary. "Jump in whenever the mood hits you."

"You're doing just fine by yourself," Rick responded. "Besides, this is your fight. I wouldn't want to seem like a chauvinistic pig."

"I don't want to ruin this dress," Gary explained. Now that's something I can understand.

"All right," I said to Ortega, pushing my chair back. "Bring it on."

I could hear Rick say with a loud sigh, "Oh, no. Did she say 'bring it on'?" Before Ortega got to me again, Rick was out of his seat and in between Ortega and me.

"I wouldn't take another step, pal," Rick warned.

Ortega said, "Screw you," and took a swing at Rick.

Rick stepped away from his punch, and Ortega missed. The next thing I knew, Ortega was on the floor. Two men, I assumed they were bouncers, rushed over to where Ortega was on the floor and started to help him up. By this time, men from several other tables decided to join in the fight.

Gary grabbed one guy and landed a good right cross. When he did, his dress tore in the seam on the side. "Damn," he said, holding the seam together and looking at it as the guy got up and took another swing at him. Gary just knocked him down once more with ease.

Another guy came after Rick; and when he grabbed onto Rick, I tried to jump on his back as I had seen done in a movie. It's not as easy as it looks. I ended up sitting on the floor rather suddenly. Rick was pushing that guy away and dodging punches from another. It was a free for all. I don't think anyone knew whom he was fighting. I started to hit some guy with my purse but remembered it was my good Gucci bag.

After dodging tumbling bodies, I crawled under a nearby table, still gripping my Gucci bag and notebook, because it was getting a little rough. I reached into my pocket for my new cell phone, but it wasn't there. Then, I saw it. It had fallen out of my jacket and onto the floor. Before I could retrieve it, a man with a very large shoe stepped on it. I moaned thinking about another trip to Verizon.

After what seemed like a long time, I saw an arm that I recognized reach under my table and grab my sleeve. As Rick pulled me out, one of the bouncers headed in our direction. He looked as if he was going to start trouble, but Rick held his hands up in a gesture that said we were leaving. Rick took hold of my arm and led me toward the door.

"Wait," I yelled. I reached down to the floor and picked up the pieces of my cell phone, putting them into my purse. Uncle Dutch would want them as proof that it wasn't my fault this time. At least, that's how I saw it.

Rick kept pulling me out the door. I was struggling with him and proclaiming loudly, "There's Gary. Wait a minute."

Rick just kept a firm hold on my arm and kept heading for the door as he said, "Come on, Slugger, time to go. Enough fun for one night."

Gary caught up with us near the door. His shoes were off, his dress torn, and his wig tilting to one side. "I'm sorry about the dress, Gary."

"Oh, it's okay, Maggie. I haven't had this much fun for a long time. Besides, this gown is last year's line anyway. But, I think it's time to go." He turned to wave at his friends who were still seated at their table, chatting and sipping their drinks despite the chaos around them.

They waved at us, and I waved back. Rick never let go of my arm.

I noticed that the cop at the bar never left his spot. He just kept watching. From the looks of his shoulders, though, I could swear he was laughing.

"I'm a little tipsy. How's that possible?" I asked. "I only had one glass of wine."

"Yeah," Rick replied. "You only had one glass, but the waitress kept filling it up."

"Oh. No wonder. You know, Ortega's an obnoxious man. I could have knocked him out, though, if you hadn't gotten in the way. "

"Lucky for him that I did. He ought to be happy I got you out of there. You need some coffee. We'll stop at Starbuck's, and, then, I'll drive you home."

We never got to Starbuck's or Rick's car because about the time we reached the door, Metro officers came through and blocked the exits.

Chapter 6

I was sitting on a bare cot in jail, holding my head, and trying to think of Johnny Cash songs about prison life. All I could think of was Elvis' *Jailhouse Rock*, and that was a little too upbeat for my mood. I must have had a little too much to drink since my head was swimming and my eyes couldn't focus. Looking up through a fog, I saw a pair of great ankle-strap shoes, Jimmy Choo, I think, standing beside me. The rest of the ensemble didn't fit the shoes. The heavily made up woman was wearing fishnet stockings and a short green, tight sequined skirt. A yellow strapless knit top finished the outfit. Her strawberry blonde hair was done up in a fifties beehive.

She spoke. "What are ya' in here for, honey?"

I licked my fuzzy teeth and squinted at her. "A fight."

"No kiddin'. Who won?" She jutted her hip out, leaned on one foot, and chewed on one of her bright red, chipped fingernails.

"I'm not sure. What are you here for?" I thought I would repay the opening conversational gesture.

"Knifin' a john. The bastard. I guess he won't be beatin' on any workin' girls soon."

"Is he dead?" I was alarmed at the thought I might be in jail with a murderer.

"Nah. I just wounded him. I got awfully close to his privates though. Another inch and he wouldn't be lookin' to hire anymore girls ever." She sat down beside me and crossed her long, fishnet-adorned legs.

"Hi, I'm Maggie." I stuck my hand out to shake.

She looked at my hand as if introductions weren't appropriate in jail, but my mother taught me to use manners on all occasions. She hadn't specifically mentioned jail, but I was pretty sure they applied here, too. Finally, she said, "Nice to meet ya'. I'm Heather. You like the name? I'm trying it out this week. I think guys like the name Heather. Sounds kind of feminine."

"Great shoes, Heather."

"Yeah. Shoes are important. If you pay a lot for your shoes, you can cut down on the rest of the wardrobe."

I agreed and nodded. The head movement hurt, though.

"Boy, honey, you must have a doozy of a headache. Drink too much?"

"I think I had too much wine."

"Oh, wine's the worst. Stick to watered down whiskey," she advised.

"I'll do that next time." I genuinely hoped there would not be a next time.

I looked across the cell and could see someone lying down on a cot. Her back was turned, but I could tell she was big.

"Who's she?" I whispered.

"I don't know. She's been like that since I came in."

A very tall, big-boned, light-skinned black woman rolled over and glared at us. "Don't be talkin' about me behind my back." She was wearing tight black leather pants and a red short-sleeved sweater that was a few sizes too small. She had on red platform shoes. I didn't think she needed the extra height, but this wasn't the time to give her fashion tips.

"Oh, we weren't," I replied quickly, not wanting to antagonize her.

Heather sauntered over and gave her the eye, standing with one hand on her hip. I thought it was a rather challenging position.

The other woman sat up straighter in bed and said, "Whatta ya' lookin' at?"

"Nothin'."

The woman on the cot stood up and was clearly a foot taller than Heather. Heather didn't flinch, though.

"You'll think nothin' when I grab that ugly hair and knock the sequins right off that hooker skirt, you skinny little ho." She moved toward Heather.

"Who are you callin' a ho, you ho?"

"Well, if the shoe fits."

With that, feisty little Heather grabbed the woman's hair and pulled it. The woman was so much bigger than Heather, though, that her head hardly moved. She did, however, take both arms and squeeze Heather around the middle. Gasping for air, Heather had to let go of her hair, and they both toppled to the floor. The big woman pinned Heather to the floor.

"Take back what you said about me being a ho."

"I ain't takin' nothin' back," cried Heather.

"Then, I ain't lettin' go."

Despite my headache, I stood up and yelled, "Ladies, ladies." I stomped my foot loudly and dramatically.

Both stopped dead in their tracks and stared at me.

Then, the big woman looked at Heather. "Ladies? Did she call us ladies?"

Heather looked at her and smiled. "She sure did."

"Come on ladies, stop it. We're in enough trouble," I begged.

"I ain't lettin' her up until she takes back what she said. I ain't no ho, and I ain't gonna have some skinny-assed ho call me one. I'm an engaged lady. Well, I was. Maybe the wedding will be called off now."

"Okay," said Heather, breathing heavily. "You're no ho. Now, get off me."

The woman let Heather up and sat back down on her cot.

I stuck my hand out toward her and introduced myself.

She shook my hand and explained that she was Alvinia. Then, she turned to Heather and said, "Hey! Sorry about my temper, but I don't hold with anybody callin' me names."

"I know what you mean," Heather conceded, straightening her skirt and twisting her top back into position. "What are you here for?"

"I found my fiancé…uh, he might not be my fiancé anymore… in bed with a skank. I beat the shit out of him. If we still get married, we'll have to wait until he's out of the hospital." Alvinia paused to think. "I shoulda been easier on him. He's pretty scrawny."

"Why would you want to marry him now?" I was truly puzzled. Some women just surprise me.

"Oh, he's weak and can't help himself. Besides, he's got a job. I ain't been engaged to no guy with a job before."

A jailer who came to the cell interrupted us by calling out, "Maggie Hall?"

I identified myself, and he said, "You're getting bailed out. Come on."

I turned to Heather and Alvinia, explaining that I was a local columnist. I gave each of them a card and told them to call if they ever had a scoop for me. I was always looking for a good source. See, this is what I mean about growing up in Vegas. Every experience can lead to a good story.

I left with the guard, picked up my belongings, and headed into the waiting area. There was Mom. She was my one phone call. I suppose I could have called a lawyer, but Mom is more persuasive with people. She was wearing a light green St. John's pantsuit. The top had frogs on it. It was one of my favorite outfits. This, apparently, was Mom's idea of the outfit to wear when bailing loved ones out of jail.

It must have worked because when I entered the waiting area, she was in a deep conversation with the officer at the desk.

"Maggie," she exclaimed, giving me a big hug. Then, she looked me over. "You're kind of messy dear."

"I know, Mom. It's not been a good night. Can we go into detail later?" I knew she would demand the full story as a trade for bail. I guess it's only fair.

"Of course, dear. By the way," she gestured toward the officer at the table, "this young man is the son of Tommy and Mary Ellis. I sold them a house about nine years ago. He was much younger then."

The officer smiled at me and said, "Hi." Nobody but me seemed embarrassed by the whole situation.

Thinking of my associates in crime, I asked, "Did you bail out Rick and Gary, too?"

"Sure. They should be on their way. Right, Billy?"

"They are, Mrs. Hall."

"Oh, don't be so formal. Call me Angela. Here's my card, too. I only do real estate part time for my friend Suzy now, but call me if you ever need anything. Do you mind my asking, do you own or rent?"

"I rent for the time being."

"Well, you're never too young to own something—invest in your own future."

He took her card and put it in his pocket. Now my head was really hurting. Hearing footsteps, I turned to see Rick and Gary entering the waiting area.

Rick entered the room as hot and handsome as ever. In fact, he looked rested after his jail stay. Gary appeared as disheveled as I was. He was carrying his red wig and his hair had a stocking holding it tight to his scalp. His gold dress was torn, and his shoes were in his other hand.

Rick smiled charmingly and shook hands with Mother. "Mrs. Hall, I presume. You're my savior."

Mother smiled back, grasping his hand a little longer than necessary. My head hurt again, and I wanted to tell Mom to turn off the charm. Rick's young enough to be her son.

Mom turned to Gary whom she knew since we had been friends for a few years. "Gary, Gary, Gary. I've seen you look better."

"Well, Mrs. Hall, you look as great as ever."

"Why thank you, dear. I've had this outfit for so many years, but it's held up well."

I had to hold my head again. "Can we go?" I asked.

And with that, the four of us headed out the door. We all rode with Mom. She dropped Rick and Gary at La Tigra to get their cars. She, then, took me to the *Gazette* for my car. On the way there, she had the good taste not to ask what happened. Mom knew I would tell her in my own good time.

Chapter 7

When I got up the next morning, I still had a slight headache. After dressing, I gingerly made my way downstairs and found Kitty on the family room floor cutting yellow ducks out of construction paper. Next year will be her first as a "real" teacher. In her upcoming second-grade classroom, apparently, it will be the "Year of the Fowl."

Mom's house is Italian Tuscany marries Santa Fe Southwest. It is painted that adobe apricot with teal shutters. To take advantage of the views of the strip and downtown, the house was designed in a horseshoe shape with the sides fanning out a bit like a bowl. Each rectangular room juts out from the other so that all spaces have views of the terrace, golf course, and city. The back of the house is predominantly glass to take advantage of these views. On the first floor, the foyer and formal living room are at the curve of the horseshoe. To the left are the dining room, family room, and kitchen. On the right side of the house are Mom's quarters—a bedroom, bathroom, sitting room and office, and the biggest closet you've ever seen. I know that if Mom has a financial crisis she can sell her shoes and hats. The extra income would keep her in bonbons for years. All of the main rooms have French doors leading to the multi-leveled terrace in the back. Outside are the pool, spa, and gardens. Beyond the property and down the hill is a large pond on the country club's golf course.

On one side of the house upstairs are my rooms, including my office, and on the other side are Kitty's rooms and her office. A balcony wraps around the back of the house upstairs with access from each room. Three other elaborately decorated bedrooms upstairs are for guests. Is it any wonder that Kitty and I still live here?

Margaret, our Scottish housekeeper, was sitting on the sofa with her feet on the coffee table, watching TV. She was wearing a flowered housedress, socks, and pink fuzzy slippers. Margaret is a wee Scottish lady in height. And, a not-so-wee Scottish lady in width. She is, at least, seventy years old and has been with Mom for over 30 years. I was just a kid when Margaret first worked for us a few hours once a week doing normal housecleaning. Now, she works for Mom three days a week. At seventy, though, Margaret usually needs Mom's help cleaning the house. Mom has talked about getting an assistant for Margaret. Often, Margaret comes over on days she doesn't work for us because she likes our big screen TV better than her little TV. She also doesn't have to cook if she comes over. Working for Mom has great benefits.

"Where's Gram?" I asked.

Perturbed and with hardly a glance in my direction, Margaret just said, "Hush, my soap's on, dearie," and Kitty didn't answer.

I wasn't about to disturb Margaret during one of her soaps. So, I turned to Kitty. Then, I saw her earphones. I lifted the earphones, draped them around her neck, and repeated myself. It's a scene I go through frequently. Some mothers might suspect they're being shut out. Not me. I just think she's considerate for not foisting her musical tastes on me.

"In her studio," reported Kitty, returning to her ducks.

She raised her head again. "Oh, Mommy Dearest," she purred. "I need to borrow a dress. I was wondering if I could wear that blue DKNY sundress you just bought."

I hadn't even worn that dress myself yet. But, how could I say "No" to Kitty? That could crush her now when she's so vulnerable. On the other hand, maybe she was clever enough to know that I couldn't refuse her anything given her current circumstances. So, she was taking advantage of me and asking to wear my new dress. Hum…could she be that devious? Note to self: stop over-thinking things. "What's the occasion?" I asked.

"I have a date with Frederick."

Mom fixed Kitty up with Frederick a few months back. Kitty had been seeing him regularly since then. He certainly seemed to take Kitty's mind off Rod.

"Where are you going that you need my new dress?"

"Out to dinner. He's going to pick the place, but he said, 'Dress up.'"

"Are you two getting serious?"

"I can't go into detail now. I have to finish up here. I told one of the other teachers that I would meet her at school, and we could plan bulletin boards for the second-grade hallway. We're thinking of doing them on *Wildlife in the Wetlands*. That way we can tie in my ducks and her frogs. Some of the other second-grade teachers are using fish this year. So, that will work nicely. I just need an answer, Mom. 'Yes' would be the right answer." She smiled sweetly, or was it devilishly?

Ducks, frogs, and fish. "How much did your education cost me?" I asked.

"Nothing, Mom. I got a scholarship, remember?"

"Oh, yeah." I forgot she was smart. That means she could be devious, then, too. "Sure, you can borrow the dress. Just don't stretch it out."

She gave me the oh-right smirk. I could see I was being dismissed; so, I took my best shot. "Getting all your ducks in a row?"

Kitty just rolled her eyes, shook her head with that only-you-can-be-so-corny look, and put her earphones back on. Kitty is what's called cute. She's about my height and slim—no hips or boobs. Her hair is auburn, a trait from Mom's Irish side of the family, but it's a shade darker than mine, with a short, spiky cut. She has green eyes and a flashy smile. The smile has pretty much gotten her everything she's wanted since she was a child.

"You used to think I was funny," I yelled, but she couldn't hear me.

Margaret replied, though. "I never thought you were funny." Her eyes didn't leave the television screen.

I turned my attention to Margaret. "Is this a work day for you?"

"No need to get snippy with me, dearie. I didn't drop your column from the paper."

Having been rebuked by our seventy-year-old, mooching housekeeper, I went outside to the studio. After Dad died Mom needed a creative outlet; so, it's been sewing, pottery, glass fusing, origami, yoga, flower arranging, decorating, cooking, and any other art that captures her creative spirit.

Mom was in the studio up to her elbows in gummy, gray clay and sitting at the potter's wheel. I must have surprised her because, when she looked up from the perfectly shaped bowl she was working on, she bumped it. It started spinning out of control. At that moment, she looked a little flustered.

Mom and Dad made lots of money in real estate, but Mom still likes to think of herself as a free spirit. So, she has two distinctive personalities. Sometimes you just have to know which personality is in residence. Her ritzy personality dresses in smartly tailored pants suits, Chanel dresses, or St. John's anything. Her free spirit comes out in her studio, in the kitchen, or in her garden. It's anything but chic and smart casual. Today she was a free spirit. She had on loose fitting, wrinkled cotton pants, and a top with as many holes as fabric. Clay was on her clothes, the walls, and her hair. She was smiling though.

Angela is about 5 feet 6 inches tall with a trim figure. She believes in resurfacing or lifting any part of her body. She says, "God made plastic surgeons for a reason." Her deep-set eyelids and high cheekbones are all hers though. At 59 years old, she is what's called "striking."

Her hair is short and frosted, requiring many trips to the hairdresser. She was a natural redhead, but too much white hair made her switch to blonde. I am always surprised at how much information she can pick up for my column at the hairdresser's. For instance, when Jack Hughes, president of the Desert Sands Hotel and Casino, left his wife and ran off with his secretary and the casino's money, Mom reported the event to me two days before it was released by Metro. My column was titled *Desert Sands Storm Brewing*, and I had the jump on everyone

"Hi! The clay goes nicely with your hair, Mom. Bad clay day?" I asked.

"It's not good." She had stopped the potter's wheel and sat on her stool with her arms leaning across her legs. She held her hands outward so the clay and water would not drip on her. "Nothing's working. I've ruined two bowls and a cup, and it's still morning. I think it's time to quit. Maybe I should take up watercolors? I would have to be able to draw for that, though, wouldn't I? What's going on?"

"I just wanted to thank you once more for springing me from jail. You're due that explanation when I have time."

I took a seat on a nearby stool. "Kitty and Frederick sure are seeing a lot of each other. Tell me again how you met him."

"Oh, remember I told you he was a client. He's a nice young man that just bought a great house in Seven Hills. It's a custom house, has four bedrooms, is five thousand square feet, and looks over the golf course."

Mom describes people based on the house they live in. Seven Hills is an upper middle class to upper class community near Anthem. Winding streets run along hills and valleys. A variety of subdivisions, both tract and custom, are throughout the Seven Hills community. Elegant lights line the streets, and medians are lush and green.

"Anything else?"

"Well, apparently, he's a real computer whiz. Las Vegas Resort Hotels and Casinos, Inc., hired him to run their information management department. I'd say from the house he bought from me, he's making good money. And he needs a haircut, but other than that I think he's nice enough looking."

I didn't think he needed a haircut, and, not only was he "nice enough looking," but he was personable and seemed kind. All in all, I was glad that Kitty was seeing him. I had to admit to myself, though, that I wasn't necessarily pleased to think that she was getting serious again so soon.

I started to walk out but remembered the rest of my mission. "I also wanted to let you know that I probably won't be home for dinner."

"But, sweetheart, I planned to make that dish I saw on the Food Network yesterday. It's a Spanish paella with fresh clams, shrimp, and chicken. Then, I made that strawberry Jell-O cake you like so much."

See what I mean! Why would I want to move? "Sorry, Mom, but save some of the cake for me."

She wasn't despondent long. "Maybe I can invite that nice Scott Andrews over. I'm sure he'd appreciate a good meal." Was that a dig? With Mom you could never tell. Scott was a new high school principal in town. Mom had just sold him a house up in Summerlin. She was right. Real estate was a great way to meet men.

Did I mention that I was in real estate for a while? I was too "candid" for the real estate business my father said. I thought "honest" was a better way to put it. I told a prospective buyer that the last owners of this house I was showing had been real pigs. I even suggested the potential buyer check the plumbing. No telling what was stuck in the pipes. Anyway, we lost the sale, and I lost my job. My father said, though, that he was just trying to get me to "be all that I could be; reach for the stars; achieve my true potential." It became clear to me that he meant, "Find another job." See, my dad was a natural-born salesman.

"Sounds like a plan, Mom. I have to go."

She looked at me to check out what I was wearing. At age 39 the way I dress still reflected on my upbringing. She must have approved because she waved and started pounding on the clay.

ᘺᘧ

For the second time in two days, I drove to the Verizon store on my way to the *Gazette*. The same clerk was behind the counter when I walked in. I took the remnants of my cell phone out of my jacket pocket and dumped them on the counter in front of him.

He held up his index finger. "Just a minute." Then, he yelled into the back office area. "She's back and you have to see it this time."

A young woman who was clerking on the other side of the store rushed over to us, and a man about my age came out of a back office.

The woman cheerfully said, "Hi. My name's Paula. This is our manager, Dave Hawkins." Paula leaned on the counter with her chin in her hands and stared at the remains of my cell phone.

"Hello, Paula, Dave." I looked a little closely at Dave. He looked familiar.

"When Joey told me your name, I thought you might be the Maggie Hall I knew," he said. "Remember me? We went to school together. Junior English and chemistry? I sat right behind you."

"Oh, right. Now I remember you. Dave Hawkins. You played football. Pretty well as I recall." I stuck out my hand to shake.

"That's right, but I got a knee injury that kept me from playing in college. I ended up in business management at UNLV. I asked you out in high school, but you didn't accept."

"I know," I explained. "I was pregnant and thought it best not go out on dates."

"That's all right. I asked Cindy Metari out after that, and eventually we got married."

"I remember Cindy. Cute girl with dark curly hair. She had a pretty smile." I didn't want to tell him that Cindy had a reputation for playing around with anyone she could snag.

"That's her. She also slept with anyone in pants and maybe some in skirts," he said. "That didn't stop when we got married. So, now we're divorced."

"Oh," I sighed sympathetically. "Sorry to hear it."

"That she slept around or that we're divorced?"

"Both, I guess."

"So," Dave said, adopting his managerial tone, "tell us about your phone."

"Well, it got in a fight." The four of us just looked at the cell phone parts on the counter and nodded.

The acne-faced kid, Paula, and Dave all said, "Hum." Then, Dave asked, "How did that happen?"

I supposed it must be a slow day for them today.

"You want the whole story?" I asked.

"That would be great," Dave said. They all nodded eagerly.

"Well, I was on assignment for the *Gazette*. Big, big story… "

By the time I recounted my tale, I had taken a little literary license, but look how bored they had been until I walked in this morning.

"Wow," exclaimed Dave. I could tell he was speaking for everyone. "You need to take your phone to safer places."

"I suppose it's silly to ask if you can transfer the numbers I just entered into this phone."

They all just looked at me. I took that to mean, "Yes, it was silly to ask."

"So, what will it be? The newest iPhone?" Dave queried.

This must be a standard question, I thought. "No, been there, done that routine with the kid. I'm not easy on my phones so why get an expensive one. I'll take the older model. It's better for Uncle Dutch's wallet."

I could see Dave thought this was a good idea. He was a financially conservative guy.

After they gave me my new phone and case and entered the information into their computers, Dave walked me to the door.

"Are you seeing anyone?" He held the door open for me.

"Oh, I'm almost engaged, Dave."

"That's too bad. I would have asked you out. It figures that a good-looking woman like you would be in a relationship, though. Well, let me know if you break up or anything."

"Sure enough, Dave. Nice seeing you."

෫ ෬

Arriving at the *Gazette,* I was still carefully holding my cell phone as I went to my cubicle. Someone turned up a CD player and blasted the theme from *Rocky* through the newsroom. Reporters have such a wonderfully biting sense of humor. I wondered how they had found out about last night so fast. They weren't that good as reporters; so, Rick must have told them. I decided I had better go explain myself to Uncle Dutch.

As I walked into his office, his secretary Bridget said, "They'll all be calling you Rocky, now."

"How did it get out?"

"I don't know," she said. "Everyone was already talking about the scuffle at La Tigra by the time I got here this morning."

"Is Dutch in?"

"He's in, but watch it. He's in a bad mood."

"What's new?" I opened his door and cheerfully called in, "Hey, Uncle Dutch. You're looking pretty sharp today." A compliment never hurts when you're about to explain how you got into a fight and ended up doing hard time.

Later that morning, satisfied that my column was nearly finished, I sat at my desk planning whom I would interview next and painting my nails slut red. The rough draft of my column lay on my desk under my nail polish. I painted, planned, and re-read at the same time. I like to think of it as multi-tasking.

Garbarino Strips for FBI

George Garbarino, owner of La Tigra, where a veritable bevy of beautiful bottomless and topless girls perform nightly, is doing a dance of his own. Yes, Garbarino is stripping and baring his breasts for the FBI.

Agents have been investigating Garbarino who yesterday reported to Yours Truly that he bribed none other than county commissioners Bruce Pritchard, Joann Kirkoff, Ernest Ortega, and Raymond Angelo. Angelo, he admitted, was his go-between in the negotiations.

Garbarino claims he gave donations to these commissioners' campaigns. Also, Angelo collected donations from outside contributors for the commissioners' campaigns. He then reimbursed these contributors with money from Garbarino. Garbarino also gave payments to Pritchard, Kirkoff, Ortega, and Angelo after they were elected to office. These payments bought their votes on a zoning issue that was favorable to La Tigra.

Not only politicians have been bad boys or girls, Readers. Garbarino also claims that Clark County Metropolitan Police Officer Coop DeMarco was bribed to give advanced warnings about vice raids. It's great work if you can get it.

Ernest Ortega, seen at La Tigra the other night, refused to answer questions about Garbarino's accusations. He's not saying he did, and he's not saying he didn't. What do you think? Should we re-elect him next election, assuming he's not in jail?

When I finished reading, I was thinking about what angle to take in my next column: the complicated FBI sting or the county commissioners betraying their electorate. I was also thinking that I wouldn't mind seeing Rick walk through the door.

Instead, I looked up to see Uncle Dutch standing in front of my desk along with the most scrumptious looking man I'd ever seen. It was lust at first sight, and I forgot all about Rick for the time being.

Uncle Dutch looked at my nails and polish and said, well not so much said as growled, "What are you doing?"

"My nails," I snapped back. It seemed obvious to me. "Don't worry," I continued, starring through Uncle Dutch to the hunk behind him.

By this time, I had returned the brush to the polish and screwed the cap back on. "My column is done and quite good, even if I do say so myself. And I do." I was craning my neck to get a better look at my unknown visitor and blowing on my polished nails.

"No, your column is not done."

"Yes, it is." I wrinkled my forehead because I was sure he was about to make a point.

Uncle Dutch gave me his editor's know-it-all smile, pointed at the stranger, and said, "Talk to him." With that he walked out.

The handsome stranger was about 6 feet 2 inches tall, bronze-skinned, with close-cropped black hair. He had a hint of a beard already and it was hardly 11 o'clock in the morning. He was wearing jeans and a great black t-shirt that definitely showed me the arms he was destined to hold me with. My eyes started on his formidable chest and began working their way down. It was as if they had a will of their own. Finally, they reached his jeans. He filled out his jeans well. I was lingering a little too long, looking where I shouldn't. He knew what I was thinking because he finally tried to direct my attention elsewhere. It wasn't easy, though.

"Marie Magdalene Hall?" he asked with a grin. People always smile when they say my full name. He also might have been smiling because he caught me leering at his jeans. Surely, I boosted his ego, but he didn't look as if his ego needed boosting. His voice was deep and his eyes were seductive. There I was staring again.

"Yes," I said, in the most alluring voice I could find. I was fumbling and stuffing my nail polish into my center desk drawer.

"I'm Coop DeMarco, FBI."

Now he really caught my attention. The man in the shadows at the bar in La Tigra. The FBI part was puzzling. "May I see your credentials?" I asked.

He showed them to me, and they looked all right. Though, to be honest, I could never tell the real ones from the fake ones.

"I thought you were with Metro?" I asked, referring to Georgy's comment that he was paying off a Metro vice cop named Coop DeMarco.

"Nope," he said and sat down, uninvited.

That didn't really enlighten me. I was still confused.

"You and Richard Steele met with Rita Ortiz Sunday, and then you and Mr. Steele drove to La Tigra and met with George Garbarino." He said this as a statement and a question. I was pretty impressed with his interviewing technique. "At the club, you were sitting with Ernest Ortega and John Barber."

Two can play the strong silent type though. "No," I replied.

"Ms. Hall…"

"Maggie please," I interrupted.

"Maggie, we have you on videotape."

"I just mean your statement isn't completely accurate. Yes, Mr. Steele and I met with Rita Ortiz. Yes, Mr. Steele and I met with Georgy…er…George Garbarino. Yes, Mr. Steele and I sat with Ortega and Barber. You left out that Mr. Steele and I had dinner in between. I just want the record to be completely accurate."

I could see a smile almost form on his lips. His eyes twinkled, and I could see a hint of dimples near his smile. I don't think FBI guys are allowed to be this amused. "Yes," he said. "At the Presidio in The District. I also left out the part where you started a fight at La Tigra."

"Right. It's pretty rude of you to mention the fight. And, that reminds me. You didn't even come over and lift a hand. Not that we needed it. Besides, if you noticed, I didn't start the fight. Ernest Ortega was calling me names and putting his hands on me. I finally got tired of being pawed and told him so. He's the one who decided to take it up a notch. I had been sitting there all evening asking my questions as politely as I could." I noticed he was just going to let me keep talking. So, I showed restraint and stopped on my own. "What's this about?"

"We know you got information from Ms. Ortiz, Mr. Garbarino, and Mr. Ortega. We just want to talk to you about what else you might know."

"Who's 'we'?" I asked. "Is somebody in your pocket?"

He gave me that smile again and said, "'We' is the FBI. We're given to talking like that. Why did you meet with Ms. Ortiz?" he asked.

"We're friends. I always meet with Rita."

"We know that. We've observed you before."

"You've been tailing me?" I wanted to show him I could use cop lingo.

"No, we've followed Ms. Ortiz."

Now I was totally confused. "Why have you been following Rita?

She's just a stripper at the club."

"I'd rather ask the questions," he said.

"That's fine. You can ask the questions, but you'll probably be more successful getting information from me if I understand what's going on too. Rita's my dearest friend."

He looked at me for a few minutes and obviously decided my plan was better. "George Garbarino was found dead early this morning."

"What?"

"George Garbarino…"

"No, no. I heard you." Looking down, I noticed that I had smeared the polish on one of my nails, but it didn't seem important. Despite Georgy's ways, I had known him a long time and had vivid memories—perhaps, not all good—of him in more carefree times. I flashed on his throwing spit wads at Father Hinley every time Father turned his back to write on the chalkboard. I pictured Rita and I listening with rapt attention to Georgy's stories about peeking onto the stage at La Tigra, unbeknownst to his father. I saw Rita and me in the back seat of his red convertible with our hair blowing, listening to 10000 Maniacs, cruising downtown Las Vegas, and laughing with joy. It couldn't be.

Pointing to my desk, Coop asked, "Is that your column?"

"Hum, yes."

"Could I read it?"

"Sure," I replied, handing it to him absentmindedly.

I watched him as he read. When he got near the end, he grinned. No doubt he enjoyed reading about himself as a corrupt cop.

When he put the column down, I asked, "Can you tell me more about Georgy's death? What happened? Why hasn't it hit the newsroom yet?"

"I don't know why the press hasn't gotten wind of the story yet, but I'm sure it's breaking now. Metro kept it under wraps as long as they could. All I know is that Garbarino was found face down in the alley behind La Tigra by one of the clean-up crew. A gun shot to the back of his head."

"I hope he didn't feel anything." I thought, Uncle Dutch is right. My column is not finished. Now I have to look into Georgy's death to see if it is connected to the bribery scandal. Besides, I owed Georgy for old time's sake.

"He probably didn't."

"Do you have a suspect yet?"

"We're not working the case. Metro is on it. We'll only come in if it's related to the bribery scandal."

"I see. Does Metro have a suspect?"

"None they've told us about."

"Any clues you can or will tell me about?"

"Nope."

I already knew I would get to Rick as soon as Coop DeMarco left. Rick could get more information with his contacts. I would be able to work the people I knew at La Tigra.

"What will you do with your star witness in the bribery scandal dead?"

"We'll manage."

"You're not very talkative."

"Silence is one of my strengths."

Hum. "What are your other strengths?" I don't always have to be professional.

He flashed me a suggestive smile and said, "Isn't it obvious?"

"Not yet," I responded. After all, two can be suggestive.

"Who might have done it?" I asked.

"I don't make guesses."

"I do. How about Ernest Ortega, Joanne Kirkoff, Bruce Pritchard , or Ray Angelo?"

"How about them?"

"Could I say they are 'persons of interest'?" I asked, looking for a quote. He wasn't falling for that tactic, though.

"You can say whatever you want. I'm not looking at anyone."

"By the way," I asked. "Why are you here?"

"I wanted to talk to you about your knowledge of the Garbarino bribery case."

"Garbarino did tell Rick and me that he bribed county commission-ers." I explained what we had learned from Georgy during the inter-view.

"Who else knew that he was cooperating with us?"

"No one that I know of. Oh, Garbarino told Rick and me that he informed Rodriquez, his club assistant manager, about the FBI investigation and how he was cooperating with the investigation. So, Rodriquez knew that Garbarino was talking. Also, Ortega didn't seem very happy with Georgy Sunday night, but he didn't say that he knew Georgy was talking."

"What about Garbarino? Did he give you any reason to believe he was in danger?

"Are you saying he knew he was going to be killed?"

"I really would like to ask the most questions. Job advancement in the FBI is more likely if I walk away from this interview with more information than you do. Well?"

"No," I said. "Georgy didn't indicate anything like that."

"Did you know about his argument with Ortega?"

"No." But, I thought, I'm sure going to ask somebody about it later.

"You said you had the impression that Ortega was upset with Garbarino? Was this before you slapped him?"

"No, he didn't talk about anything specific, before or after I defended myself. And, I didn't slap him. I doubled up my fist and hit him squarely in the jaw."

"I saw you, and you gave him a girlie slap." He smiled confidently and continued. "We can't ignore the possibility that someone might have wanted Garbarino dead because of his cooperation with us. Maybe someone like Ortega. Especially after their fight."

"Their fight? Does that mean they had a fistfight or just an argument? Because there is a difference?"

"Is that another question?" he asked.

I gave him a contrite smile. "Sometimes Georgy was kind of a creep, but I can't imagine that anyone would want to kill him unless it is tied to the bribery scandal. A lot of reputations are on the line. Georgy wasn't the violent type, and I don't think he was in tight with the wise guys. Uh oh, I just remembered that fight he had in high school. But... you know...that kid, what was his name—oh yeah, Richie—Richie threw up on Georgy in the cafeteria. I don't think Georgy was so much hitting Richie as knocking him away so that he wouldn't puke on him again." I noticed Coop was getting a glazed look in his eyes. Probably too much information. "No, Georgy said the same thing about Ortega that he said about the other commissioners. He said that Angelo collected campaign donations and, then, reimbursed the contributors; and he said that he gave money to the commissioners after they were elected. The money was in trade for their favorable vote on zoning. Oh, and Ortega got some perks when he came into La Tigra."

Changing the subject, I said, "I thought you were a detective with Metro on the take to Georgy?"

I think he gave up because he answered my question. "I've been undercover."

"Oh." I pondered his answer, thoughtfully.

"I assume your new column won't require me to demand a retraction to reinstate my good name. My mother hates to see my name and dirty cop in the same sentence in the newspaper?"

"That would seem to be in order," I admitted.

We got up to leave and Coop said, "You know, Ms. Hall…"

"Maggie," I reminded him.

"You know Maggie. Watch yourself investigating this story. We don't know what's happened yet. When somebody gets killed, it's never good. Just be careful until we find out what's going on."

Hum… Does he care about me already or does he take his job protecting the general public very seriously? "I'm always careful."

"I could tell that at the club the other night."

℠℞

I hurried to Rick's desk with the news of Garbarino's death and the fact that Coop DeMarco was an undercover FBI agent rather than a dirty cop. Rick was going to visit his Metro sources, and I was going to nose around La Tigra. We both thought that the best explanation for Georgy's murder at this time was his cooperation with the FBI on the bribery scandal. We would both explore that but keep our minds open to other motives. We'd meet back here later today. For once we didn't trade *double entendres*. Was it the news of Georgy's death, the scent of a hot news story, or lingering thoughts of Coop DeMarco?

Having satisfied my professional obligations, I called Rita to tell her about Georgy. We spent a few minutes reminiscing about him before

Rita realized that she might be out of a job. I then grabbed my purse, considered clearing off my desk, thought better of it, and hurried out of the office.

℘℃

An hour later, I found myself at La Tigra again. A sign on the door noted that the strip club was closed. The door, however, was unlocked; so I walked into the bar. The same bartender was there and I walked up to him. The place was quiet and subdued. In the light, though, I could see that the tables were older than I had thought, the carpet was frayed, the candle holders were covered with grime, and the stage looked smaller. Things don't always look better in the light of day. I told the bartender that I was here about Georgy. When I reminded him that I was an old friend, he called to the back, telling me that Georgy's dad was here.

When Mr. Garbarino came to the door where I had just recently seen Georgy standing, I extended my hand. "I'm so sorry to hear about Georgy, Mr. Garbarino. I don't know if you remember me, but I'm Maggie Hall. George and I went to high school together."

"Sure, I remember you, Maggie. You were always a polite young lady."

Mr. Garbarino looked older and sadder. I didn't know how much of that was the years between or Georgy's death.

We walked into what had been Georgy's office a few day's before. Mr. Garbarino pointed out a seat, indicating that I should sit there. He took the chair behind the desk and was quiet for a few minutes. Then, he asked, "What brings you here, Maggie?"

"Well, I am an old friend of George's, but I'm also a columnist at the *Gazette*."

"I know. Your Uncle Dutch owns it, doesn't he?"

"Yes, he does."

"A good man."

"I recently met with George about the FBI's investigation a few days ago. I'm here now as a columnist; so, if you don't want to talk to me, Mr. Garbarino, I'll understand and be on my way."

"No, I'll talk to you, Maggie. Just do George justice in your column.

55

He had his faults. God only knows, he wasn't the best husband. A father knows. But he was a good son."

"George and I were friends once, Mr. Garbarino. I'll keep that in mind. Have the police told you anything about his death?"

"Just that he was found this morning by Clarence Hoyle, the janitor here. Whoever did it, shot him and left him lay outside the club in the back alley. They said he was shot sometime in the early morning. About 4:00 or 4:30. They'll know better later. The cops told me that George was shot in the back of the head. He probably didn't feel a thing, they said. I don't think the cops found much evidence." A tear was falling down his cheek, and he wiped it with the back of his right hand. "Georgy should have lived a long life. You know?"

"Yes, he should have, Mr. Garbarino."

He was silent now, and I took that for a message to leave. I stood and handed Mr. Garbarino my card. "Call me if you want. And, again, I'm very sorry for your loss."

Mr. Garbarino took my card and reached into his pocket. He handed me his card. "My cell phone number is on it," he pointed out. "If you need anything…anything, call me. I want you to look into George's murder. The more people looking into it, the better."

"I'll do that," I assured him, taking his card.

Chapter 8

I was sitting at my desk at the *Gazette* Tuesday morning. Surrounded by discarded food wrappers, scattered papers, and a nearly finished doughnut, I was rereading my revised column that appeared this morning. The *Review-Journal* had the story of Georgy's murder, but I scooped them on the angle that Georgy was cooperating with the FBI on a bribery scandal.

Garbarino Stripped and Stripping

George Garbarino was stripped of his life yesterday early in the morning before the sun came up. He was murdered in cold blood, one shot to the back of the head. Clarence Hoyle, a long-time janitor at the strip club, found his body in the alley behind La Tigra.

Garbarino, owner of La Tigra, where a veritable bevy of beautiful bottomless and topless girls perform nightly, made a business hiring dancers, but did you know he was doing a dance of his own? Yes, Garbarino was stripping and baring his breasts for the FBI before he was brutally silenced.

Agents have been investigating Garbarino who recently reported to Yours Truly that he bribed none other than county commissioners Bruce Pritchard, Joann Kirkoff, Ernest Ortega, and Raymond Angelo. Angelo, he admitted, was his go-between in the negotiations.

In addition to money Garbarino contributed to campaign funds, Angelo allegedly collected donations from outside contributors for the commissioners' campaigns. He then reimbursed these contributors with money from Garbarino. Garbarino also gave payments to the commissioners after they were elected to office. These payments bought their votes on a zoning issue that was favorable to La Tigra.

Ernest Ortega, seen at La Tigra the other night, refused to answer questions about Garbarino's accusations. He's not saying he did, and he's not saying he didn't. What do you think? Should we re-elect him next election, assuming he's not in jail?

Now I need to ask myself, "Is Garbarino's murder related to his song and dance for the FBI? Who gains from his death?" The answers might be in my column, Readers.

As a postscript, Readers, Yours Truly has known George Garbarino since high school. While I did not sanction some of his admitted nefarious doings, I do remember a high school chum who could bring a smile to our faces with some of his antics. He was a savvy businessman and a beloved son. Let's pause to remember a popular Las Vegas High School Wildcat. Go Wildcat!

When I lay my column on my desk, making a space for it by moving aside my coffee and the remaining bite of a chocolate glazed doughnut from Krispy Crème, I sensed someone standing over my desk. I sighed, and my heart skipped a few beats. It was the hunk.

"Hi." I said, lamely. Why didn't I ever look busy when he was here? "What's up with the FBI? Any news you want to share?"

He hesitated, looked around, and then said, "Come on. I'll take you out and buy you a cup of coffee. I think everyone is listening around here."

"We're reporters," I explained. "That's what we do. We listen. But, sure coffee would be great."

I grabbed my purse, brushed the remaining doughnut and crumbs off my desk, and straightened some of the papers. I wanted to look organized. I think I failed.

We went to a nearby Starbucks and sat outside. I ordered my usual Mocha Frappuccino. Agent DeMarco had a coffee, black. What a man!

He looked at me for a few minutes and apparently decided to get to the point. "Ernest Ortega, the commissioner you almost took out single-handedly the other night, is missing. He cleared out yesterday."

"You said before that Georgy and Ortega had a fight. When?"

"Sunday night."

Hum, I thought. A new column is coming to mind. Now I need to look into Ernest Ortega's disappearance to see if it is connected to the bribery scandal and Georgy's murder. "Do you think he killed Georgy and ran?"

"Do you?" Coop replied.

"All I know is what was in Rick's article and my column today. Rick said his sources told him that no evidence was found at the scene. No witnesses. No clues. The bullet in Georgy was too damaged for a match later."

"Yeah, Metro's stumped."

"You said that Ortega 'cleared out.' What did you mean?"

"I mean Ortega packed and left his house. He's nowhere to be found."

"Is the FBI investigating Georgy's murder now that Ortega might be involved?"

"As it might relate to the political scandal. I'm looking under all the rocks. Right now, you're one of my rocks. I thought you might have uncovered something working on your column."

"I wish I had, but no. I still need to interview Pritchard, Kirkoff, and Angelo. I'll probably meet with Rodriquez and Mrs. Ortega also. I'm still reporting on the bribery scandal, but I'll be covering Georgy's murder also."

"I'd feel better if you weren't involved."

"You might feel better, but I'd be out of a job. Say, have you found another informant yet for the bribery scandal?"

He didn't answer.

We had thrown away our empty cups and headed to our cars.

We stalled for a while at mine.

"I'll probably be stopping by to see you with more questions." He gave me a very suggestive smile and leaned in a little close for FBI agent to columnist. I could feel the chemistry between us. It was powerful, magnetic, and instinctual. Maybe I was in heat, and he was drawn to me like a savage beast. Or, maybe, he hadn't had sex for a while either.

"That's great," I responded," because I'll be thinking of some terrific answers." I gave him my best come hither look.

"Are you always this way?" he asked.

"What way?" I slipped into my car. I might have winked at him.

"You know. See ya."

In the car I was whistling. If he didn't ask me out on a date, I was losing my touch.

Chapter 9

I returned to the office to find Rick at his desk. "Hi," he said. "Monroe says the cops took you out of here in handcuffs. What's the charge this time?"

I ignored the slam. "No charge," I sat on the edge of his desk, happy that I had worn a short skirt this time. "I just had coffee with Coop DeMarco, the FBI agent working undercover."

"That's interesting. He probably would have been safer just handcuffing you."

I ignored the slam again, struck by my maturity. "He told me that Ernest Ortega disappeared yesterday. Georgy and Ortega had a fight the night Georgy was killed and before Ortega disappeared."

"I'll talk to my friend at Metro again. I'm going to owe him a lot of doughnuts. This story is getting sticky," Rick said. "Garbarino dead, Ortega missing, and county commissioners facing charges. What's the FBI's case with its star witness dead?"

"I don't know. I can't get DeMarco to talk, but I'll keep working on him." I smiled my I'll-get-him-to-talk-or-my-name-isn't-Maggie-Hall smile.

Rick responded with "I'm betting on you. Let's touch base later in the day."

"Fine. I'm going to see if anybody knows about the fight between Georgy and Ortega. I also need to arrange to meet with Ortega's wife, Raymond Angelo, Joann Kirkoff, and Bruce Pritchard."

"Good. Don't get into any fights today."

"You can trust me to be professional." Then, I sat there a few minutes lost in thought.

Finally, Rick said, "Stop staring at me. It makes me uncomfortable."

"I'm not staring at you."

"Yes, you are."

"Okay, I was, but I thought you had a little something on your face."

I gestured as if I were wiping something off my lip.

"Is it still there?" Rick asked, wiping his mouth.

"Yes, closer to your lip." I touched the right side of my lip.

"Did I get it now?"

"Oh, I can see now that it was just a shadow."

Rick frowned at me as I left, but I swayed my hips and looked around at him until he smiled.

I heard him mutter, "Childish," as I turned again to leave.

Rick needed information now if his follow-up story was to be in to-morrow's edition, but I could wait. My next column was due Thursday for Friday's paper.

As I walked away from Rick's desk, I was still flush with thoughts of Coop DeMarco and here I was hitting on Rick. Let's face it; I'm a slut.

Later I was working at my desk when a dark shadow fell across it. I looked up to see Monroe standing there. Uninvited, he took a seat.

"What do you need, Monroe?"

"Whatever happened to pleasant greetings between colleagues?"

"You've never been pleasant, Monroe."

"And you have?"

"I'm always nice. Get to your point."

"The office is taking bets," he said.

"How much do you want?" I reached into my purse. I was always up for a bet. And, in this office, we bet on everything. Once we bet on how long it would take Aunt Ann to make Uncle Dutch fire a new secretary. She was young, bouncy, hot, and flirtatious with Uncle Dutch. Monroe won the bet. She was fired one hour after Aunt Ann saw her. It took so long because Uncle Dutch was on the phone with someone else; so, Ann had to wait to get through to him.

"Nothing. I'm here to settle the bet."

"What's it on?" Now I was curious.

"Your sex life. We have two bets going. One is on how long it's been since you were laid, Hall. We have two months to two years. I'm the two years."

"Who took two months?" I asked. Wouldn't that be nice?

"Rachael, but she doesn't know you very well."

"What's the other bet?" After all, I was curious.

"How long it will be before you get laid again."

"Get lost Monroe before I tell my uncle."

"What do I care? He wouldn't fire me. I'm the best reporter he's got."

"No," I explained, "You're the sleaziest reporter he's got. Don't confuse the two."

Monroe walked away and yelled to everyone. "She won't say. We'll have to ask her mother." My mother wouldn't tell them. At least, I was pretty sure she wouldn't.

Just then my cell phone rang. It was Rita. She sounded upset and told me to meet her at Panera's.

As I was leaving the office to meet Rita, all the reporters were hanging their heads and not looking at me. I could tell they were smiling, though. They were enjoying the new bets. You'd think reporters would have something better to do, like telling the world about some tyrannical dictator and his plot to seize the government or a guy who just lifted a banana at the local grocery story.

≔≕

On my way to Panera's I called Uncle Dutch."How did you like my revised column?"

"Don't fish for compliments. It's unbecoming. But, if you must know, it was good. What angle are you working on now?"

"Well, I just learned that Ernest Ortega has been missing since yesterday. He's now my number one suspect for Georgy's murder. I'm going to talk to Rita to see if she knows anything about a fight between Ortega and Georgy. I need to keep pursuing the connection between the bribery scandal, Georgy's murder, and Ortega's disappearance. I think it's likely they are all linked. I need to see Mrs. Ortega, Pritchard, Angelo, and Kirkoff soon."

"Are you working with Steele on this?" he asked.

"Yes, and I want to thank you for that, Uncle Dutch."

"Maggie?"

"What, Uncle Dutch?"

"Never mind. It wouldn't do any good." I loved to throw Uncle

Dutch off his game.

"Yes, Steele and I have been exchanging information. By the way, do you think I'm underpaid?"

"No, honey. I think you're overpaid."

See, I told you he was cheap. "We'll talk about this later, Uncle Dutch."

I could hear him sigh. "I look forward to it. Bye."

I, then, called Brian in research at the *Gazette*. Brian was kind of a geeky guy who sat at a computer all day surrounded by reference books, old newspapers, and any other information he could get his hands on. His job was to keep us accurate. It was a formidable job.

"Hi, Brian. It's Maggie."

"Hi, Mags. It's always great to hear from you." Brian meant it. He was 24 and had a crush on me. You know, the older woman thing.

"Brian, I need some information, and I need it quickly."

"Let me have it, Doll."

"Doll? Have you been reading Mickey Spillane mysteries again, Brian?"

"He's my favorite author."

"I need to know Ernest Ortega's wife's name, address, and phone number. Ortega's a county commissioner. Then, I also need addresses and phone numbers for Bruce Pritchard and Raymond Angelo, ex-commissioners, and Joann Kirkoff, a current commissioner. Get the office number for John Barber, assistant district attorney. That's it."

"I'll get back to you soon. In fact, I'll drop what I'm doing and work on your stuff. Should we meet for coffee or a drink when I get the information?"

"No, Brian. Just give me a call."

"Just so you know, Maggie. I'm not in on the office bets, but I could help you break your dry spell."

"Brian, that's disgusting. I'm almost old enough to be your mother."

"My mother doesn't look like you. If she did, I guess I'd have a serious Oedipal Complex."

"This conversation is over, Brian. Talk to you later."

Chapter 10

I got to Panera's before Rita so I ordered two iced teas. Another frozen mocha today would have been too much. I could pinch an inch of fat at my waist.

Rita came rushing in, and for Rita she looked bad. Only half of the guys turned around to stare at her. She was wearing jeans and an off-the-shoulder white blouse. Her shoes were white beaded slip-ons with a small heel. Rita's hair was hardly combed and it was pulled back in a ponytail. She was wearing no makeup and looked as if she had been crying.

She sat down, flung her large Dooney and Burke purse on the table, and took a long swig from her iced tea before sitting back in her chair. Rita can be dramatic, probably a direct result of dancing on stage for so many years.

"It was awful," she said. "They came to the house, a well-built, good looking guy with dark hair wearing jeans and this tight black t-shirt and this other guy who looked like an accountant. They asked me to go to their office for questioning. Oh, the well-built guy was the same one that was supposedly working for Metro and being paid off by Georgy. That was a big mistake on Georgy's part. Anyway, I had to go to head-quarters with them. If you don't go, you look guilty."

"Are you guilty of something?"

When I asked that, Rita gave me a really nasty look. It was the same look she gave Marianne Martin in high school just before decking her with one punch. Marianne deserved it. She had gone out with Rita's boyfriend. What was she thinking?

"Do you think I'm guilty of something?" she snapped at me.

"Of course you're not," I said quickly. After all, she was my best friend, and I didn't want to end up on the floor like Marianne Martin.

"You're right! I'm not, but I don't want to look guilty either. They're investigating Georgy's murder and his bribing those commissioners.

And now, Ernest Ortega has disappeared. They asked me what I knew about it all. You know I've never so much as walked on grass if the sign says 'Do not walk on the grass.' Do you think they think I'm involved in all this?" She finally took a breath and another drink of her iced tea.

"I think they're just fishing for information, Rita. They probably think that because you work at La Tigra you might know something. By the way, I just found out that Georgy and Ortega had a fight before Georgy was murdered. Do you know anything about that?"

"Only what I told that good looking FBI guy, Coop something."

"DeMarco," I filled in.

"Hum," Rita gave me an inquisitive look. "Boy, was he good looking. I was too upset to get his full name. Anyway, I heard about the fight from Rhonda because I wasn't there. After the cops left Sunday night, Ortega came back to the club."

Rita could see my grimace. "Sorry, Maggie. I didn't mean to bring up a sore point. Anyway, somehow Ortega hadn't been arrested. He probably bribed a cop. Rhonda saw Ortega storming out of Georgy's office. He didn't look happy. She said he was a little roughed up. His clothes were disheveled and his skin was splotchy by his jaw. Like he'd been punched."

She paused here to tap her finger on her jaw. "Jaime Rodriquez was right behind him, and they stopped to talk in the hallway for a few minutes. Then, Ortega left. Rhonda couldn't hear what Ortega was saying to Jaime because she wasn't close enough, but Ortega was using a lot of hand gestures."

"Tell me about Ortega. Was he at the club a lot? We obviously saw him there Sunday night."

"Yeah, he was there a lot, always with one or another of the girls. Of course, Ray was at the club all the time, too. Georgy kept them both well supplied with girls and booze."

"I think I'll go in and talk to Rodriquez after we leave here. By the way, Rita, leave the good-looking FBI guy alone. I saw him first."

"When did you see him?"

"Monday morning. Actually, I saw him the other night at La Tigra, but that doesn't count because I didn't meet him and I couldn't see him very well."

"Okay," she said. "That beats me. I didn't meet him until early this morning. He's all yours. How about Rick?"

"No, leave him alone, too."

"That's not fair, Maggie. You can't have both."

"Well, I haven't decided who's the man for me yet. They may have to fight a duel. So, we'll see who's left standing. You can have the fallen knight."

"Thanks. You're very generous. But, I'm putting you on a time schedule. If you don't decide soon, I'll go after one of them."

Rita's such a good sport.

"By the way," asked Rita, "what did the FBI want with you?"

I told her about my two conversations with Coop. Now she was really upset when she found out that the FBI had been watching her.

We left Panera's saying that we'd talk to each other soon and reminding each other that we had spa time coming up.

₭ℂ

Once in my car, I prepared myself to call Brian at the *Gazette* again.

"Hi, Doll. Whatcha need?"

"Hi, Brian. I need a home address and home and work phone numbers for Jaime Rodriquez, the assistant manager at La Tigra." When he pulled it up, I told him to text it to me. "Do you have the other information I asked for?"

"Not yet."

Then, he was strangely silent.

"What's going on, Brian?"

"Why, what do you mean, Mags?"

"No flirting; no planned trysts, no sexual innuendoes?"

"I'm playing hard to get. Is it working?"

"No, but it does make me curious."

"Okay, then, it might be working a little bit. I'll keep it up, unless it doesn't work and then I'll just have to meet with you so I can see your legs or hold your hand or …"

"Enough, Brian," I interrupted. "I've got the idea. But I think the playing hard to get thing might work. So, just keep it up. Bye."

Using the numbers that Brian gave me, I called Rodriquez, but he didn't answer at home or the club. I really needed to talk to him so I called Mr. Garbarino on his cell.

"Can you help me get in touch with Rodriquez, Mr. Garbarino?"

"What do you need him for, Maggie?"

"I heard that George and Ernest Ortega had a fight the night of George's murder and that Rodriquez was in the room at the time. I'd like to talk to him about it."

"Sure, I'll make certain he calls you, Maggie."

A few minutes after I hung up with Mr. Garbarino, Rodriquez called me. I told you. Old connections are important in Las Vegas. He agreed to see me as soon as I could get to La Tigra.

Chapter 11

I pulled away from the curb where I had been sitting making my phone calls. While I am a good multi-tasker, it doesn't pay to drive and talk on the phone if you can help it.

When I arrived to meet with Rodriquez, the club was still closed. I had to bang on the door this time.

The male bartender greeted me as if we were old friends. I guess we were. He had seen more of me than some of my dates had. Jaime was in his office and told the bartender to let me come into the back. A man I thought I recognized let me into the hallway. Then, I placed him. He was one of the bouncers the night of the fight.

"Expecting trouble?" I asked.

"You never know," he said. He was a big guy, but he looked as if he might be putting down too many pancakes.

"It's nice to see you again." I figured I might as well be friendly. After all, a fight could break out here at anytime, and I might need his help. It pays to stay on the good side of the security guys.

"Yeah, nice to see you, too." I'm not sure he was sincere.

He stopped in front of an office door and knocked. "Jaime," he yelled in, "the reporter broad is here."

"Send her in," Jaime called back.

I looked at the bouncer guy. "You know, it's not nice nowadays to call a woman 'a broad.'"

"Yeah? I didn't know that."

He opened the door and motioned for me to go into the office. Well, I hoped I had given him a helpful social pointer.

"Bye," I said. "See you around."

He didn't look particularly happy to hear that.

I walked into Jaime's office and introduced myself.

"I know who you are," Rodriquez said. "I've read your column."

It was nice to hear that my column had broad-base appeal. Rodriquez was pouring himself a drink and asked if I wanted one.

"No, thanks."

I told him I was investigating the bribery scandal that Georgy had been talking to the FBI about before he was killed. I added that now I was looking into Georgy's murder and Ortega's disappearance, too.

"Did you know about Georgy's payoffs to county commissioners?" I asked.

"No, I understand that most of that went on before I came here."

"Did you know that Raymond Angelo was Georgy's go-between?"

"I saw him in the club a lot. I told you that I didn't know about the bribes. I help manage the club. That's all."

"Do you think that there is a connection between Georgy's murder and his talking to the FBI about the bribes? After all, Ortega, Kirkoff, Angelo, and Pritchard would have been angry. Their reputations, to say nothing of jail time, were at stake."

"I don't know."

"Do you know of anyone else who might have had it in for Georgy?"

"No."

"What about Ortega's disappearance? Isn't it a little coincidental?"

Rodriquez didn't have a chance to answer because just then a stripper came in without knocking and interrupted us. I knew she was a stripper because she was missing most of her clothes. In fact, I wear more clothes when I take a shower.

"Jaime, I need…" she started to say. When she saw me, she stopped. "Oh, hi. I didn't know you had company." She looked a little frazzled. She was fairly tall with a huge bosom, most of it showing. I'm a B cup; I think she's much farther along in the alphabet. She had long legs that I would kill for. Besides being indecent looking, though not for a stripper I suppose, she appeared tired and worn out. Dressed as she was, stacked as she was, and rough as she was, she still had a little girl look about her. Maybe it was her voice. Her voice reminded me of a five-year-old who wasn't getting her way. Her blonde hair was long and straight and pulled back into a ponytail. Her eyes were big but looked as if no one was home. I don't think she was a deep thinker, but maybe I'm stereotyping.

"I'm really busy right now, Laurie. Come back later." Rodriquez didn't sound too pleased.

"Sure," she said, backing out of the door, "but I gotta see you real soon, real soon."

"Sorry," he said to me. "The girls all come to me with every little problem. What can you do?" He shrugged as if he was resigned to being a big brother.

He didn't look the big brother type. Rodriquez was short, with dark slicked-back hair. He had a black mustache, and his eyes stood out behind thick, curly lashes. I read somewhere that Nevada produced more gold than any other state in the U.S. and was third in the world behind South Africa and Australia. If that's so, Jaime was decked out in most of Nevada's gold supply; it was around his neck, on his wrists, and on his fingers. I was reassessing my belief that you can never wear too much jewelry. His suit looked too shiny for a natural fiber.

"So, what about Ortega's disappearance?" I repeated, getting back to the interview.

"I don't know about Ortega's disappearance. But, I would think that scandal and murder are good motivators for running. But, I don't know."

"Do you know where he is?"

"How would I know where he is?"

"Tell me about the fight between Ortega and Georgy Sunday night?"

"I don't know about it."

"You were in the room with them. You must know."

He looked surprised that I knew he was in the room during the fight.

"It wasn't much. Ortega accused Mr. Garbarino of talking to the FBI. Mr. Garbarino told him to get out of his office. Ortega had a few choice words. Maybe some threats. He took a swing and missed. Mr. Garbarino decked him. I helped Ortega out of the office and out of the club."

"How did Ortega know about the investigation into the bribes and Georgy's talking to the FBI. I had a feeling he knew about it before I talked to him Sunday night."

"Are you implying that I told him? I said I'm not involved in any of this."

"I'm not implying anything. It just seems to me that an assistant manager should know a lot more than you seem to know." I think I need to work on my tact. The direct approach isn't always best when you try to wheedle information from someone.

Rodriquez started to get angry. "I'm through talking with you."

"Do you know anything about Ortega's disappearance?"

"I said I'm done talking to you. Talk to Commissioner Kirkoff. See if she knows where he is."

"Why Kirkoff?"

"Why not?" he said. By then, he had stood, walked around his desk, and taken my arm. He led me to the door, opened it, and pushed me through it. I guess our interview was done. Note to self: Jaime Rodriquez is a hot head.

Chapter 12

As I walked out to the parking lot to get into my '97 BMW, Coop was leaning up against it. His arms were crossed on his chest, and he had a scowl on his otherwise handsome face. When I saw him, my attraction was validated. He was a hunk.

"What are you doing here?" he asked. "Didn't you see enough action the other night?"

"I'm doing my job." I reminded him that I was a columnist. "I'm a pretty good one too. If you don't count that story I did when I first started. That was a disaster. I accused some guy of embezzling funds to pay off his gambling debts. Come to find out, his wife was the one with the gambling problem. She seemed so nice. He was just caught up in helping her. He really did embezzle funds, though. I was right about that. I think he really, truly loved her." Oops, he was getting that glazed look in his eyes again.

"Better yet, what are you doing here? Stalking me? That's illegal. What will they think down at FBI headquarters when I have to turn you in because you're having sexual fantasies about me?"

"Look, I told you," he said, ignoring my taunts. "I don't like what's happening here. One man's dead and another is missing. A number of people had a reason to want Garbarino dead, and Ortega's among them. He's on the run, but he's not leaving a trail to follow. Something's not right. Until we find him, you should be careful."

"La de da!" I batted my eyes. " I didn't know you cared."

"There's a lot you don't know about me." He reached over and opening my car door. I slid in, realizing he was way too close for comfort.

Some things I probably wouldn't want to know about Coop, I thought. "I'd like to remedy that. How am I going to get to know more about you?" That was a big enough hint for me to throw his way.

"Later." He'd almost closed the door when he hesitated and then leaned into the car. He was so close I was afraid he could hear my heart beating.

"How would you like to go for a ride tomorrow—in an effort to get to know me better? I just bought a sweet 2004 Sportster. I'd like to take it out."

"Sure," I replied quickly before he changed his mind. "It's not to the FBI office to be interrogated like my friend Rita, is it? I was just kidding about the stalking thing."

"No," he smiled. "We'll go out into the desert. A picnic. Dress for rough terrain."

"Sounds like fun." Do I look like an outdoor girl? If so, I need some serious spa treatments. "What time?"

"I'll pick you up at about 10:00 in the morning. I don't have to be to work until later in the afternoon. Where do you live?"

"Anthem Country Club. Just ask for the Hall's at the gate."

Before he closed my door, he said, "You bring the food."

He turned to leave before I could mention that I didn't cook. Oh, well. Lucky for me that Mom does. What a day! A hunk and a sports car. I was salivating already.

As I was driving home, my cell phone rang. "Maggie here."

"Hi, Mags. It's Brian."

"Hi, Bri," I pulled over to the side of the road so that we could talk.

"I've got your info. Are you sure we can't meet somewhere?"

"I'm sure, Brian. Stop trying to get me out. Like I said, I'm old enough to be your mother, at least, an older sister."

"I like older women. I want to be nurtured."

"I'm not the nurturing type. I'm more the kick you in your balls type."

"I can do that, too." Now he was begging.

"Brian, give me the stuff I asked for. Start texting now."

When I got home, I went to my desk and used the numbers Brian had given me to phone Pritchard, Kirkoff, Angelo, and Judith Ortega. Only Mrs. Ortega was home. I made an appointment with her for late tomorrow afternoon. She told me to call again ahead of time. I also made an appointment to meet with John Barber at his office.

⁍⁖

Later that night Kitty and I were sitting in the family room. Once Kitty started college and I became more involved in my job, we made sure that we spent at least one night each week doing something together. It didn't matter what it was as long as we did it together. Tonight we were waiting for Rita. She quit her job today, having found out that Jaime Rodriquez would be running the club. He wasn't her idea of a good boss. Rita was coming over for some TLC and female companionship. Our plan was to watch Bette Davis and Paul Henreid in *Now Voyager*, one of the great love stories of all times. Just the right movie when tragedy strikes. The doorbell rang and Rita stood there looking despondent.

"Hi," she mumbled and brushed past me.

She didn't wait for my response. She just walked into the room, gave Kitty a brief nod, and flopped down on the couch. She hadn't looked this sad since her divorce. Rita was briefly married to a guy who used her money to buy some van for a carpet cleaning business. Then, he just lay on the couch watching TV all the time. Rita finally figured out he really wasn't interested in running a business, and he was a bum. After she kicked him out, she enrolled at UNLV. While she was in school, she started stripping part time. It was a night job, and she needed the money for books and tuition. Those science books can be very costly.

Did you know I was in the carpet cleaning business? After Rita's separation and divorce, I used the van for a while to try out the carpet cleaning business. I discovered that too many homes were dirty and downright nasty. Besides, I didn't much like manual labor.

The three of us ate popcorn as Paul Henreid put two cigarettes in his mouth. He lighted both and handed one to Bette. He kept the other cigarette dangling seductively off his lips. I melted. I might have to start smoking. We cried because Bette and Paul could never be together, shot down all men except Paul Henreid, and all-around had a good time for the rest of the evening.

When the movie was over, Rita wiped her eyes and said, "I needed that. Where's Angela, by the way?"

As if on cue, Mom came in from her studio. She had washed up, but clay still clung to her arms and a few places on her face. She greeted Rita warmly. Mom always liked Rita. "How's your Mom and Dad?" She remained standing while she quizzed Rita because she didn't want to get the furniture dirty with her clothes.

"Fine. They just got back from a cruise."

"Do they still love that house I found for them?"

"They sure do. Mom's in a furniture shopping frenzy. She's going room by room. Dad just keeps shutting himself in his study, refiguring the bills."

"If your mom needs a shopping buddy, I'm available. I've cut back my hours at the office. And, you know how I love to shop."

"I'll let her know, Mrs. H. I think she'd like some company."

"What was it tonight, girls? *Gone with the Wind; Now, Voyager;* or *Casablanca?*"

We said in unison, "*Now, Voyager.*"

"Perfect," she said.

Then, it came. We didn't have to wait too long. "I'm so happy you aren't taking off your clothes at that horrible club anymore, Rita? I know you're out of a job but that wasn't much of a job."

"Yes, Mrs. H, I'm out of a job." Rita was never offended by my mother's direct approach. She was probably afraid that Mom would stop cooking gourmet meals and inviting her over.

"Why don't you get your real estate license and come to work for my friend Suzie. You meet nicer men in the real estate business, dear." Mom had been trying to get Rita out of stripping for years.

"I've been thinking about it."

"Have you really?" I asked. This was the first I had heard, and I'm her best friend.

"Yes, I have," said Rita. "I won't work for Jaime Rodriquez, and I don't care for any of the other club managers. This whole scandal and murder and my being hauled in by the FBI is too much. Anyway, the glamour's gone."

"First of all, you weren't hauled in by the FBI." I needed to give Rita a reality check.

"It was a small exaggeration, but you know what I mean."

"And, you never found stripping glamorous."

"Oh, that's right. I was in it for the money. I forgot. I thought I liked the sleazy clothes and gaudy jewelry."

"Well, I guess there were some perks," I said.

Before Rita left, Kitty got up and gave her a big hug and reminded her that life would get better. The young are so optimistic. I reminded her that she had a large savings account, parents that she could move in with if things got bad, and the brains to find a new job. I'm sure Rita was happy that she came over to our house for comfort.

Chapter 13

Kitty answered the door when Coop came to the house the next morning. Mom was waiting for him in the living room also, along with Margaret. It's a big deal around here when a man comes calling for me. I should have been dressed earlier, but I was too busy finding just the right shade of lipstick. Fool!

By the time I reached the upstairs landing, it was apparent that Mom had been grilling Coop. She had probably already covered family history, heritage, jobs, and income. Now, she was asking him what kind of house he lived in. That was the real test question.

"I bought one of those custom houses off Pecos. It's older and badly in need of repair; so, I got it for a good price. I've slowly been doing the work on it myself. It takes a long time, though."

Wow! He passed several tests at once. He got a good deal on a house, and he can do his own renovation work.

Kitty was most concerned about the nature of his job with the FBI. Did he carry a gun? Had he ever used the gun? Did he travel much? It's no wonder I never have a date.

"Hi," I said cheerfully, running down the stairs to save whatever chance I had.

"Hi yourself." He turned around to face me and was about to smile when he looked at my clothes. He shook his head. "You can't go out in those clothes."

"Why not? This is a great outfit." I had on these cute yellow plaid shorts with a skimpy top and sandals that tied around my ankles. Mom, Kitty, and Margaret agreed that the outfit was great. What was Coop's problem?

"Well, for starters, we're going to be walking in the desert. And for another thing, I don't think you'll be very comfortable on the bike dressed that way. So I'd say you need long pants, a t-shirt, and much better shoes. Socks would be good, too. Don't forget sunscreen."

I noticed he had on jeans and a t-shirt again. He was wearing old, worn hiking boots. I guess he did this outdoors thing frequently. Suddenly, what he said dawned on me. "Did you say, 'bike'?"

"Yes, bike."

"The big kind? With an engine?"

"That's the one."

"You said sports car. You said we were going for a ride in your sports car."

"No, I said we were going for a ride on my Sportster, my Harley 1200 Custom Sportster XL. It's a beauty."

Mom, Kitty, and Margaret all smiled sadistically. They were picturing me on the back of Coop's motorcycle riding through the desert. I was picturing me in the hospital.

"I'll be back." I looked at the four of them and raced upstairs because Coop seemed a little concerned about being left alone in the room with the three furies. Come to think of it, he might have been a little shocked, too, since I had forgotten to tell him about Kitty.

When I got back downstairs, he immediately jumped up to go. When we walked outside, any doubt I had disappeared; he wasn't lying. A bike was parked in front of the house. It was big and black and red; it looked powerful and mean.

"Put this on." Coop handed me a black helmet.

Oh, great. There goes the hairdo I'd worked on all morning. "I've never been on one of these."

"I can tell. Nothing to it. Just hold on tight." Then, he showed me where to put my feet.

By the time we left the house, it was closer to 10:45, and I was scared. We drove up to the Mount Charleston area and then took some dirt road off the main highway. I spent most of the time sucking in dust, dodging bugs, and holding on. The holding on part was just fine. He had great abdominal muscles, firm to the touch. Every once in a while, I touched the hard thickness on his chest, arms, and shoulders just for fun. As I was getting used to caressing his body in the name of bike safety, we stopped.

"What happened?" I asked. "Is something wrong with the bike?"

"No. Now we hike."

"Great." I tried out my most sincere smile. I looked around and didn't see a path, just cactus and lots of prickly looking bushes and plants. "Where's the trail?" I asked.

He smiled as if I had told a joke. "No trail. We'll just go hike that ravine."

"Great," I said again. "Do you do this often?"

"Whenever I can. I saw this canyon when I was on the road a few weeks ago and wanted to explore it." He grabbed a pack from the bike and the basket with our lunch. We headed out. I can only guess what is in the backpack. K-rations, snakebite oil, flares, first-aid kit, hemlock in case we get lost and never found.

We hiked for what seemed like an hour; okay, it might have been a half hour or even fifteen minutes. Then, Coop stopped, put down his bag, and opened it. He took out a large old blanket and spread it on the ground. With an exaggerated gesture, he indicated that I should sit down. Which I did. I had earned it.

He grabbed the picnic basket and asked, "What's in here?"

"Let's open it and see," I responded with my raised, inquisitive eyebrows and a perky smile. I didn't want him to know I would be as surprised as he was.

Then, he opened the basket and took out two wine glasses, small plates, thermoses, and croissants. In a plastic container was Mom's curried chicken salad.

"Great!" I exclaimed. I tried to cover my surprise, which surely gave away the fact that I hadn't cooked or packed the lunch, with "I'm happy it's still fresh."

I put one croissant on each plate, slathering it with chicken salad. Coop poured the coffee for both of us and a mimosa for me. I supposed he was the designated biker and was abstaining.

"I just love roughing it in the dessert," I said. "Do you do this elegant picnic thing often, too?"

"No, I'm out of town a lot; and when I do get on my bike, I usually keep riding. You don't seem like the biker babe type, though."

"Thank goodness. I was starting to worry about my image."

"Don't worry. Your image is in tact."

"Now what image is that?" I asked.

"You know. Hard hitting, heavy drinking, verbally meandering, highly sexed journalist."

"Really? Good. That's what I was going for. And, what's your image?"

"Good looking, well-endowed, powerful, highly professional FBI agent."

"You don't think much of yourself, do you?"

"I thought we were here so you could get to know me better. I just wanted to fill you in on the important facts."

I asked, "Why are you out of town so much?"

"My job."

"Where do you go?"

"If I told you, I'd have to kill you."

We sat for some time eating our sandwiches and drinking our coffee. I gave Coop my history about Kitty. He talked a bit about life in the FBI.

I managed to slip in a few questions about Georgy's murder and the bribery investigation. "How are you going to prove your case with Georgy dead?"

"I guess I'll have to find someone else to talk."

"Anyone in mind yet?" I questioned."

"No one you need bother your pretty little head about." He grinned, obviously happy with his sexist comment.

In between getting each other's life histories and my asking probing questions, I was giving him my most alluring smile, looking into his eyes longingly, and swirling my mimosa in the glass as seductively as I could. Finally, gaining my courage, I asked him when he thought I might get to know him better as promised.

"Now," he said, pulling me over to him and kissing me—long and hard with a lot of tongue. He continued to pull me closer until our bodies were touching, and we were lying on the blanket holding onto each other. The heat was starting to get to me, and it wasn't coming from the desert sun. After all, we were in the shade. Coop rolled over onto me and pushed my legs open with his one knee. He was looking directly into my eyes while starting to unzip my jeans, and I was just getting ready for more fun on the blanket when I heard a cell phone ring."

His hand stopped where it was, and we reluctantly let go of one another. It wasn't my ring.

"Damn!" He answered his phone and said gruffly, "Coop." Then, he nodded his head a lot and said "Uh huh" frequently. Finally, I heard, "Okay. I'm on my way."

"What?" I asked.

"Business." I could tell I wasn't going to get more detail. "I'll be gone for a day or two," he explained.

"Are you emotionally available?" I asked while we gathered up what was left of our picnic.

"What's that mean?"

"I don't know. I read it in a magazine."

"What magazine?"

"Cosmo."

"Start reading other magazines."

"Is that your answer?"

"Yep. That's my answer."

We got on the bike and bumped along the dusty road again, and Coop took me home. He walked me up to the door and flung an arm around my hips, drawing me in tight. His other arm leaned against the door and above my head. Smoothly, his hand slid from near my waist and trailed under my shirt, pushing my bra up. He cupped my breast and squeezed, warming me instantly. As I moaned shamelessly, he bent down to kiss my nipple. Then, he raised his head and pressed his lips to my mouth. I parted my lips letting his tongue come in. I was thrusting into his groin, and I could tell he liked it.

"Stop," he said, gripping me by my shoulders. "I really need to find more time off work."

"No argument here. I wish you'd finish what you start."

He laughed. "Be careful what you wish for."

Chapter 14

When I went inside, I decided that I'd better get to my work today, too. So, after showering and changing clothes, I called Judith Ortega, Ernest's wife, and asked her if we were still on for later this afternoon. She said, "Yes," and we firmed up the time.

"I read your column all the time," she said on the phone. "I really liked the series you did about street walkers on the strip. What was it called?"

She had a distinctive Southern drawl, dragging her words out slowly. That series was called *Pussy Galore*. I could tell Judith had good taste in reading material. It was an in-depth series about the underworld of Las Vegas.

Judith said she wasn't doing anything later this afternoon; so, she would prepare afternoon tea for us. Oh, boy, tea with a real Southern lady. If it weren't for the fact that her husband was missing and I was trying to get her to confess that he took bribes and murdered Georgy, this could be a terrific visit.

Knowing that Judith was serving tea, I changed clothes one more time. For the occasion, I wore a short, straight khaki skirt, a crème-colored, silk halter-top, my brown lightweight blazer, and tan "sensible" heels.

Ernest and Judith lived in the northwest part of the valley off Cheyenne. So, I drove down Eastern and got onto 215. The drive took longer than expected because I ran into some traffic. I exited on Cheyenne and headed further west, surprised to see all the new homes having been built. A few years ago nothing but cactus and yucca grew here. Every so often I had to dodge orange cones, which were slowing the cars down. With all the people moving into Las Vegas, over 6,000 each month for years now, the impact on roads and construction is enormous. Road construction and repair are so extensive that orange road cones should be the state flower. They're pervasive, drought tolerant, and colorful.

Judith met me at the door when I drove up. She took me into the living room. The house was elaborately decorated, but a little fussy for my taste. Two couches faced each other in front of the fireplace and were covered in peach flowered fabric. The drapes were in the same fabric while the chairs in the room were a complimentary stripe. The rug was a soft, thick oriental.

Judith is average height. She looks like a Southern belle and speaks with that soft, lazy-sounding drawl. Her hair is blonde, short, and swept back from her face. I think she is probably ten to fifteen years older than I am. She wore a straight black skirt with a white blouse. I think I saw the same skirt in Neiman's. Very pricey. The collar of the blouse was turned up in the back and accentuated her long neck. Her earrings were big diamonds… big, big diamonds. Around her neck was a gold chain with a diamond enhancer. I wondered if her stones had been purchased with ill-gotten gain. She was wearing black pumps. What a lady!

Her eyes were red and swollen. I guessed she had been crying a lot.

When we sat down, she offered me tea and these cute little sandwiches. She said some were cream cheese and cucumber; others were cream cheese, carrots, and ginger; and some salmon salad. *Petit fours* were on the plate also. What a great food day this was turning out to be.

I told her I would try one of each. After all, they were so small.

While explaining to Judith that I was doing a column on the investigation into George Garbarino's bribery of county commissioners Bruce Pritchard, Joann Kirkoff, Raymond Angelo, and her husband, I also slipped in that I was looking into George Garbarino's murder and her husband's disappearance. I tried to sound sympathetic about any role her husband might have had in all the incidents. I don't know if I pulled it off.

She admitted she had seen my column the other day. "I don't know what else I can tell y'all. I really didn't know what was going on until Ernest disappeared. Then, the FBI came and started questioning me about Ernest and his relationship with Mr. Garbarino."

"Did you know George Garbarino?" I asked, stuffing a small cucumber sandwich into my mouth.

"Dear, me, no! I belong to Junior League, for heaven's sake. It's not as if we run in the same social circles."

"Did you know that your husband was taking bribes from anyone? Perhaps, Raymond Angelo?" I paused to stuff a salmon salad sandwich in my mouth and lick my fingers.

"Well, I knew Raymond, of course, because he was a commissioner also. He seemed like such a nice man, too. In fact, we had gatherings for Raymond, Joann, Bruce, and the others while they were all on the commission. Once, we had this Hawaiian luau where we roasted a pig in a pit in the ground out back. We even had a small group playing Hawaiian music. It was quite lovely, but I didn't know anything about any bribes."

"Did Raymond and your husband appear to be close?"

"Not any closer than any of the other commissioners."

"Did you notice any extra money coming in?"

"Oh, my, no. But, I wouldn't. I never handled the finances."

"Do you think that your husband's disappearance is related to the bribery investigation or to George Garbarino's murder? Or, can you think of any other explanation for his disappearance?"

"I can't say Ernest has been happy as a commissioner. The job is so stressful; but after the last election, life seemed a little calmer. Then, the last few weeks, Ernie has been upset about something. He's been on the phone all the time. And, he goes into his study to talk. He never talks out here where I can hear him."

"Who was calling him?"

"I only knew who was calling if I answered the phone first. Raymond called sometimes. And someone named Johnnie or …no… Jamie I think. Ernie talked to Bruce Pritchard also. Once they got into a terrible argument on the phone. Lots of yelling. I could hear Ernie's voice out here. That was a while back, though."

Johnny or Jamie could have been Jaime Rodriquez at La Tigra, I thought. It was likely that Ortega told the other commissioners that Georgy was cooperating with the FBI. That means they all had knowledge of Georgy's activities and had motivation to want him dead. But to the best of my knowledge, other than Ortega, there were no missing commissioners. Hence, he still remained the best suspect in Georgy's murder.

"When did Raymond call?" I asked.

"The last time he called was the morning that Ernest disappeared. Let me think. Yes, that's right. I was about to go to the salon for my weekly nail appointment when the phone rang. I answered it, and Ray Angelo was on the line. He asked for Ernie. Ernest was still on the phone talking to him when I left for my appointment. They seemed to be arguing, but I couldn't really hear very well."

"When did you realize your husband was missing?" I asked.

"When I got back from the salon, Ernie was not at home. I didn't think anything about it at the time; but when he didn't come back by dinner and he didn't call, I began to worry. I kept leaving messages on his cell phone, but he didn't return my calls. I called Metro later that evening. They asked if clothes or anything else was missing. That's when I went upstairs and checked his closet. Most of his clothes were gone. And, all of the suitcases were gone. We had two big ones and a few smaller bags." She pulled a handkerchief out of her sleeve and dabbed at her eyes. I hadn't seen a handkerchief since my Grandma's.

"Was anything else missing?"

"When the FBI found out that perhaps Ernie was gone, they asked me about money; and sure enough when I checked, our bank accounts were empty. I also checked to see if our gun was gone. It was. Ernest bought that gun because there had been a couple of home invasions in the valley this year. He said it would make us safer. Personally, I thought the burglar alarm was all we needed."

"What kind of gun did you have?"

"I don't know anything about guns. I have the receipt, though. That's what I had to show the police and FBI. I'll get it if you would like to see it."

"That would be great." While Judith was out of the room, I took the opportunity to dive into the plate of tea sandwiches and *petit fours*.

Judith showed me a receipt for a Smith and Wesson 9mm semiautomatic pistol.

"Why did Pritchard and your husband argue on the phone?" I asked.

"I don't know. I couldn't hear them, and Ernie wouldn't tell me."

"What was his conversation with Raymond about?"

"Again, I couldn't hear Ernest well enough to tell, sugar."

"What do you think happened to your husband?"

"If you ask me, I think someone came into the house, Ernie got the gun out, the intruder took the gun away from him, and then kidnapped him. Maybe it's the same person who killed Mr. Garbarino."

"Why would someone want to kidnap him?"

"Because of the ransom, maybe because Ernie knew something about who killed Mr. Garbarino, or maybe because someone is upset about a decision he made on the commission?"

"Why would your bank accounts be empty then?" I asked, puzzled with her thinking.

"Well don't you see, they made him withdraw everything from the bank. It happens. I've seen it on the television."

Hum, I thought. "But would they have made him take his clothes?"

"They probably did that to throw off the police."

I thought it was a bit of a stretch, but apparently she needed to believe this. Despite what Judith thought, the FBI investigation and Georgy's murder seemed the most likely reasons for Ortega to leave. And, he had a gun that he took with him. I was curious, though, about Raymond being the last person to speak to Ortega and their argument, about why Jaime would call him at home, and about his argument with Pritchard.

"Ernie loved me, you know, sugar. We had our rough times, but things were better, and he loved me. He wouldn't just leave. Even if he was in trouble, he wouldn't just leave." The handkerchief came out again.

I didn't want to tell her that it happens all the time. I also didn't want to tell her that her husband was scum. Judith was a little haughty, but I liked her.

When I left Judith's place, having eaten all of the little sandwiches and most of the cakes, I drove to John Barber's office.

ℴℴ

I made it just in time for my interview with Barber. A busy secretary waved me into John's office, never looking up from her computer while she pushed an intercom button. I gave my hair a flip and bounced into his office all perky-like. My smile was meant to be disarming.

These were good moves for a columnist on the trail of a hot story.

John stood up, came around his desk, and put out his hand. "Nice to see you again, Maggie. I understand you want to talk to me about George Garbarino and Ernest Ortega."

John looked at his watch. Since I'm a great study of human nature, this gesture indicated to me that this meeting would be short.

"Yes, I have a few questions since you seemed to know both of them well and you were one of the last people to see Ortega before he left town. Also, you were one of the last people to see George Garbarino alive." I took out my notebook and pen, giving that professional newspaper reporter appearance. I hoped I would have something to write.

"You were one of the last to see both of them, too," he reminded me. "About Ernest Ortega, I wouldn't say I knew him well; and, if you remember, I left La Tigra before you did. By the way, I hear you got into a fight after I left." He smiled in that I-told-you-so way.

"You could say that." I didn't elaborate. "Why were you with Ortega that night?"

"As I said, I came by to see George and on my way out stopped for a drink with Ernie."

"Being an assistant district attorney and hanging out at La Tigra isn't a good idea, is it?"

"My work takes me to strange places."

"Oh, were you working a case?"

"I can't really say, Maggie."

"On a couple of occasions that night, Ortega implied you might be involved or that you knew something about the zoning scandal."

"Ernie was drunk, remember. I wish I could give you something for your column, Maggie, but anything I know is confidential for now."

"Did Ortega tell you he was leaving town?"

"No, he didn't say a thing."

"What did you see Georgy about?"

"That's confidential and deals with a case I'm working on."

"Do you know anyone who would want to see Georgy dead?"

"No, no, I don't." John stood and extended his hand again. When I took it, I noticed it was sweaty this time. He apologized one more time for not being able to share any valuable information.

I got nothing useful from John Barber to put in my notebook. I drove to the office because I needed to talk to Rick. I tried Ray Angelo again and got him at home finally. We set an appointment for tomorrow.

Chapter 15

When I got to the office, I went in search of Rick. I found him in his cubicle. He was working at his computer. I sat in the chair across from his desk and crossed my legs. Boy, was I glad that I wore my short khaki skirt. The heels could have been a little higher for maximum effect, but you work with what you've got.

"My friend at Metro is involved in the disappearance case," he said, looking up from his computer. "He said Ortega took money out of his accounts at the bank on Monday. The police are examining surveillance camera footage."

"Could they tell it was definitely Ortega?"

"Yes. And, apparently, the clerk at the bank also knows him."

"Was anyone else lurking about?"

"Why do you ask?"

"Judith Ortega has a scenario."

"What's Judith's take on all this?"

"She thinks hubby was kidnapped."

"Really?"

"Really. She said Ernest Ortega truly loved her. I guess we knew him better than she did. Anyway, if he was kidnapped, someone would have been with him at the bank."

"No one shows on the tape, and the clerk didn't notice anything strange."

"So, Judith Ortega's rather far-fetched explanation is not looking too good. I don't think Ortega was kidnapped."

"I think that's a pretty sound conclusion, as conclusions go."

"Have they found out where Ortega is?" I asked.

"No. My source said they haven't found a trace. And, that's strange. No evidence he used credit cards, no bookings on an airline or bus. He hasn't rented a room, at least with his name. And, his car hasn't shown up anywhere."

"What about friends? Have they been contacted?"

"Yes, the police are going down a list of friends and acquaintances, but no luck there. No one admits to knowing anything about his leaving or where he is. He's vanished. What about you?"

"When I spoke to Judith this morning, she claimed she doesn't know George Garbarino, and she doesn't know about any bribes from Raymond Angelo."

"She doesn't know anything about the money?"

"She says she doesn't, sugar." I was trying out Judith's Southern drawl.

"Do you believe her?" Rick looked at me strangely. Perhaps my drawl was having an effect.

"I don't know. It's possible. She is this haughty, but charming Southern belle. We even had little tea sandwiches and *petit fours*. She did say that Ortega was showing signs of stress the last few weeks. A while back Bruce Pritchard and Ortega argued on the phone."

"What about?"

"I don't know." I explained, "Judith couldn't hear the conversation. Raymond Angelo was possibly the last person to speak to Ortega, and they had a disagreement on the phone. Again, though, Judith couldn't hear the conversation."

"Ortega must have spent a lot of time on the phone."

"Oh, and Jaime Rodriquez probably called the house."

"What would he want with Ortega?"

"I don't know. Judith wasn't even certain it was Rodriquez. She told me that Ortega's clothes are gone, along with the suitcases. They also have a Smith and Wesson pistol that's missing."

"That's interesting. What did you find out about Garbarino's fight with Ortega?"

"He and Ortega did have a fight in Garbarino's office. Ortega knew that Georgy was talking to the FBI."

"That's enough to make somebody mad."

"Yeah, I guess Ortega took a swing and missed; so, Georgy cold cocked him.

Rick's eyes kept going to my legs throughout our conversation and it was getting distracting.

"You like my legs?" I asked, as I crossed them again and hiked my skirt up a little. I'm shameless.

"Why do you ask? Fishing for compliments?"

"No, you keep staring at them. Well, actually, more leering."

"You have great legs."

"But we still won't ever go out?"

"I'm not a leg man."

"Then, why do you keep staring at them?" I was swinging my crossed leg very enticingly, I thought.

"I'm learning to appreciate new things." He shot me a winning smile.

Just when Rick was getting interesting, Uncle Dutch walked in.

"Hey, you two," he said. "Working on the Garbarino murder and the commissioner's disappearance? I love it when my employees collaborate professionally." But he was looking at us as if we had been caught at something we shouldn't be doing.

I blushed and said, "We sure are. And so far, we've found out nothing on Ortega's disappearance. No one's found any meaningful evidence on Georgy's murder either." I jumped up and said I had work to do.

Back at my desk, I called Coop on his cell phone. He had given me his number when we went out.

"Miss me, already?" he asked. He was way too smug. I had to stop being so easy.

"No," I replied. "I just wondered if you had anything on Ortega yet."

"Not a thing."

"Was Raymond Angelo really the last person to talk to Ortega?" I asked, trying to verify what Judith had told me. Uncle Dutch would be proud of me.

"How do you know that?" I took that for a "yes."

"What gave you the idea to tap Raymond's phone?"

"What tap?" I took that to mean he wasn't going to tell me. The tone in his voice, though, told me Georgy had been right about the wiretap.

"What did Raymond and Ortega talk about on the phone that last day?" I continued.

"Did Raymond and Ortega talk?"

"What did they argue about on the phone?"

Silence.

"What did Pritchard and Ortega argue about on the phone?"

"Did they argue?" he asked.

"Are you going to answer all my questions with a question?" I pursued.

"Why shouldn't I?"

"Because I'm a very cute and clever columnist. And, I promise to keep your name out of my column."

"You are very cute and clever. But if I don't tell you anything, I can make sure my name is not in your column."

Changing the subject, I said, "I met Judith Ortega today?"

"I suppose that means you're still on this story?"

"Of course, I'm still on the story. I have a column due."

I could hear his sigh over the phone. He probably looked a little disgusted too. "Does my warning mean anything to you?" he asked.

"Sure, it does. It means you care what happens to me."

Silence.

"Anyway, Judith said Ortega took his clothes with him. Have you found him or his clothes?"

"Judith must know."

"Judith said their gun is missing, too."

"Is it?"

"Judith says she doesn't know anything about her husband taking any bribes."

"Doesn't she?"

"Judith says their money is gone."

"Really? That Judith sure says a lot."

"You are really very frustrating. How's the Garbarino murder investigation going? Do you have anyone yet to take his place as an FBI snitch?" I asked.

"Gotta go," he said. "You know, I don't usually talk to reporters."

"I'm not a reporter. I'm a columnist."

"I don't usually talk to columnists."

"Yes, but I'm no ordinary columnist. I'm the columnist who's going to make you a happy man."

"I'm looking forward to it. You know I'm already a happy man. You'd better aim for ecstatic. See you when I get back." And with that he hung up.

I spent a little time sitting at my desk and thinking about Coop. I could almost taste his kisses. Then, I spent more valuable time re-reading and organizing notes and researching for background. I tried Pritchard, Rodriquez, and Kirkoff again. Still no answer at their numbers. And I didn't expect them to return my calls. Most people aren't that excited to talk to a newsperson. I made a plan for tomorrow; so, I decided to get home in time for dinner and to see if I could spend some time with Kitty

Chapter 16

In the morning, rather than go to the office, I got up and headed to my 10 o'clock appointment with Raymond Angelo. He owned a small construction company and told me he was out on a job in the southwest part of the valley near Southern Highlands. I arranged to meet him in his trailer at the site.

Ray was standing at a table, looking over some plans, when I walked in. Two other guys were with him, and he told them to leave us alone for a few minutes. They looked me over, and one gave me a long, low construction worker's whistle. Usually I don't mind, but they were pretty sorry looking guys. I think one was missing some teeth.

Raymond had changed since high school. He looked more confident, but then again, Georgy wasn't here to steal the limelight. Ray had the same dark wavy hair he always had; maybe it was shorter. He used to be a little on the chubby side in high school. Now, he looked fit and tan. His tan may have been sprayed on, though. He wore dress slacks and had his shirtsleeves rolled up for work.

After he walked over to me, Ray took one of my hands in both of his. It must have been a gesture he learned while he was in politics; it dripped with sincerity. "You look wonderful, Maggie. How long has it been?"

"A long time, Ray. I think the last time I saw you, you and Georgy were leaving the junior prom mooning everybody from your car. It made a lasting impression on me."

"Georgy, yeah. I'll miss him. We did a lot of kid stuff like that. Everybody called me Mooner for years. I've grown up a lot since then, but I still have a great ass. From what I can see your ass isn't so bad either."

"Thanks, I think. I hear you're still in trouble, Ray."

"There's trouble all right, but not of my making."

"When did you get into the construction business?" I asked.

"After I lost the election. This opportunity came up, and I took advantage of it."

"Who are your partners?"

"They're what you might call silent partners."

Hum…Note to self: remember to look into Ray's silent partners for a future column. "I work for Uncle Dutch at the *Gazette* now, and I was doing some columns on the bribes you guys took from Georgy. And, now of course, I'm looking into his murder. He told me you were working for him while you were a commissioner. That adds up to bad news, Ray."

"Have a seat." He indicated a couch at one end of the trailer. "Can I get you something to drink?" I had the feeling Ray was taking a long time to think about his answer.

"Sure, water would be good."

Ray went to a small fridge in the corner to get a bottle of water. Binders were on shelves everywhere, and plans were spread out all over the table. Ray's desk looked pretty messy. This really did look like a construction office.

Ray took a seat near the couch where I sat. He sighed and shook his head. "You know Georgy and I were friends a long time. We met before high school, in middle school. I don't think you were there with us. At least, I don't remember you then."

"No, I wasn't," I agreed. "I was still at St. Anne's."

"Oh, yeah, I forgot. You were a good Catholic girl. Well, not too good. There was that thing with Artie in high school."

"That thing with Artie in high school, Ray, turned out to be my daughter, Kitty."

"Is that her name, Kitty?" he asked.

"Yes."

"Wow, how old is she?"

"She's almost 22 years old. Are you interested in my life story or are you stalling?"

"Stalling, I guess. I just don't want to say anything bad about Georgy. We were friends for so long. Besides, my lawyer said, 'Do not talk to anybody.'"

"Yeah? Who's your lawyer?"

"Not Petey."

"That's good." I paused. "If you were going to say anything bad about Georgy, what would you say?"

"I'd say the FBI was squeezing his balls, and he'd say anything to keep from going to jail."

"Anything? Including turning on you?"

"Not just turning on me, but making up stuff to get himself off the hook. Georgy never was too loyal. Remember that time in high school when I got suspended for stealing clothes out of the girls' locker room?"

"Sure, some of the clothes were mine. I had to walk around all day in my gym clothes. I didn't have a date for months."

"Well, Georgy turned me in. He told Mr. Becker it was all my idea and that he tried to stop me. He got a slap on the wrist, and I got a ten-day suspension. But, you know me. Once my friend, always my friend. I forgave Georgy."

I didn't point out that he forgave Georgy because Georgy's dad was loaded with dough and that Ray knew a good thing when he saw one. Mr. Garbarino made his money by opening some of the first strip clubs in Las Vegas a long time ago.

"Getting a suspension in high school is a little different from going to jail because of political bribes. Let's be clear about this, Ray. Are you telling me that you never took money from Georgy while you were a commissioner? Are you telling me you didn't work for Georgy? Are you telling me that you never used Georgy's money to bribe Pritchard, Ortega, or Kirkoff?"

"That's right, Maggie. Well, I've worked for Georgy off and on, but not while I was a commissioner."

"Ray, did you collect donations for Kirkoff's, Pritchard's, and Ortega's campaigns?"

"Sure, I helped them out. Nothing illegal about that."

"Did you then use Georgy's money to reimburse the supposed campaign donors?"

"No way, Maggie."

"Did Georgy buy you that nice Rolex you're wearing?" I admired his watch.

"No, I bought this for myself. Sort of a non-reelection gift."

How about a car?"

"I bought my own car."

"Ray, the FBI has phone tapes of you talking to Pritchard, Ortega, Kirkoff, and various donors. They have pictures of you meeting with them. They probably have your bank account transactions. They have witnesses who can attest to the watch and car. But you still deny any involvement."

"Well, I don't deny that I went over to La Tigra for a little fun occasionally, and I'd do dinner and drinks with some of the other commissioners, but I never took a bribe or asked others to take one. I don't know what the FBI has on tape, but it can't involve me."

"How did you vote on the zoning that helped Georgy build La Tigra where it is?"

"Look at my record. I was always in favor of very liberal zoning laws. That issue was no exception."

Boy, Ray had me convinced. I couldn't figure out how he lost the last election, being the honest, hard working politician that he was. The FBI had obviously victimized him. In fact, I was tempted to start a donation for his legal defense. "Ray, just saying, 'I didn't do it,' isn't going to work."

"That's my story and I'm sticking to it."

"So, if you're innocent of the charges, Georgy's allegations must have made you even angrier. Angry enough to murder him, Ray?" I probed.

"Maggie, I'm hurt you'd even suggest that I could murder my best friend."

"But, your best friend was selling you out."

"Nothing new there, Maggie. He was my best friend, and I'll miss him no matter what."

"Okay, let's talk about Ernest Ortega." I changed the subject.

"How about that? Ernie, disappearing, just when all of this is going on."

"I talked to Mrs. Ortega. She says you were the last person to talk to Ernest."

"Was I? I didn't know that. I know I talked to him Monday morning."

"What did you talk about?"

"What do you think we talked about? We talked about Georgy dragging us into this mess."

"Did you already know about the investigation or did Ortega tell you?"

"Ernest told me that George was talking to the FBI. That was the first I heard of it. Boy, was he upset."

"Did Ernest have anything to be upset about?"

"I don't know. You know, maybe, he was a little crooked. Maybe he took money he shouldn't have taken from Georgy. I didn't trust Ernie all that much. He was always thinking about himself. He liked Georgy's girls and booze too much. But, personally, I don't know about anything else he did, if he did anything. And I'm not saying that he did."

Ray's lawyer had to love him. "Ray, did you and Ortega argue on the phone? If Ortega decided to talk, he could implicate you in the scandal and attest to Georgy's statements."

"We argued because Ernest was thinking about talking to the FBI. Sure, he could hurt me if he decided to talk, but I think Georgy was doing enough talking all on his own, don't you? Ernie couldn't hurt me any more than Georgy could."

"What do you think happened to Ortega?"

"I think he ran while he could. He's pretty chicken shit."

"Do you think he murdered Georgy?" I asked.

"I don't know. He was pretty edgy."

I had to admit, Ray made sense.

"Did he tell you that he was going to leave?"

"No, but he wouldn't necessarily take me into his confidence."

"Do you know anyone else who might know something about Ortega's disappearance, someone he might take into his confidence?"

"I'd talk to Jamie Rodriquez over at La Tigra. They seemed pretty tight."

"Really? You're not the first person to suggest that Ortega and Rodriquez might have a connection."

"Yeah, I saw them together quite a few times."

"Ray, is there anything else you can think of that I might want to know?"

"Just that you look great, Maggie. Seeing anyone?"

I was taken off guard, but I quickly recovered and said, "Yes." I couldn't see us together ever. "In fact, I'm almost engaged," I added. He looked kind of sorry to hear that.

Recovering he asked, "Do you fool around on the side?"

"As tempting as that sounds, Ray, no. I don't. And my-almost fiancé is big, mean, and very jealous. Did I tell you that he carries a gun?"

"No, but almost everyone I know does. No need to tell him we talked, Maggie," he smiled.

Ray stood as I got up to leave. He turned around and pretended to moon me. "Just for old time's sake, Maggie," he laughed.

What a sense of humor! When I smiled at him, though, his eyes had lost their laughter.

"That would have been more fun with Georgy here," he lamented.

I knew then he would really miss his best friend. I was more determined than ever to find out who killed Georgy.

₭₠

Too many people were connecting Jaime Rodriquez and Ernest Ortega. What was their connection? I phoned Judith before I left the parking lot to ask where she and Ortega lived before they moved to Las Vegas. They were from L.A. Then, I called Mr. Garbarino again.

"Did Ortega and Rodriquez know each other well?" I asked him.

"Hum…Well, now that you mention it, they seemed to know each other. It's not like they hung out or anything, though. It's just a feeling. And I wasn't around that much recently."

"Where's Rodriquez from?" I asked.

"He came here from our club in L.A. He was in training there as an assistant manager, and he did a good job. When the position opened here, we thought he deserved a shot. He's worked out well." Mr. Garbarino paused. "Where are you going with this, Maggie?"

"Oh, I don't know. I'm just checking everything."

"You know, he's going to run the club for me. If he had any connection to my son's death, I don't want him anywhere near here."

"I have nothing that connects him to Georgy's death, Sir. I'm just checking on his relationship with Ortega."

"Okay, keep me informed, Maggie."

"I'll do that, Mr. Garbarino.

I disconnected. I had a stab-in-the-dark kind of idea and called Judith again to ask her about it. When she said, "Yes," I told her I would stop by soon.

Chapter 17

I went back to the *Gazette* and looked to see if Rick was in his office. I couldn't find him there or in the lounge area where the coffee pot was. While in the lounge, I poured myself a cup of coffee. It was getting pretty strong by this time of the day. I thought of knocking on the men's room door but decided against it. I already had a reputation in the newsroom for being a little tenacious. No use overdoing it. I asked around for Rick, but nobody had seen him for a while.

So, I sat at my desk and thought about what was now being called the G-sting case, Georgy's murder, and Ortega's disappearance. A novice to the newspaper business might have thought I was just sitting at my desk doing nothing, but that's not true. The real work in writing a column is the thought that goes into it before it's written.

Thinking also requires munching on snacks. Just for this purpose, I had a number of snacks in my desk drawer. I reached for the red licorice, salted peanuts, and Snickers candy bars. I get the small candy bars because they have fewer calories in them. Since they are small, I can eat more of them.

Anyway, I was sitting there thinking, munching, and drinking. George Garbarino said he bribed Ray Angelo, Bruce Pritchard, Joanne Kirkoff, and Ernest Ortega for zoning consideration. Raymond denied he was bribed. Who would believe him, though? Anyway, FBI tapes, according to Georgy, said differently. And, the named commissioners did vote in Georgy's favor. Then, Georgy was cooperating with the FBI to save his own skin. Ernest Ortega found out about the investigation somehow, and they had a fight. All of those commissioners had reason to kill Georgy. Other than Ortega, however, did the rest of them even know about Georgy's talking to the FBI before he was murdered? If I believed Ray, Ortega didn't tell him about the FBI investigation until after Georgy was dead. Then, Ortega disappeared with his gun, making him look guilty. And, Rodriquez might know more than he's saying. Raymond was the last person to talk to Ortega, and they talked about the investigation. Judith heard Pritchard arguing on the phone with her husband, but she doesn't know what it was about. Could it have been about the investigation? If it was, then, Pritchard knew about Georgy's cooperation with the FBI before he was murdered. Also, why did Rodriquez suggest that I talk to Kirkoff? With those questions still unanswered, I wrote my column.

Scam, Bam, and on the Lam

*Here's the **scam**, Readers. Ernest Ortega is one of four county commissioners or ex-commissioners being investigated by the FBI for taking bribes from the late George Garbarino, La Tigra strip club owner. The others are purported to be Bruce Pritchard, Raymond Angelo, and Joann Kirkoff.*

Garbarino wanted and got their votes on a zoning issue that paved the way for his club to be built on its current site.

Angelo, sporting a Rolex watch that Garbarino said came from ill-gotten gains, denies taking bribes, and Pritchard and Kirkoff cannot be reached for comment yet. Our politicians have let us down. They sold us out.

*Then, **bam**! George Garbarino is murdered outside his own club, the very club that was built on ill-gotten gains. No evidence, no witness, no suspect in custody.*

*Now, Readers, Ortega's on the **lam**. That's right, Ernest Ortega is missing. Is he running from the FBI and information gathered by one agent who was working undercover; is he avoiding being questioned for another crime, say murder, for example; or is there some as-yet unknown cause?*

But, hear this, he didn't leave empty-handed. Ortega packed his gun, emptied his bank account, and ran.

I don't know much, Readers. But I do know this: George Garbarino was an old school chum. I promised his father, longtime Las Vegas businessman and strip club owner, that I would investigate his murder. So, whoever you are, the FBI is looking for you, Metro is looking for you, and most of all, this tenacious columnist is looking for you. Take my word, and I do keep my word, you will be found.

I suggested the editors use the headline *Scam, Bam, and on the Lam* because I'm big on rhymes. After all, I was an English major. I also like alliteration whenever possible. My favorite column title was *Casino Cage Catches Cash*. Several cashiers had figured out a clever way to skim money from their well-known casino. They made away with a lot of money before a small slip-up revealed their plot. It just shows you that crime does not pay. Well, maybe for a little while.

I turned in my column, finally reached Joann Kirkoff, and scheduled a meeting with her for Saturday afternoon. Saturday was the only day she could see me. She had a very crowded schedule. I still couldn't reach Pritchard.

Georgy's funeral was this afternoon at the Guardian Angel Cathedral behind the Wynn Hotel. The Guardian Angel was a Las Vegas landmark and a fitting site for saying goodbye to a native Las Vegan. The small, un-air-conditioned cathedral was overfilled with well-wishers, many of them LVHS alums. I found Rita outside talking to a group of ex-boyfriends, chatted with them for a few minutes, and then took Rita's arm to go in search of seats. Father Hinley was presiding over the mass. He was old and a little shaky now. Apparently, senility allowed him to forget that Georgy splattered the back of his robe with spit wads. Anyway, he remembered Georgy as a beloved Las Vegan. Many attendees had Georgy stories to tell, stories I had forgotten. He was legend. Funny how someone fares better in death than in life. Suddenly, Georgy didn't seem sleazy or creepy anymore, just quirky and funny. I was thinking that I would miss him. And, I hadn't even seen him for years. Except for Ray, none of the accused commissioners was present.

After the funeral, I went home for dinner. Mom had prepared a smoked salmon appetizer with *coq au vin* for the entrée. Too bad Kitty would be on another date with Frederick. More for me. I found out when I got home, though, that Margaret would be dining with us. Margaret eats more than her weight.

ജ ℃

After dinner Mom said she wanted to see me in the family room. Then, she dropped a bombshell.

"Margaret's going to be moving in with us for a while," she said in a whisper.

"What?" I shouted.

"Margaret's going to be moving in with us for a while."

"That's what I thought you said."

"Lower your voice. I have everything arranged. She'll stay in one of the spare rooms. The green one I think. It's so pleasant."

"When is she moving in?" I asked, apparently loudly again.

"Mom said, "Hush. She'll hear you.""

"I don't care if she hears me."

From the kitchen, Margaret yelled in, "I do hear you."

"See," Mom said, "She can hear you. She's already brought her things over."

"Why is she moving in?" I heard my own voice, and it was shrill.

"I can still hear you," Margaret yelled again. "I have a wee bit of a gambling problem. Nothing serious. I'm working on it."

"Can't she work on it someplace else? Mom, she doesn't like me."

"I don't dislike you, though," Margaret yelled back. "Most of the time you're just fine."

"Why don't you just come in here, Margaret," I yelled back.

"No, dearie, I don't want to interfere in a private, family conversation between you and your mother. That would be no way for me to start my visit."

"What did Kitty think?" I whispered to Mom. "You did tell Kitty, didn't you?"

"Oh, yes," Mom said. "Kitty thought it was wonderful."

"Well, of course. That's because Margaret likes Kitty. She's nice to her."

Mom just gave me her patronizing you're-such-a-child smile.

Margaret yelled in again, "I like her better because she's nicer."

Chapter 18

I had a sleepless night, interrupted by nightmares of Margaret coming after me with an axe, Margaret going out on a date with Coop, and Margaret borrowing my favorite Donna Karen black dress and stretching it out of shape. I got up Friday morning and decided to take the day off. I was tired, my next column wasn't due until Saturday night, and my uncle was editor. Besides, today was the day that Rita and I were going to the spa. I thought I'd ask Kitty if she wanted to go, too. A spa treatment would be good for all of us. I realized that Coop had not called. He hadn't seen me enough to be tired of me. What's up?

Kitty was delighted to go to Mandalay Bay with Rita and me. So, I called their receptionist and got appointments for Kitty. She could come as long as she settled for an Aroma Therapy Massage and an Ala'Ea Salt Glow. Those were the only appointments the receptionist could arrange so late. I was getting a Seaweed Wrap Body Treatment and a Mandalay Deep Cleansing Facial, and Rita was getting a Swedish Massage and an Ala'Ea Salt Glow. We thought we'd meet for lunch at Mon Ami Gabe at the Paris and then head over to Mandalay Bay. It's great to live in Vegas.

Mon Ami Gabi sits at the front of the Paris Hotel. You can dine inside at elegantly set tables or outside on a terrace that sits a little above street level but right on the strip. Colorful umbrellas accent tables on the terrace. The inside dining area is darker and, in my estimation, more appropriate for business dinners or luncheons. Sitting outside gives you a view of the strip, all the tourists walking along the crowded street, cars driving slowly by, and the Bellagio with its fountains that shoot up every fifteen minutes. Of course, everyone walking along the strip can see you too; so, Mon Ami Gabi is a place to see and be seen. There are no reservations for the outside dining area, so we waited in the patio bar, looking out the French doors, until a table was ready.

We ordered a bottle of Beaujolais to split and began our meal sharing the Country Style Pate. Each of us ordered one of the steak frites that we love. I ordered the Steak au Poivre, Kitty got the Steak Classique, and Rita went with the Steak Roquefort. Each is a very thin steak fried to perfection. Thin, crisp fries compliment the steaks. After gorging ourselves, we sat looking across the street at the Bellagio fountains that danced periodically to music, and we were prepared for our beauty treatments.

Following lunch, we drove to Mandalay Bay. We were frequent visitors at the Mandalay Bay Spa. It was luxurious; it was decadent; it was delightful, and it was also expensive. But the afterglow was worth it. Coop and Rick wouldn't be able to resist when the spa ladies got through working their magic on me. I could choose between them.

Leaving our valuables, as if we had any, at the desk, we got our rubber shower sandals. We found our lockers with the robes inside and began to undress. Kitty and I silently acknowledged that Rita had the best body. Rita and I also silently recognized that Kitty had the firmest, trimmest body. I suspect the two of them agreed that I needed the most work.

After we changed and grabbed towels, we headed for the showers. We always obeyed the instructions to shower before entering the spa, steam room, or sauna. We started in the steam room and, then, headed to the spa. This was our usual pattern. Why change a good routine?

The spa room is elegantly tiled with ceramic and marble. Three spas are available for guests. One very warm long and narrow spa features cascading water. On each side of it are two other spas. One is filled with cold water and the other with hot. Water shoots out of the mouths of fish into these spas. I'm sure that even the Romans didn't get to experience such decadence.

We chose the long, narrow spa first and, getting in, moaned with contentment. The jets bubbled hot water all over us. Surrounded by marble, tile, and statuary, surely we were living a grand life. It could hardly get better, I thought, settling back in the spa.

"Okay," said Rita. "What's your worst moment this month? I mean worst personal moment. The worst moment obviously would be Georgy's murder, but let's go with worst personal moment. If you think of it in the spa, it goes away."

I would have to choose the second worse thing since my daughter was present, the first thing being interrupted hot sex with Coop on a blanket in the desert. "The fact that Uncle Dutch pulled my column."

"I can top that problem." Rita said. "My worst moment was some guy jumping up on stage and grabbing me. The security guards were too slow getting to him, and he planted a big, wet kiss right on my lips. I brushed my teeth for an hour. I had to use Listerine for days. I hope I don't catch anything like hoof and mouth disease or distemper. And, after suffering through all that, I quit my job and am unemployed."

We looked at Kitty.

"What?" she said. "I've had a great month." Ah, youth.

"I win," exclaimed Rita. She doesn't care why she wins or what she wins, just that she wins.

Then, we leaned back and let the spa do its work.

After relaxing silently for a while, I turned to Kitty and asked, "How's it going with Frederick?"

"Great! We went to this terrific restaurant in the Bellagio, Le Cirque, I think it's called. The food was extraordinary, and the room was gorgeous. It's done in rose and yellows. The chairs are covered in this really rich looking striped fabric. We split a lobster salad, and I had sea bass that was wrapped in potatoes. He had a roasted chicken that was tasty. I got a bite of it. Dessert was best, though. We shared a strawberry crepe, and they flambéed it right at the table. Frederick, and he prefers to be called Frederick, had difficulty making reservations, he said. I guess it's a very popular restaurant."

Rita and I looked at one another and smiled. "Popular?" I exclaimed. "It's one of the best restaurants in town. Mom's right. He must be doing very well financially, or he just spent a month's salary on your dinner."

"Really?" Kitty shook her head, thoughtfully. "How sweet."

"Was it a special occasion?" I probed, always the journalist.

"Yes, kind of."

Rita and I both turned to Kitty. I was cautious, but Rita blurted, "Well, spill. Don't make us pull it from you."

"Well," said Kitty, "I was going to tell Mom more privately, but this is good."

Now I was just plain nervous.

"Frederick has asked me to move in with him."

"What did you tell him?" I asked, holding my breath. I wasn't ready for this situation. Kitty was still my little girl. We were a pair. Kitty and Maggie.

"I haven't given him an answer, yet, Mom. I was waiting to talk to you. What do you think?"

Rita was being unusually quiet. After a long pause, I said, "I..uh, don't know what to think yet. Let me think about it. My first thought is that you're too young to be out on your own, Kitty."

"I wouldn't be on my own, Mom. I'd be with Frederick," she reminded me.

"Of course," I responded, but I couldn't say anymore. My mind felt cluttered, stalled. "We'll talk more later."

"Good," Kitty said. She suddenly seemed unburdened. I, on the other hand, seemed more burdened.

Rita just looked at me with a sad understanding.

Then, I turned to Rita, wanting desperately to change the subject. I was good at pushing things off until I could deal with them. "By the way, what do you know about a girl who works at your club named Laurie?"

"Ooh! What a skank." I think Rita was happy to change the subject, too.

"How so?"

"Well, first of all, the boobs aren't real. And, I would swear they keep getting bigger. Pretty soon she's going to topple over. When she gets old, as we all will, she'll be walking on them if she doesn't hoist them up in a sling. You know how ugly that can be."

"Has she been at La Tigra long?"

"About a year or more. She's a pretty hardcore stripper. Really into the life, you know. I'd bet she's a prostitute on the side. Jaime's always hooking her up with guys or some party that's going on in town."

"What about drugs? She looked pretty strung out to me. I saw her when she came into Rodriquez's office the other day."

"That fits. Sometimes she's real down and jittery; other times, she's Ms. Bubbles and can't stop talking. Not that I'd hold that against her. We all know people who can't stop talking." Rita looked right at me.

"Are you referring to me?" I asked.

"Yes, but you have important and interesting things to say. Besides, you make a good living out of talking."

"Thanks for the compliment, I think. Could Jaime be her connection?" I was thinking that I would have to ask Kitty later if I talk too much.

"It wouldn't shock me. He didn't do anything openly but that was because of Georgy. Georgy didn't want any drugs around, and he made that very clear. I don't know if he was afraid to lose his license or afraid of his dad. If Jaime's involved with drugs, he wouldn't have flaunted it around me because he knows I'd tell Georgy. And, Georgy fired more than one employee for getting involved with drugs."

When it was nearly time for our treatments, we dared each other to try the cold plunge. Kitty was the only one brave enough to go into the cold water. It must be an age thing. We dried off and headed to the quiet lounge. Each of us grabbed a bottle of water and tried to be quiet. As we sat in the lounge, I kept looking at Kitty. She was such a child. No, no she wasn't. She grew up in front of me, and I didn't notice. Now she wanted to leave.

I was called first to go into the room for my seaweed wrap. I never had one before, but I heard it was relaxing. Anyway, this girl, I think she said her name was Angie, had me take off my robe and get onto a table. She exfoliated my skin first and, then, put a pre-warmed seaweed body wrap blend all over me. At least, that's what she said it was. Next, she took a plastic sheet and electric thermal blanket that were partially under me and began wrapping them all around me. My arms were tight to my side, and my feet and legs were immobilized. I ended up like a giant sushi. Only my head and neck stuck out from the blanket.

Angie began telling me about the treatment. She stood very still and delivered her prepared speech. "The pre-warmed liquid seaweed body wrap blend is rich in sea minerals and biotrace elements. It increases metabolic…"

I interrupted Angie because I was curious if she understood what she was saying. "What's a 'biotrace element?" I asked.

Angie sighed, frowned, tipped her head in my direction, and didn't answer my question. She had to start all over again, though. "The pre-warmed liquid seaweed body wrap blend is rich in sea minerals and biotrace elements. It increases metabolic rate and activates the exchange of substances, thereby eliminating toxins. The amino acids aid in tissue development, and mineral salts act on cell vitality." When Angie finished her lines, she seemed quite pleased with herself and happy that I hadn't interrupted again.

"Thanks, Angie. That explains it clearly. Basically," I summarized, "this will rid me of all my impurities."

"I suppose," she said, not content with my summary.

"Try this," I said. "It's like going to confession, except it's for your body and not your soul."

Apparently, Angie hadn't grown up Catholic because she didn't even crack a smile. I think she took this seaweed wrap thing very seriously.

Angie said she was going to leave me for a while so that I could go "into my special place." There was no way I could go to my special place all wrapped up like this, but I didn't share that with Angie. She'd already shown me that she had no sense of humor.

After about five minutes, I realized I didn't like not being able to move my legs. Then, I realized I didn't like not being able to move my arms either. I kept telling myself to relax, to find that special place Angie talked about, and to get in touch with my inner being. But my inner being was screaming to get out. It was getting a serious case of claustrophobia.

"Angie," I called.

No response.

"Angie," I called a little louder.

Still no response.

"Angie, get in here, Right now!" I screamed.

She came running in. "What's wrong?"

"Loosen the blankets. Quickly! I…I feel trapped." I must have been squirming like a beached mermaid.

Angie tried to hurry. I could tell she was watching her big tip wiggle away.

"This does bother some people," she said, looking a little sorry for me. "Sometimes I have to wrap the blankets very loosely. Are you all right?"

"Sure, I'm fine now." What a relief! If some people don't like the blankets that tight, why didn't Angie ask me if I wanted my blankets looser. She definitely was not getting a big tip.

After the failed seaweed wrap, I returned to the quiet lounge before my facial. I had some time to spare since I cut short Angie's tip and the seaweed wrap. I was looking through the latest issue of *Vogue* and had my feet up on an ottoman when Kitty came into the lounge.

She returned from her Aroma Therapy Massage and picked up a magazine. A young woman came around and brought us small cups of juice. We both chose cranberry.

"How was your massage?" I asked Kitty.

"Great. I didn't realize my muscles were so tense. The oils were divine. Here smell me, she said, sticking an arm under my nose.

I sniffed her arm, detecting a lavender scent. I told her about my frightening experience at the hands of the sadistic and cite-from-rote-memory Angie.

Karen came to get me for the facial. She seemed nice and gentle. When we got to the room, I lay on the treatment table as indicated. Karen washed my face and used a few unknown ingredients on it. I can never remember what they use even though the therapists tell you as they go. She turned on the warm water mister. Wow! That was wonderful. Now I could relax. The blanket was loose around me; I had on heated mittens and footies. Normally I would feel great, but thoughts of Kitty's bombshell kept puncturing my tranquility.

After about five or ten minutes, Karen came back in and started in on my face some more. She talked a lot, but she was good.

I was so content right up to the point when she said, "You really have some serious skin problems. Do you sit in the sun without sunscreen?"

"No." I was indignant. I thought my skin was in great shape.

"Well, your skin is really dry. You'll just keep getting more wrinkles."

"What do you mean by 'more wrinkles'?"

"Well," explained Karen, "you have these around your eyes already." She was touching near the edges of the sides of my eyes.

"But, they're not very bad are they?"

"Oh, no. Not now. But you can never be too careful. And, your pores are dirty and clogged. Do you wash your face, at least, three times a day?"

"Of course I wash my face. Maybe only twice a day, though." I lied because sometimes I only washed my face once.

"That might be the problem," Karen said after careful consideration.

I stopped and thought for a moment. "Could I get clogged pores from being on a motorcycle in the desert?"

"Could be," she said. "If you get enough dirt on your face."

Karen and I were quiet for a while. We were both disappointed that I hadn't taken better care of my skin.

Karen sighed and said she'd do the best she could. I could tell I was a big challenge for her. She said she would have to do some extractions. Now she was starting to sound like an unlicensed surgeon. I spent much of the remaining facial time saying, "Ouch," as Karen removed blackheads and unsightly clogs in my pores.

She kept exclaiming, "That one's big. Oh, I got it." I had the feeling she was enjoying this more than I was.

I left my facial feeling a little worse than when I had gone in. I imagined that my wrinkles were increasing because of my concern over aging skin problems and a daughter who might abandon me.

Kitty was already in the locker room starting to get dressed.

"How was the facial, Mom?

"Not good. I've got sun-damaged dry skin with big, dirty pores, and Coop's motorcycle may be the culprit. I'm also getting old and wrinkled."

Sliding right over my response, Kitty said, "My salt glow was great. Not only did I get a massage with it, but also the salt glow stuff is oily and lemony smelling. My skin feels wonderful."

Just then, Rita came in. "How was it, girls?"

"Not good, I said. "I've got sun-damaged dry skin with big, dirty pores, and Coop's motorcycle may be the culprit. I'm also getting old and wrinkled."

"My salt glow was so relaxing, and you'll never guess what."

"What?" I said. It was obvious nobody cared about my skin.

"No, you have to guess."

Kitty was tired of this game. "Rita, we'll never guess. Now tell us."

"My masseuse was a man. And what a man!"

"You're kidding," I said.

"Of course, I'm kidding. It never hurts to dream. But it was great all the same."

Chapter 19

Saturday morning over a breakfast of homemade biscuits, bacon, and scrambled eggs with a red sauce that Mom made, Kitty told Mom about Frederick's invitation to move in with him.

"You're too young. You belong at home with your family."

Kitty and I looked at each other. That was that, for Mom. I suspected that wasn't the end of it for Kitty, though.

"Have you heard from Rod at all?" I asked.

"Nope, not a word, but I don't expect to."

"Good thing, too," said Margaret. She must have just come downstairs while we were talking. She was in her nightgown, a robe, and slippers. Toilet paper was wrapped around her head. We all stared. She was quite a sight. "He was no good for you, Kitty," Margaret continued, getting out a plate and helping herself to the biscuits, bacon, scrambled eggs, and the sauce.

"I thought you liked him, Margaret?" Kitty's eyes were wide with surprise.

"Not really," she said with her mouth full.

"What do you think of Frederick?" Kitty asked.

"Oh, he seems nice enough." Margaret turned to Mom. "Oh, Angela. That sauce is wonderful. You have such a talent for cooking. I wish I could do half as well. Is there any coffee?"

Mom beamed and rushed to pour Margaret a cup of coffee. Boy, was Margaret buttering her up.

"Why are you just getting around to telling me how you didn't like Rod now?" Kitty exclaimed.

"Oh, I didn't want to hurt your feelings, dearie," Margaret explained. Kitty accepted that answer.

When it became obvious that no one else was going to, I finally had to ask, "Margaret, why do you have toilet paper around your head?"

"It's a beauty secret, dearie. It keeps the curls in overnight. I'm surprised you haven't seen it in all those fancy fashion magazines you keep your nose in all the time."

Hum, I was sorry I hadn't thought of wearing toilet paper.

Kitty and I finished breakfast, and we stood up to leave.

"Don't forget to put the leftovers away, and put your dishes in the dishwasher," reminded Margaret.

I was about to say something since I had assumed Margaret was getting paid to clean up, but I didn't want to get on her bad side. Margaret could really hold a grudge. She might look like a nice little old Scottish lady, but I knew better. When I was a child, she would confiscate a toy if my room were too messy. For example, I had two tiny Snoopy dogs that I would dressed up in these cute little outfits, some with hats and shoes. One day one of my Snoopy dogs was missing. It was the same day that Margaret had stood in my bedroom doorway, aghast at the sight in front of her and lamenting that she would never get my room clean.

Somewhere I know that Margaret has a gigantic box filled with my old toys. Snoopy's been stuffed in there all these years, along with some tinker toys, Light Bright parts, and puzzle pieces. Missing puzzle pieces are aggravating. Just when you are about to finish the puzzle, you realize that you are missing some essential pieces. I want all of my stuff back, but I'm afraid to confront Margaret.

෩෬

While I was upstairs getting dressed, my cell phone rang. It was Coop.

"Hi," I said. "Are you back in town?"

"Yep. How have you been getting along without me?"

"About the same as I was all those years before I met you."

"That bad?"

"I've had a very exciting life, I'll have you know."

"Without me?" He sounded indignant. "That can't be."

"You're awfully sure of yourself, aren't you?"

"Only when it comes to you."

Okay, now I was getting a little angry. "Just tell me what you want before I'm really upset with you."

"Are you free tonight?"

"Let me check my calendar," I said. Then, I waited a few seconds with my hand over the phone. I thought maybe he should sweat a little. I returned to the phone, figuring he had suffered enough. "As luck would have it, this is about my only free night."

"I can't believe it. Did you really check your calendar?"

"You caught me. I can't get away with anything. I'll bet you're one of the best agents the FBI has."

"I'll pick you up tonight at about 8."

I was a fast learner, though. "Bike or car?" I had to plan my wardrobe appropriately.

"Car. It's a special occasion."

"What's special about it?"

"You might get lucky," Then, he hung up.

Now I was excited and only a little infuriated.

I called him back.

When he answered, I asked, "Dressy or casual?"

"Sexy," he said and hung up again.

I called him back again. When he answered, I hung up. "Got him," I said to myself, feeling a little more satisfied.

I finished dressing and decided to keep busy until my appointment with Joann Kirkoff and until this evening when Coop was due. I called Rita from my desk to find out Laurie's phone number and address. Rita said she needed to phone a friend who works in the office at La Tigra.

I straightened up my office while I waited for Rita to call me back. Finally, the phone rang.

"She lives off Eastern in those apartments across the street from Valley High School." Rita gave me her phone number and the apartment number.

I went back downstairs before I left to talk to Laurie. I found Mom and Kitty still in the kitchen. Apparently, Mom was giving Kitty advice on men. I knew her advice had worked for me. That's how I ended up pregnant in high school. They were discussing Rod again.

Mom had just put a large piece of strawberry Jell-O cake on a plate in front of Kitty. Then, she put a scoop of ice cream on Kitty's plate, alongside the cake.

"But you said he was perfect for me. Didn't anybody like him?"

"I did before I got to know him, honey. It never would have worked out. You would have had to dump him eventually."

Kitty took another bite of cake and ice cream.

Mom looked at me and put another scoop of ice cream on Kitty's plate. She returned the cake to the refrigerator and the ice cream to the freezer saying, "Maggie, I was just explaining to Kitty that it's too soon after Rod to move in with Frederick. She needs to give herself some time."

I nodded in agreement. It was good advice.

"Could I have some cake and ice cream, too, Mom?"

"You know where it is, sweetheart." Turning to Kitty, she continued, "I know he's a nice young man and able to afford that great house in Seven Hills."

Just then Margaret walked into the kitchen. She must have smelled the cake and ice cream because she opened the fridge and looked around. "That's the best thing," she interjected. "Give yourself some time." She was rummaging through the refrigerator looking for the cake. When she found it, she took it out and went in search of the ice cream.

"Margaret, would you get me some, too?" I asked.

"No. You've put on a few pounds," she scolded.

"Don't you have work to do?" I asked while Margaret put a big piece of cake on a plate and started to add a scoop of the vanilla ice cream.

"Aren't you old enough to move into a home of your own?" she responded. When she was through, she put the ice cream and cake away.

Kitty obviously didn't like the attention being taken off her. "Well, I told Frederick I would think about it." She spoke with a piece of cake in her mouth, and her words were a little muffled.

ഔൽ

I got into my car and drove to Laurie's place, happy to have something to do other than think about Kitty. The apartments were badly in need of repair. They weren't the way I remembered them. Years ago, I had a friend who lived there. At the time, they were new and freshly painted.

I found Laurie's apartment and rang the doorbell. I wasn't too sure the bell worked, though, because I couldn't hear it. So, I knocked on the door. I knocked several times, harder each time. I was just about to walk away until I heard somebody having a little trouble opening the door.

"Yeah?" The door opened a crack. "What da ya want?"

It was Laurie, and she looked like the morning after a really bad night. She had on dirty, threadbare stretch pants and an old thin sweater that was missing its buttons. It was held together with a very nice decorative pin, though. Laurie's face looked swollen, and her hair was stringy. I could tell she had looked a lot better once. She was barefooted, and her eyes, what I could see of them as she squinted against the light, looked bloodshot.

"I'm Maggie Hall," I said. "We have a friend in common, Jaime Rodriquez." I pushed past her into the room while I was talking.

Laurie just looked at me for a minute. Then, she shrugged. "Come on in."

I glanced around for a place to sit, but the room was pretty messy. Assorted empty beer bottles and soda cans were everywhere. Remains of fast food were spread about the table and floor. There was an odor in the room, but I couldn't place it. I think it was the smell of decaying food, unnamable pests and vermin, and stale smoke. But, I had never gotten a whiff of them all together. One chair looked fairly okay, so I scooped the papers from the seat onto the floor. I sat down.

"Who did you say sent you?" she asked. "Jaime?" Her hands were shaking pretty badly, and her eyes were darting all around the room.

"He didn't send me," I explained. "We just both know him."

"Have I seen you around the club?"

"Yeah, I was there yesterday when you came into Jaime's office."

She hesitated for a moment. "Sure, I remember." I'm not certain she did. She sat down on the floor, cross-legged.

"Well, I went to see Jaime to buy some stuff from him yesterday. I paid him, and he was supposed to send me my stuff later. It's later and I haven't heard from him. I was wondering if you know anything about it?" Not knowing what was going on, I thought, "stuff" was about as specific as I could get. I was hoping Laurie was as dumb as she looked and fell for my story.

"I tried to reach him all last night and this morning, the son-of-a-bitch. He's supposed to get me my fix, but he's not answering his phones. I saw him coming out of the club, but he got in his car and drove away before I could catch him. I had to go to a friend for a little help, but it's not enough. If you see Jaime first, tell him to call me, too." She stood up now and started pacing about the room.

"What other girls at the club could I contact to find Jaime for us?" I asked.

"Geraldine, maybe Linda. Hell, I don't know. The guy that runs the lights buys from Jaime, too, I think. Just don't talk to Rita, though. Jaime says to stay away from her. She'd tell George." She stopped suddenly, looking sadder. "I guess that doesn't matter anymore."

"Do you know anything about Georgy's murder," I asked.

"No."

What would Georgy have done if he found out Rodriquez was selling drugs?" I asked.

"He would have fired him. George hated drugs. Once when he found them…" She looked at me and stopped talking.

"He what?" I asked.

"Oh, nothing." She shook her head. "It doesn't matter anymore," she repeated.

I changed the subject. "Do you know Ernest Ortega?"

"No."

"Think carefully, Laurie. He's a county commissioner who comes around the club."

"Oh, him," she remembered. "Yeah, I saw him a couple of times." She was running her fingers through her hair and looking all around the room. I had the feeling she wanted to run.

"Do you know anything about his disappearance?"

"No, I didn't know him that well."

I thanked her for talking to me and told her I would have Jaime call when I found him. Then, I left. She was in such bad shape that she didn't even ask how I had found out where she lived. At least, I was now pretty sure that Jaime was dealing drugs at the club. I didn't know any more about Georgy's murder or Ortega's disappearance though or whether Rodriquez and his drugs were connected to the murder and disappearance. With Rodriquez dealing drugs and Georgy feeling the way he did, I could add Rodriquez to my short list of suspects. I needed to tell Coop that Rodriquez might be dealing drugs. If I found out more I'd call Mr. Garbarino, too. I don't think he would want his manager using the club to deal.

Chapter 20

It was time for me to meet with Joann Kirkoff, so I headed over to the Sunrise Mountain area. She lives in one of those tract houses on the side of the hill in the eastern part of the valley. This area is high above the city just as Anthem Country Club is. The view of the city from Anthem is breathtaking, and the view from the Sunrise Mountain area, though a different perspective of the city, is equally beautiful.

I found Joann Kirkoff to be an attractive lady, even if she had a bit of a hausfrau-like look. She was wearing a yellow print dress with cap sleeves and plain brown flats. She had a warm smile, though. I'm sure this smile helped her win her commissioner's seat. She didn't look like someone who would be interested in politics; in fact, she didn't even look as if she read the newspaper or watched TV news. Of course, being up on local and national events might not be a requirement for politics.

"Come on in," she invited, turning that smile on me. She was holding two small and matching mop-haired dogs, one in each arm. I could never remember whether they were Shih Tzus or Lhasa Apsos. They were both yapping at me.

Did I mention that I briefly worked at a pet store? I forgot to lock the cages once and all the dogs got out. We had quite a time catching them. The other clerks and the owner were running all over the store chasing the dogs. Not me. I got out some treats, sat down, and waited for the dogs to come to me. One by one, they were re-incarcerated. I got fired any way. I thought I should have kept my job since I was so clever at catching the escaped inmates. I guess a job at a prison is out of the question.

I explained again to Joann Kirkoff who I was and told her about my column. I was right. She didn't read the papers and wasn't embarrassed to tell me so.

"I've been investigating the charges of bribery that the FBI is looking into, the charges that involve Commissioners Ortega, Pritchard, Angelo, and you," I explained. "I'm also looking into George Garbarino's murder and Ernest Ortega's disappearance. I'd like to know if they are connected." About this time, she set the dogs loose. They made a beeline for me, sniffing all around me. I didn't trust them; they had beady little eyes and sharp teeth.

"I can't really talk to you about the FBI investigation. My lawyer strictly forbids that I talk to anyone about the false allegations."

By this time, one of the dogs had started to hump my leg. I was trying to get the dog down without drawing too much attention. I kind of felt sorry for the dog. I know what it's like to go without sex for long periods of time.

"Get down, Oodles," she scolded. "That's Oodles," Joann explained. "He has the red jeweled collar around his neck. The other cutsie wootsie with the blue jeweled collar is Toodles." I could understand their anger now. Who would want to be called "Oodles" or "Toodles"? As my name had done to me, their names had probably scarred them for life.

"Come here," she called to them. Toodles ran over to her, but Oodles got in a few more humps before he gave up and ran to Joann. I think Oodles smiled at me, though.

Brushing off my leg, I said, "I understand that your lawyer doesn't want you to talk about the allegations, but I think there might be some things you can talk about. I just have a few questions. I really need a comment for my column. Otherwise, it sounds so bad when someone hasn't had a chance to respond." I smiled at Joann. I could use a winning smile, too.

"Well, I'd like to talk about all of it, you understand. The whole thing's ridiculous, really. I don't know why this George…what's his name…Garabaldi, or something… would even say these things about me. I've always represented my constituents in the most honest and forthright way possible. I would never think of being dishonest. After all, I'm the commissioner who makes it a point to protect the values of the families in this valley. That's been my election platform, and I'm proud of it." Her smile had pretty much faded by this time.

Oh, she was good. Just the appropriate mixture of indignation and innocence.

Oodles or Toodles, I had forgotten who had on what color collar, had begun to lick his genitals, making a loud sucking sound. He was having a great time. Just as I was thinking about how lucky dogs were, Joann interceded and gave him a little smack on the head. He stopped. I was embarrassed for her. I understood. It's not always easy being a parent. There was more than one occasion when I should have smacked Kitty on the head. I just never could bring myself to do it.

"Did you know George Garbarino? His last name is Garbarino, by the way."

"No, not that I recall, but then again, when you are a commissioner, you meet so many people. So, I might have met him but not remember it."

"He did contribute to your campaign this last election."

Both Oodles and Toodles took this occasion to begin barking at me and nipping at my pant leg.

"Oh, you're such exuberant doggies. Cut it out, now," commanded Joann. "You have to be so firm with them." Joann turned to me. "We go to dog obedience school once a week. They used to be such bad boys."

I smiled and said I could tell the training was working. I lied.

"Did he contribute to my campaign? So many good people did contribute, you know. But I am not acquainted with all of them."

"Raymond Angelo helped raise money for your campaign. Correct?" I asked.

"Yes, he did. Raymond helped many of us raise money for our campaigns. Having grown up in Las Vegas, Raymond has many contacts. He went to those contacts and was quite successful."

"Are you aware that he returned money to some of the donors? George Garbarino's money?"

"Of course not." She was petting both of the dogs rather vigorously now.

"The FBI has you on tape talking to Raymond Angelo about accepting pay for your vote on the zoning issue."

"I certainly talked to Raymond often enough. He was a commissioner, also, you know."

"Did your conversations include your talking about voting in favor of zoning to help Garbarino?"

"I'm sure we talked about zoning, but certainly not money for my vote. That wouldn't be legal." She definitely could not be shaken, and I knew I had a knack for shaking people.

"What about the tape the FBI has of you and Raymond eating out. On the tape, they have you accepting an envelope from Raymond."

"Well, Raymond and I conducted many business meetings over dinner. He easily could have handed me an envelope. If he did, that envelope probably had background information in it on some important issue with a vote pending. We need such an awful amount of information in order to make an informed vote on the commission. I can't tell you how much I have to read. I ask so many questions to make sure I understand, too. Serving the public is a great responsibility that I take very seriously."

For someone who couldn't talk about the case, she sure did have a lot to say. Like I said, I don't have much trouble getting people to talk. I can't vouch for their honesty, though. And, I didn't believe much of what she was saying. She was starting to sound as if she was campaigning, and I'm not even in her district.

"Ms. Kirkoff, do you have any idea why someone would want George Garbarino dead?"

"Heavens, no. Although someone who goes around spreading all those lies might anger a few people."

"Do you know of anyone in particular who was angered," I asked.

"Oh, no. I just think it likely."

I decided to take another tack. "Did you meet often with Ernest Ortega for business dinners, also?" I tried a shot in the dark. I wasn't getting any real answers from her about the investigation into the bribery charges. Maybe, she knew something about Ortega's disappearance. After all, Rodriquez suggested that I talk to her. Maybe he knew something.

She turned white when I asked her this question. She stopped petting Oodles and Toodles. Her eyes dropped to the floor, and she also began wringing her hands together. I was confused for a moment. Why would this question make her more nervous than questions about bribery? Ah, I thought, that's why Jaime wanted me to talk to Kirkoff. Of course! Ortega must have told him something about Kirkoff. What could he have told Rodriquez? Now, knowing Ortega's penchant for women…

Oodles and Toodles must have felt the charged emotions in the air because they began to growl at me. Apparently, they blamed me. Joann gave them a signal to stop. To give them their due, they did stop on command. Maybe they weren't as spoiled as I thought.

"Ms. Kirkoff," I was about to lie and hoped Oodles and Toodles wouldn't snitch on me. "I talked to Mrs. Ortega. She knew about you and Ernest. In fact," and I might have been pushing my luck here, "Ernest told her everything, and she told me." I looked at the two dogs to see if they were about to bite me, but they just sat staring at me. They didn't look happy, though.

I waited to see if I had gone too far.

She still sat there wringing her hands. "I know he told her about us," she finally said, softly. I almost couldn't hear her. And, she had her head down and was speaking into her hands. Then, she looked up, and I could see anger flash in her eyes. "He had to tell her. She is such a bitch. He didn't love her, but what could he do?"

Wow! I struck pay dirt. Too bad I'm not a gossip columnist. "What happened, Joann?" I asked. After all, now we were talking woman to woman.

"Ernest and I had a brief affair. I was lonely, and he was very sympathetic after my marriage ended. Howard and I had been married twenty years when he ran off with that girl who worked in his office. I was devastated. Oh, I had Oodles and Toodles; but other than them, I was alone. I turned to Ernie for comfort, and he was very understanding. We would meet for lunch or dinner, and he would give me the man's viewpoint on issues. At some point, we realized we were in love. I would tell you, though, Judith found out after we had seen each other only a couple of times. Ernie came to me right away. I agreed that our affair should end. I didn't want to cause any trouble for him after he had been so nice to me."

It amazed me that she was so clever in denying the bribery charges but so naïve when it came to love. She was willing to tell me everything. I told you, people talk to me. In fact, I could hardly stop her from talking. Women! Even her dogs seemed to know better. Oodles and Toodles were just staring at her as if to say, "Now you've done it."

"Ernie and I went to that little hotel on the strip, the one with the swimming pool where you can see the swimmers underneath the water."

"Oh, right. The one they're tearing down soon."

"Yes, that's the one. We thought that no one would check there and that we would look just like tourists. We checked in only twice. It was after our last time there, the same night, I believe, that Ernie called me on the phone. He said he needed to see me right away. We met at that Denny's restaurant on Maryland Parkway. He said he had to tell me in person; a phone call just wouldn't do. While he held my hands in his, he told me that Judith found out about us. I never knew how. I never asked. He said she was furious. He almost seemed frightened of her. She threatened to leave him and ruin him. He said he knew she would get all his money, and she would have no problem smearing his reputation. His good name and his position meant everything to him. He made sure I understood that he didn't regret what we had done; he said he would always treasure our time together. Wasn't that caring?" she asked.

"Hum," I agreed, but not enthusiastically. Her description wasn't of the same Ortega that I'd met. I would describe him as someone who takes bribes, drinks, food, and girls from Georgy; cheats on his wife; smooth talks vulnerable women into bed; picks on poor defenseless columnists in strip clubs; and has a drug dealer for a friend. Hum, sounds like some guys I've gone out with. And now he's missing. Who wouldn't want the guy gone?

"That woman ruined him. He was just looking for a little happiness. Anyway, that's the last time we saw each other alone."

Joann definitely sounded scorned, but her contempt was reserved for Judith not Ortega. She took two small treats out of a nearby bowl and gave one to each dog. They yapped for more, and each got one more treat.

"You wouldn't know anything about Ortega's disappearance, would you? Like, maybe, where he would go or what happened to him?"

"No, as I said, I never saw him alone again, and I never even spoke to him on the phone privately. All of our dealings were concerning the commission after that. He did always seem to smile at me so sadly, though."

I thanked Joann and left. Oodles and Toodles sent me on my way by biting at my heels as I walked out. I felt sorry for Joann; Oodles and Toodles were going to be trouble when they got into their teens. I know about these things. She needed some serious family/doggie counseling.

↪↫

I still had plenty of time, and I was curious about Ortega's affair. I also needed to pick up that item Judith and I had talked about on the phone. On the chance that she would be home, I decided to drive over to see her again.

On my way I tried Coop again, but there was no answer. I also called Rita because I wanted to see what was going on with her job search.

"Hi, Maggie," Rita said.

"What's going on?" I asked.

"I'm at La Tigra right now. They opened again after Georgy's funeral. I had to come over here to clear out my locker, and I stopped in to see Mr. Garbarino. Petey's over here, too, and you'll never guess what Petey asked me?

"What?"

"No, you'll never guess. Come on and guess."

"Okay," I said, coming up with the most outrageous situation I could think of. "Petey offered you a job."

"You guessed." She was clearly disappointed.

"What! I was just joking around. What kind of a job did Petey offer you?"

"He said he was always impressed with how smart I was, and he's been looking for someone to work as an investigator for him. I've taken some law classes and I'm good with research. Besides, I have a very analytical mind, probably from studying science. I'll have to do some legwork, but I'm sure I can handle it."

I wasn't sure they were thinking about the same kind of legwork, but I knew Rita could definitely handle Petey. A 10-year-old girl scout could handle Petey. "What's the job pay?"

"Not as much as my job at La Tigra, especially with tips. But I was serious when I told your Mom I was thinking of getting out of this business. I've got some money saved, my mortgage payment is okay, and

I'm tired of taking my clothes off. Like I said, this is the ideal time. Jaime is going to take over more control at the club. Petey's still going to work on the bribery investigation with the Feds. Mr. Garbarino wants him to continue dealing with them. Mr. G. is trying to keep his places here open, but who knows what will happen."

"When do you start?"

"Right away. I'm going over to the office now and get acquainted with his secretary. I'll check out my new office. Isn't it great, Maggie? I'll have an office."

"It sounds like a real opportunity, Rita. I'm happy for you. Gotta go. I'm at Judith Ortega's house. Talk to you later. By the way, I have a date with Coop tonight."

"Exciting! Do you need to borrow anything hot to wear? I won't need most of my work clothes now. I don't think they'll fit in at Petey's office. I've got some old feathers and pasties I won't be using. I have scads of slinky, long dresses that tear off easily. My shoes might be too big for you, but I have a couple of g-strings. Maybe you would be finicky about wearing them. They're clean, though."

I laughed. "I'll keep them in mind. Bye." Rita sounded more cheerful than she had in ages.

Chapter 21

As I was walking up the sidewalk to ring Judith's doorbell, a car pulled up to the curb. It was a dark sedan and could be government issue. Two men got out. One was Coop, and he didn't look happy to see me. I didn't know the guy driving, but he could be the accountant-type guy who helped question Rita.

I walked over to the car where they were.

"What are you doing here?" Coop asked. I thought there was a little too much FBI agent in his tone.

"Nice to see you, too," I said, not letting his tone affect my greeting.

"Roger, this is Maggie Hall. Maggie, Roger Fleming. He's my partner. Roger, don't say a word to Maggie. She's a columnist at the *Gazette*."

"Nice to meet you, Maggie." Roger offered his hand. He was much more pleasant than Coop.

I looked at Roger, and then I looked at Coop. Coop was in jeans and another t-shirt that made me want to rub my hands all over his arms and chest. Out of respect for Roger though, I showed remarkable restraint. I just sighed. Roger, on the other hand, looked like an FBI agent; he was a dark-skinned, black man, and he wore the regulation FBI sunglasses. He had on a navy-blue pin stripped suit with a cream-colored shirt and subtle tie. His hair was cut short, and he was clean-shaven. A very professional look.

"Why don't you have to dress like Roger?" I asked Coop.

"I haven't had time to change. Something came up." Coop sounded defensive.

"And not everybody can look as debonair as I do." Roger flashed an FBI smile.

I wondered what Coop was doing for the agency where he had to dress as Super Stud. I had the good sense not to ask.

"Like I said, why are you here?" Coop asked again.

"Oh, I came to talk to Judith again."

"Not now, we're going in."

"I was here first."

"But we're bigger, we're armed, and there are two of us. And besides, if you don't do what I say, I might arrest you," Coop threatened. Maybe it wasn't a threat.

I could tell Roger was a little confused. He probably didn't like arresting unarmed women. He must have been good cop to Coop's bad cop.

"Will you use handcuffs? I've always wanted to try handcuffs," I said to Coop.

"Maybe, but I'll definitely use a gag for your mouth."

"Oh," I teased. "Now you're just getting downright dirty. And in front of Roger."

His partner just kept looking back and forth between us. I'm not sure he was enjoying himself. Coop just looked at him and shrugged like "What can I do?"

"I tried to call you a few minutes ago." I changed the subject.

He checked his cell. "Damn," he said. "It's off." He turned it back on.

"What kind of an FBI agent are you?" I asked. "My cell phone is always on, and I'm just a columnist." I didn't feel the need to explain that my cell phone was usually in some state of damage.

"A damned good one."

"I could have had valuable information for you," I told Coop.

"Do you?"

"Yes, but it's not about the case."

"What's it about?"

"Well, I was wondering, which color do you think is sexier, black or red?"

"Red. Definitely red."

Roger was not appreciating our conversation now. Finally, he spoke to both of us. "Take this talk to the back seat of the car where it belongs. I've got work to do."

"What kind of a girl do you think I am, Roger?"

"I don't know, and I'm not finding out."

"Damn straight, Roger. Stay away from her. She's very dangerous." Coop narrowed his eyes when he warned his partner.

I thought that was an exaggeration, but I kept my mouth shut for a change.

ဆက

Just then, the front door opened, and Judith gracefully walked down the sidewalk towards us. She was in another tailored skirt with a crisp, linen shirt. I admired people who got linen to stay so wrinkle-free? Today she was wearing a pearl necklace and matching earrings. A lovely pearl broach was pinned at the neckline of her shirt. I never look that good at home.

The three of us approached Judith.

"Maggie, I wasn't expecting ya'll, was I?"

"No, Judith. I just had a few follow up questions I needed to ask. I ran into Agent DeMarco and Agent Fleming in front of your house." Before anybody could stop me, I added, "You don't mind if I stick around while they talk to you, do you, Judith?"

Coop was snarling. Though he was standing behind me, I heard him.

"Of course I don't, sugar. In fact, I insist on it. Ya'll haven't found out anything about Ernest, have ya?" she asked Coop and Roger.

"Sorry, no we haven't, Mrs. Ortega," volunteered Roger. "We'd rather talk to you alone, though."

"I have nothing to hide, and I'd rather have Maggie around. In fact, I can insist, can't I? I mean, it's my house, and I can just not talk to ya'll. Yes, that's what I'll do. I insist Maggie be here too," she said emphatically, but in a very sweet, Southern way. "If she can't be here, then you just have to come back later. Of course, I don't know if I'll be able to talk to you later." She smiled and winked at me.

You have to hand it to Judith. She isn't the pushover she appears to be.

Coop and Roger couldn't do much except consent, especially since they wanted to talk with her.

As we started to walk toward her house, I turned to Coop, "I have to talk to you for a minute before we go in."

132

"Not now, Maggie," he whispered.

Yes, now," I said quietly, smiling.

When I finally got him to the side, I spoke as softly as I could. "Ernest had an affair with Joann Kirkoff. That's one reason I'm here to see Judith." I knew he'd just find out inside if I asked Judith about the affair. This way, I thought he might ask Judith about it, and I could keep my good relationship with her intact. You have to be clever when you're trying to manipulate the FBI.

"How do you know?"

"I was over at Joann Kirkoff's."

"What were you doing there?"

"I have a thing going with one of her dogs. He was having his way with me."

Coop decided not to pursue my relationship with Kirkoff's dog, but I could tell he was jealous.

When we got inside, Judith had everyone sit down while she went into the kitchen to get glasses of iced tea. I was disappointed. No little sandwiches or *petit fours*.

"I'm afraid I can only spare less than an hour. I have an appointment at the hair salon."

Life goes on even if your husband has disappeared. Besides with all the reporters and cameras, keeping up one's appearance was important.

She turned to me. "Ya'll know, Maggie, how important an appointment at the hairdresser is. I never cancel an appointment."

"Boy, do I. I just had a facial and a seaweed wrap at Mandalay Bay. What a treat that was. Well, not the seaweed wrap. Have you ever had one?"

"I can't say I have? Did ya'll not enjoy it?"

"No, I hated it. I was wrapped up tighter than a sushi. Have you ever been to the Mandalay Bay Spa?"

"No, I haven't. When I want a massage or facial, I go to my salon. They have a lovely facility."

"Uh, can we get started then since we have limited time," interrupted Roger. I think Coop knew better.

"Sure," said Judith.

"Fine by me," I said. "Consider me the mouse in the corner."

That got a look from Coop and Roger. They both flashed the official FBI smirk. I gave them the official *Gazette* columnist sneer right back. A journalist should never appear intimidated by the law.

Roger had taken some papers out of his briefcase. He laid them on the table. Roger struck me as a very organized man. The inside of his briefcase was neater than any part of my desk or office. I bet he knew where everything was.

"These are some of the bank records from an account shared by you and Mr. Ortega. We have a few questions."

"Okay, but I know so little about our finances. In fact, I don't know what I'm going to do with no money in the accounts. I have a little in my own savings, but not much. I'm going to have to move back to where my family is soon or get a job. Even if I get a job, I don't think I can keep up this house."

She looked so sad sitting there. I expected her to pull her hankie out of her sleeve again.

"Three years ago, there is a deposit for $2000. Then, a few months after that, another deposit for $4500. These deposits are shortly before the vote on zoning that affected La Tigra. Then, over the next few years, there are monthly deposits of $1000 or $2000 each. What do you know about all of these?" asked Roger.

Was that part of the bribe money, I wondered?

"I don't know anything about them. Ernest was a tax consultant. Perhaps, they were fees from clients," Judith speculated.

"Would you know what clients?" pursued Roger.

"I'm afraid not. I never looked at our accounts. I don't even know how much money is missing. Ernest gave me money twice a month, and, then, whenever I needed some. I started a little savings account with the money Ernie gave me. He was very generous."

"Why are these deposits important?" I asked.

All three of them looked at me. Then, Coop and Roger looked away. Their look said, "Mind your own business." That didn't stop me, though.

"And, how much is missing from their account?" I continued.

Coop looked at me again and said, "A lot." Then he looked back at Judith. "You see, Mrs. Ortega, these dates for the deposits just happen to coincide with the dates that other deposits were made to county commissioners' bank accounts. These records seem to confirm what George Garbarino told us about his payoffs to your husband, Pritchard, Kirkoff, and Angelo. But, your husband got bigger payoffs."

"Oh," said Judith. "That sounds very bad, but I don't think Ernest would have done anything wrong. Ya'll just have to know him."

Once again, I didn't challenge Judith's assessment of her husband. Love is blind.

"Have you heard from him?" asked Coop.

"No. I surely expected to, though. And if he was kidnapped, certainly his kidnappers should have contacted me by now."

"Why would they contact you, Judith, if they already have all the money?" I thought the question was logical.

Judith had to think about it. "Why, I suppose they think I could sell the house and the car to get more money or borrow against them."

"Okay," I agreed.

Roger pulled out another stack of papers. He knew right where they were in his briefcase. I had the urge to clean up my desk when I returned to the *Gazette*. He glanced through the pages and pulled out one page. "Mrs. Ortega, these are phone records of calls going in and coming out of your house. We have identified all the calls. Quite a few of the calls are from Garbarino's phone at La Tigra."

"Yes, Ernest was on the phone quite a bit when he was home." Judith said.

Roger showed her on the sheet. "A call came from Garbarino's phone the night of his murder."

"He must have talked to Ernest."

Roger nodded and put the phone records away.

"Mrs. Ortega, is there any chance that your husband would have cleaned out his closet and your account and be planning to meet someone else, like Joann Kirkoff?" Coop asked.

I tried to look stunned for Judith's sake. She looked pretty surprised, too; but after a few seconds, she just broke down and started to cry.

"I'm so sorry," she finally sobbed. "This has been very hard on me. I'm all alone and have no one to talk to." She was quiet for a few moments, pulling herself together. "About Joann Kirkoff, though. I won't say I haven't thought about it, but I really don't think Ernie would run away to be with her. He slipped up awhile back, but their affair was over." She turned to me, "You remember, sugar, I said we had some rough times, but we came through them. Our love and our marriage have never been stronger than in this last year. So, no, I don't think he would run off to meet Joann or any other woman. I do know, though, when he comes back, this mess will all be cleared up."

"How did Joann Kirkoff take it when Ernie stopped seeing her?" I asked.

"That crazy woman called the house all the time. She screamed obscenities at me and at Ernie. She even had those two dogs yapping at us on the phone. Ernie kept telling her it was over. Her calls came for a long time; and, then, they stopped. I think she got the message."

This version of the story certainly differed from Joann's version, and Judith was a loyal wife. I wasn't so sure about her husband, though. He wasn't as reformed as he led Judith to believe, and I think he could have done anything, particularly with the FBI hot on his trail.

Finally, Judith looked at her watch. "Dear me, it's nearly time for my appointment. I'll have to say goodbye."

"By the way, Judith, I just have to tell you that's a lovely pin," I said.

"Thanks. It was his last gift to me." She started to cry softly.

Ⅎ⁍

We finished talking to Judith and I picked up the item that I came to get. I was about to say goodbye to Roger and Coop at the curb when Coop got a phone call.

"I'll just take it in the car," he said.

Roger and I were left standing beside the car, and I thought this would be a great opportunity for me to grill Roger about Coop. As a journalist, you understand.

"So, what's it like being Coop's partner?"

"Oh, I feel sorry for him. All the ladies hit on me. He always feels left out."

"I imagine you do get your share of hits."

"Keep flattering me. It works."

"So, do FBI agents have specialties?"

"Yes, we do."

"What's your area of expertise?"

"I'm good with money matters. I go after the bad guys by going through their records. Some people find it tedious. I look at it like solving a giant puzzle. It's kind of like I never stopped being a kid."

"What's Coop's area of expertise?" I asked, trying to sound nonchalant.

Roger said, "Oh, he's an excellent undercover agent. For some reason, people have an easier time seeing him as the bad guy instead of the good guy."

I could understand that. "Does he work undercover often?"

"Often enough. He blends in, and he can act like a terrorist or a bank robber. That's handy. Also, this is the age of interagency cooperation, at least, on the surface; so, he works with other agencies when they need his skills."

"What skills?"

"Oh, just your run-of-the-mill FBI skills."

Why didn't I believe that?

Coop got out of the car and told Roger to hurry up. He said he would see me later.

Chapter 22

Back in my car, I kept thinking that I was overlooking something, missing a fact that was right there. Then, my cell phone rang and interrupted my thoughts.

"Maggie Hall," I said.

It was a woman's voice. "You don't know me, but I have some information for you." The voice was disguised. It sounded low and gravelly. It could be anybody because the *Gazette* would give out my cell number if the caller said she had information about a story I was investigating. They wouldn't bother finding out who was calling.

"What do you have?"

"Jaime Rodriquez killed George Garbarino."

"How do you know that?"

"I just know."

"Why do you think he did it?"

"I think he was caught by Garbarino dealing drugs."

"So, he killed him?"

"Yes."

"What proof do you have?" I asked, but she had already disconnected.

I pulled to the side of the road, and I checked the number that she called from. Then I phoned Brian. I told him I had a phone number I wanted checked out.

"Just a minute, Mags. I'll call you right back."

I sat and waited in my car. Finally, the phone rang again.

Brian said, "The call was made from a pay phone."

"They still have those? Where's the pay phone located?"

"There's still a few. This one's over on Sahara and Maryland Parkway in a market."

"Hum," I said.

"Does that help?" Brian asked.

"Not really. I don't suppose you're good enough to tell who was on the pay phone."

"Not without fingerprinting it. Sorry. You know, Mags, with you calling me all the time, I can't stop thinking about you."

"Get over me, Brian," I warned and hung up.

৪০৫

I headed back to the *Gazette* to write my column. I wanted to get home before 6 o'clock this evening because it would take, at least, two hours to prepare for going out with Coop. Particularly after my stunt at Judith's. If I didn't look sensational, I would probably get into serious trouble for managing to stick around while they talked to her. I thought I could pull it off, though. Lots of cleavage and a short skirt would do the trick.

When I got to the office, I ran into Uncle Dutch as I got off the elevator.

"Where are you going?" I asked. He never left this early. He must have a hot date with Aunt Ann.

"Home. Don't you have a deadline?" He looked at his watch.

"I have plenty of time. Have I ever missed a deadline? Scratch that question. Actually, I'm almost through."

"Give me the short version of your column."

"I'm thinking about calling it *Mr. Clean Cleans Up and Out*. I found out that Ernest Ortega was having an affair a few years back with another county commissioner. I won't name the commissioner because I'm not into the gossip columnist thing. He also frequented La Tigra to be with the girls and get freebies. It's likely he sold his vote on zoning. The Feds show unaccounted for deposits in his account. Those deposits match deposits in other commissioner's accounts. And, if all that's not bad enough, he cleaned out his bank account when he ran, leaving his wife almost destitute. He took his gun with him and looks good for Georgy's murder. But, now Rodriquez is looking suspicious, too. He seems to know Ortega too well, and he probably sells drugs, a fact that Georgy would not have tolerated."

"Well, hurry up and write it. You know, you don't always have to turn your columns in at the last minute."

"It wouldn't hurt you, Uncle Dutch, to say, 'Good job, Maggie. Nice work. I like your dedication to your job.' You know, something nice once in a while."

"Yes, it would."

℘℺

Rick walked into my cubicle while I was sitting at my desk about to write my column.

"Hi, Legs," he said with a smile, sitting on the edge of my desk.

"Don't say that unless you mean it," I responded.

"Oh, I mean it. How's it going with Ortega?"

I explained to him about Ortega and Kirkoff. I also told him what I knew about the bank records, including the amounts and approximate times.

"I think Jaime Rodriquez is selling drugs out of La Tigra. Georgy might have found out. I know that Laurie, one of the strippers, bought from him. Maybe some of the others did, too. She named some of the girls at the club who bought drugs from Rodriquez. Also, I got a phone call telling me that Rodriquez killed Georgy."

"Who called?"

"I don't know. It was a woman, but I couldn't recognize the voice. She called from a pay phone. Maybe we should start examining the drug connection as much as the bribery scandal?"

"Maybe. Let me call some cops in vice. Who else at the club bought drugs from Rodriquez? Maybe I could talk to them."

I gave Rick the names that Laurie had told me.

"How have you been doing?" I asked.

"The FBI is still looking for someone to testify on the bribery charges. They've talked to Papa Garbarino, but it's most likely he wasn't involved at all. So, he's a dead end. Oh, and here's an interesting tidbit. Your suspicion about Barber might be on target. John Barber, assistant district attorney, was removed from the Garbarino G-sting case and suspended. He's being accused of accepting favors from your Georgy, also."

"That might explain why we saw him at La Tigra with Ortega."

Oops, I just remembered that I forgot to tell Coop about Rodriquez.

I should probably warn Mr. Garbarino also. I don't have what I would really call solid proof yet, but he deserves a head's up. Once a Wildcat, always a Wildcat. I barely had time to flirt with Rick some more before I had to sit down and write up my column.

Mr. Clean Cleans Up and Out

*County Commissioner Ernest Ortega, accused of accepting bribes from the recently murdered strip club owner George Garbarino for a zoning vote, looks less and less like **Mr. Clean**.*

When he should have been minding his P's and Q's, he was chasing the three B's—babes, booze, and bucks. None other than the late George Garbarino supplied the babes, booze, and bucks to him. What did Ortega supply to Garbarino. Nothing much. Just his political integrity. That's right. He sold his political integrity for money. And, we, his unsuspecting electorate, should be outraged.

*FBI copies of Ortega's bank statements, viewed by Yours Truly, show that over a three-year period of time he deposited well over $30,000 into the account shared with his wife. The FBI revealed that unidentified commissioners have smaller deposits into their accounts at the same time. Yes, folks, Ortega **cleaned up**, but he wasn't the only one. Bruce Pritchard, Joann Kirkoff, and Raymond Angelo also stand accused. What? More than one dirty politician? Can that be?*

*Now, Ortega's **cleaned out** and emptied the shared bank account, leaving his wife with nothing. Well, that's not true. He left her to explain his actions to the FBI. She's a good person who has had to answer all questions put to her by the FBI.*

As you know by now, George Garbarino was murdered before he could testify in court about the nefarious doings of our county commissioners. The coincidence screams connection to the G-sting case. Then, Ortega, one of the accused, disappears. A murder and a disappearance. Hum? But, Readers, before I go off half-cocked (a clever reference to the gun Ortega took with him when he hightailed it), Yours Truly is looking into another possible lead.

Oh, and let me add that Assistant District Attorney John Barber, has been suspended from his job and accused of accepting favors from Garbarino also.

Will the list of corrupted officials never end?

Chapter 23

I sat on my vanity stool in front of the bathroom mirror putting on my makeup, just having gotten out of a wonderful soak in bubbly bath water. I even treated myself to a facial mask while I sat in the tub. I decided to pull my hair back just a bit from my face with a comb on each side. I used an excessive amount of John Frieda's curling spray, being convinced that long curly hair is an aphrodisiac for men. After all, tonight I wasn't striving for the successful-career-woman look with my hair done up in a tight bun.

I put on my sexiest black underwear, black lace panties and a strapless bra. Thank goodness I had just paid a visit to Victoria Secret's at the Fashion Show Mall. My red, silky spaghetti-strap Versace dress was about the sexiest I owned. So, I chose that. The bodice was fitted, and I added a narrow black belt at the waist. The dress came just to my knees and had a flouncey little skirt on it. I chose my stiletto black hooker-heels. I slipped on a Lagos watch and finished with old, but loved, Lunch-at-the-Ritz chili pepper earrings and matching necklace. The necklace enhanced what little cleavage I had.

Standing in front of the full-length mirror, I conducted my final assessment. Makeup subtle, check. Hair wild, check. Earrings glittering, check. Dress makes me look 10 pounds lighter, check. Shoes make legs look great, check. Overall potential limitless, check. Coop better not bring his bike.

I made certain that I got downstairs early this time. I didn't want to put a damper on the mood for the evening. Kitty, Frederick, Mom, and Margaret were sitting in the living room sipping wine, eating cheese and crackers, and apparently waiting to grill Coop again. They looked disappointed to see me downstairs before time. Kitty had probably told Frederick what fun it was to quiz my dates. I hated to spoil their fun.

Kitty prepared a list of five dating don'ts that she shared with us.

1. Don't talk about yourself incessantly.
2. Don't drink too much.
3. Don't order the most expensive thing on the menu.
4. Don't dress in a way that says you're eager for sex.
5. Don't fall down if you're wearing stiletto black hooker heels.

She added #5 to the list after she saw me. I could tell that Kitty, Mom, and Margaret thought I had already broken Rule #4. Frederick, obviously a man with good taste, seemed to approve of my look. Sometimes obvious is best.

Coop was prompt; and when the doorbell rang, I had to race everyone to the door. He was a little intimidated when all five of us answered. At least four of us said, "O Wow!" in unison when we saw him. He was wearing a gray lightweight summer suit. His body filled out the shoulders just right. His five o'clock shadow was still there with his sexy smile. I rushed on through the door, pushing Coop along the walkway in front of me. I turned to the inquisitors and gave a little wave.

"Sorry to rush, but we'll be late for our reservations," I apologized.

Coop was trying to say, "Nice to see you, again. Bye," on his way down to his car.

"You can thank me later," I said.

"Oh, I will." He smiled as he opened the car door for me. "You look sensational."

He was driving a black GMC SUV. It was a big step up in my stilettos, but I made it with a boost from my date; and anything beats the bike.

"Where are we going?" I asked.

"I wanted to try out Bouchon's in the Venetian. I've heard great things about it but have never been there. Have you?"

"No. Rita was there and said the food is divine."

Ever the dedicated journalist, I filled Coop in on what I knew about Rodriquez. I told him that Laurie, who was a stripper at La Tigra, led me to believe that Rodriquez was selling drugs. At least, at the club. Maybe elsewhere. I didn't know if Ortega was involved, but I said that Laurie was.

I also told him about my anonymous phone caller who said she thought that Rodriquez killed Garbarino. Coop made a phone call and repeated what I had told him. Then, he suggested to whomever was on the phone that Metro be called with the information.

When he disconnected, I asked, "Who was that?" He just smiled. How infuriating is that? But, I let go of that thought. Business talk was over and I just wanted to have fun tonight.

੪੫

We sat at the bar in Bouchon's while they got us a table outside on the patio. Coop ordered a domestic beer on tap. I ordered a Cosmopolitan. We decided to have oysters on the half shell at the bar while we waited. I don't think Coop needed the oysters. His libido seemed okay to me. I know mine was, but it never hurts to have a little extra help.

When our drinks came, Coop proposed a toast. "To a wonderfully sexy and challenging woman." He smiled and clinked my glass.

We drank and marveled over the exotic oysters.

When we were seated, we looked the menu over carefully.

"What do you think?" Coop asked. "Do you want another appetizer? Pate, lobster, clams, mussels, more oysters? How about the Grand Plateau with one lobster, sixteen oysters, eight shrimp, nine mussels, and crab? Wow!"

"I don't think I could handle that, and we don't need more oysters."

"You never know," Coop said.

"I don't think so. How about splitting the endive salad with Roquefort, apples, walnuts and vinaigrette?"

"Sounds healthy."

"I'm thinking of getting the sautéed salmon." I checked the price. I was okay on Rule #3. It wasn't the most expensive item on the menu.

"I think I'll get the pork roast, but the leg of lamb looks good. Nope. I'm going for the pork," said Coop.

We gave our order to the waiter and asked for a French wine, a Sancerre, which he brought right away.

I was curious about Coop, more so than I had been about any man in a long time. At least, any man I wasn't investigating for my column.

"So how did you get the name, Coop?" I asked. "Was your mother a Gary Cooper fan?"

145

"Well, I'm sure she was, but that's not where the name comes from. Mom was a Cooper from Boston. To the dismay of her very proper family, she married a regular guy, an Italian Catholic to boot. I was the first-born, and I think she hoped her family would accept the marriage and children better if she named me 'Cooper.'"

"Did it work?"

"Not entirely, but we get along okay. I'm not sure they consider the FBI an appropriate choice for an occupation. Grandma Cooper has less trouble with it than Grandpa Cooper.

"If you are the first-born, you obviously have a sibling or siblings."

"Yes, one brother and one sister."

"What are they like? Do they live around here?"

"No, they're both still in Boston. My brother's a lawyer, works for a big firm; and my sister married a stockbroker. Sherrie, my sister, has two kids, and my brother Reggie is recently divorce and no children. Thank goodness. His ex-wife, better known as The Annihilator, would have made a terrible mother. And Reggie wouldn't have been home often enough to know the names of his own children. He's a workaholic. How about you? Any brothers or sisters?"

"Just one brother. He's a year older and lives in Laguna Beach. Jack, that would be Jackson, is in real estate as Mom and Dad were."

"And you never married?" he asked.

"Nope. I was too busy raising Kitty and working to support us. Then, I started college and began writing a column for the *Gazette*. I went out infrequently, and the few serious relationships I had never went anywhere. I guess I just never had the time."

Just about then our dinners arrived. They were so good that we didn't talk much.

After we finished dinner, Coop insisted on dessert. "What looks good to you?"

"Oh, I love profiteroles."

"What are they?"

"This puff pastry filled with ice cream or whipped cream and topped with a yummy chocolate sauce."

"That will do," he said.

By this time, we had wiped out our bottle of wine, though I noticed

I drank most of it. I think Rule #2 was compromised.

I finally asked Coop, "What about you? Did you ever marry?"

"No. Kind of the same situation but without the daughter to raise. My job kept me busy, and I was probably raising myself for a long time."

"How old are you?" I asked.

"I'm 37; I'll be 38 in July."

"Hum," I thought.

"Why? How old are you?"

"A lady never tells her age, but I just turned 39. Don't ask my weight because you'll never get that out of me."

"You seem younger."

"I'm making up for my lost teen years; besides, Kitty's mature enough for both of us. What do you think of an older woman?"

"I think I could learn a lot from an older woman."

"Hum," I said. "I just bet you can."

The waiter brought the profiteroles and after-dinner drinks that Coop had ordered for us.

He gave me a wicked smile. The conversation was taking a turn. "I'm looking forward to it." He reached around the dessert and took my hand in his. Then, he leaned in to kiss me, parting my lips with his tongue. The kiss seemed eternal.

Then, I started to feel a tingle. It could have been caused by the Cosmopolitan, several glasses of Sancerre, and an after-dinner drink. I didn't think so. When my knees began to quiver, I thought it best to change the subject quickly. After all, we were in the middle of Bouchon's.

"Do you have any friends still around since childhood?" Friends showed a lot about a person.

He smiled and knew I was trying to regain my dignity and strength. So, he leaned back in his chair again. "Yeah. Most of them are spread out on the East Coast. A few guys I grew up with. We were pretty wild in school, though. After high school, I did a stint in the Navy. Then, I became a Seal. It made me appreciate life and discipline. After that I went to college and eventually joined the FBI. You and Rita seem close. How long have you known her?"

"Oh, we go back to St. Anne's where we were in grade school together. Rita's been married twice, both losers. She was the only friend who stuck by me when I had Kitty. My family was great, but some friends disappeared. Rita's a good person, nice family. Her father was maitre d' at the Sands for years. He saw them all—Sinatra, Dean Martin, Sammy. He used to talk about them all the time. When the Sands lost some of its appeal and the big stars, he went to Caesars. Rita and I grew up together when our families lived over on Fourth Avenue. Then, we went to Las Vegas High School together, along with George Garbarino and Raymond Angelo, by the way."

Recalling what Rick had said about magazines and books, I asked Coop, "What do you like, magazines or books?"

"I read newspapers, lots of them. I almost never pick up a magazine or a book."

A newspaper? I'll have to ask Rick what that means. But, I don't think it's good. I decided to try the direct approach. "How do you feel about loyalty, commitment, and serious attention?"

"I'm for them, in general."

"How about in the specific," I queried.

"Specifically? Well, I want my dog loyal; I want terribly disturbed people committed; and attention to sports, especially football, I always take seriously."

Men! I thought. I can really pick them.

We finished dessert and drinks holding hands across the table, smiling more than usual, and looking into each other's eyes.

He had the most beautiful dark, dark eyes with long curling eyelashes. I was thinking about our possibilities when he asked for the bill. I noticed a hungry look in his eyes. Knowing that he had just eaten, I was sure it was a different hunger, the same one I was feeling.

We strolled through the Venetian on our way back to the car. The gondoliers sang romantic Italian songs, and we stopped briefly to hear the wandering singers on the steps of the hotel's imitation St. Mark's Square. Coop kept his arm around me while we stood listening. He reached down and kissed me gently at the end of the song. The tingling and weak knees returned.

When we reached the car door, and before I could get in, he kissed me again. At first it was gentle, but, then, we were pressing against each other as hard as we could. I had my back up against the car and could feel him smashed against me. And oh, he was getting hard. The oysters had worked well. Finally, Coop pushed away. "We've got to hurry."

When he got in on his side, I asked, "Hurry where?"

"My house. I have some sketches you need to see."

"Drive faster." I was suddenly intrigued by his artwork.

We parked in the driveway and nearly ran to his front door. It wasn't easy for me in the stilettos.

When we got inside, Coop didn't turn on a light. He just backed me against the wall and began kissing me. I was taking the suit jacket off his shoulders and trying to unbutton his shirt at the same time. I think my leg might have been wrapped around his. We were pretty eager to explore each other even before I had seen his sketches. I could feel his one hand on my thigh, and he was pulling my skirt up. Then, he was pulling my Victoria Secret panties down, admiring them all the while. I could feel his hand on my flesh. Suddenly, I heard that sound. A phone was ringing.

I cried loudly, "That had better not be your cell phone."

He stopped. Took out his phone and stared at the screen. "What?" he shouted. "Make this good. Really good."

He started nodding and saying "Yeah."

"Where?" he asked. I heard, "Uh huh" and "Uh huh. I'll be there as soon as possible." He shoved the phone back into his pocket.

"No," I begged. "Don't tell me you have to go somewhere. What if I just take all my clothes off right now? Will you stay? I took his hand and put it on my breast."

"Don't do that. I can't stand it. I do have to go. The police found Ernest Ortega's body. I'll take you with me because there's no time to take you home right now. But you need to stay in the car and be quiet. Deal?"

"Of course, I'll stay in the car and be quiet." Didn't he know me by now? Hum, maybe he knew me too well.

"They found the body out in the desert in a canyon near Red Rock. We'll go out Blue Diamond until the turnoff and then take some dirt roads to get there."

He strapped on his holster and put his gun in it after checking the chamber, the clip, and the safety. He then slipped his jacket back on.

We both sighed and headed for the car.

"I didn't even get to see your house or the sketches," I said. "You didn't get to find out how much I love good art."

"My real plan was for you to see more of me and the bed."

"Really? I didn't get that either." I sulked. I planned to pout, too.

"Why do you think you're going along?" he said.

"Oh, boy! Are we going to play nasty in the back of the car?"

"No, but I'm taking you back to my house if nothing comes up. If that doesn't work out, I'll take you home."

Chapter 24

It wasn't easy getting to the canyon where Ortega had been found. We took Warm Springs to Las Vegas Boulevard, and then we turned onto Blue Diamond Highway. We turned off on the road leading to the Blue Diamond community, drove a short distance, and turned to the left onto a dirt road that headed up into the canyons. After a few minutes, we saw a lot of people illuminated by spotlights in one section of the canyon. Cops, plainclothesmen, and crime scene guys were busy moving around, examining areas, or standing about talking in small groups. I'd never been to a crime scene before; so, it looked pretty confusing and chaotic to me. I usually just heard about them later.

The crime scene was in a small canyon that looked like a dry riverbed or wash. Mesquite trees, yucca, and creosote bushes grew scattered. Everybody was pretty crowded into the area.

Coop parked near the other cars, told me to stay put, and got out of the car. Roger was standing at the edge of the action. When he saw Coop, he waved him over. Coop went up to him. They stood and talked for a while. I could see Roger pointing every now and again. Then, they both moved farther into the lighted area. They were talking to someone, but I couldn't see who it was from my vantage point.

Just then I heard what might have been a crime scene specialist talking to a guy in a suit, I assumed a detective. I leaned out the window and saw both near Coop's front left bumper. I ducked my head back into the car so that they wouldn't see me. The crime scene guy's voice was higher and younger. The detective had a more gravelly voice, and he sounded older.

Crime scene guy said, "That's right. The body looks as if it is Ernest Ortega."

"How can you tell?" asked the detective.

"He's wearing clothes that look like the clothes his wife said he had on when she left the house Monday morning. The size and shape of the body are consistent with the description, and the shoe size is correct. His hair color is the right shade, too."

"Anything else?" the detective continued.

"Oh, yeah," said crime scene guy, "wallet has his driver's license in it, and his cell phone's in his pocket."

"You'd think you would have mentioned that first."

"Yeah, but then you wouldn't be impressed by my deductions, my dear Watson."

"You've got that backwards," explained the detective. "You're Watson; I'm Sherlock."

"Oh, I never could get that straight. Anyway, he didn't die right away."

"How do you know?" asked the detective.

"Because he had time to leave a clue for a clever detective."

"What about a stupid detective?"

"Oh, yeah, he was even nice to you," quipped crime scene guy. "He wrote *Ja* in the dirt. Capital *J*, lower case *a*."

"You're kidding."

"Nope, it's as clear as it can be."

"Could it have been written earlier by someone else?" asked the detective.

"I doubt it. His hand was near the letters. He had dirt on his fingers. It looks as if he might have collapsed or died before he finished."

"What do you suppose *Ja* means?"

"Well, I'm no clever detective like you Sherlock; but if somebody had just shot me twice, I'd try to give the police a clue as to 'who done it.'"

"That's what I'm thinking, Watson. *Ja* could be that manager at La Tigra, Jaime Rodriquez."

"Well, we'll collect as much evidence from the area and the body as we can to help you nail this guy, if he's the one. How did you guys find out the body was here?"

"Two hikers found more than they were looking for. I guess a dead body really destroys the serenity and splendor of the surrounding environment."

"I didn't realize you were such a naturalist."

"Yeah, that's me. Have we found out how he got out here yet?" the detective asked.

"We're not sure. Possibly his car. It's not around here, but there are tire tracks. We'll spread out farther looking for the car. Les is taking molds of the tracks left by the tires."

"Did you find any good shoe or footprints?"

"Nope, nothing good."

"Where was he shot?"

"About where he's lying," said the crime scene guy, I'm sure with a smile.

"I don't mean the location. I can see the location," replied the detective.

I had the impression that these two had covered a few murders together.

"Oh, two shots, one to the back of the head and one to the back under the left shoulder blade."

"Which one was the killer?" asked the detective.

"Don't know yet. We have to get to the lab."

"Any weapon?"

"Not that we've found. We're expanding the search for it, too.

"Was the money found?"

"Nope. No money. No suitcases of clothes. We did find something of interest in one of the pockets."

"What's that?" asked the detective.

"A small amount of drugs were found in his pocket."

They moved on, and I didn't hear anything else. I sat patiently for another five or ten minutes. I tapped my fingers on the dashboard and examined my nail polish. I arranged my dress on the seat about ten times, and I looked into Coop's glove compartment just because I am nosey. I didn't find anything incriminating there. I sighed loudly, but no one was around to hear me. I was getting bored. Okay, I was getting curious, too. Here I was at a crime scene, and I was stuck in this vehicle. After all, I am a journalist. But I couldn't see too well, and I definitely couldn't hear anything now that the two men were out of range.

I opened the car door slightly and stuck my head out, looking around. I had lost track of Coop and couldn't see him. I cautiously got out of the car and wandered around the edge of the lighted area hoping to hear some more talk about the crime. Traveling in my heels was difficult, and I know they were getting ruined in the desert sand. My heels kept sinking in the sand; so, I appeared to be doing a dance as I stumbled around the area. I was attracting attention because of the way I was dressed, too. Normally, I would have been ecstatic, but I was trying to look inconspicuous and as if I belonged here. I could see some technicians sifting through an area up the canyon and to my left. I assumed from the look of it that it was where Ortega was found. His body had apparently already been taken away. I saw Roger and Coop in the distance and did my sand dance until I got near them. When I reached where they were standing, Roger just stared as Coop turned around.

Suddenly, I heard an angry bellow, "Maggie. What are you doing?"

It was Coop. He didn't sound pleased. "Oh, me? I'm stretching my legs. See my legs? They need stretching, don't you think?"

I caught Coop's attention with my legs. He looked for a few moments while I ran my hand along my leg.

Then, he came to his senses. "No. Didn't I tell you to stay in the car?"

"I don't remember. Did you? I'm getting very forgetful. Do you think I could be getting Alzheimer's or dementia? Or, maybe, when I'm around you, I can't think of anything but you."

"I don't think so, and don't try to change the subject."

"Oh, I'm undone. Hi, Roger," I said, noticing that he was smiling.

"Hi, Maggie. Red is sexier. Good choice."

"Oh, this? It's just a little something I threw on, Roger. But, thanks."

"You can't stay out here." Coop sounded firm.

"It's so stuffy in the car," I whined. "Besides, I can't tell what's going on if you make me hide in the car." I turned to Roger. "What's going on?"

"Well, it's being handled by Metro, but it seems that Ernest Ortega got himself shot. He's been out here a while the ME said. I guess it could have been since Monday. The crime scene guys are going over the area thoroughly."

That's all I heard because Coop was taking me by the arm and half dragging me back to the car.

"Watch the shoes," I said. "They don't do too well out here. And, Rule #5 says I shouldn't fall in them."

"Then, you shouldn't have gotten out of the car." In order to save my shoes, I think, he picked me up and carried me tucked under his arm. "What's Rule #5?"

I could tell he didn't really want to know.

"You wouldn't understand. I didn't tell Roger goodbye." I was trying to lift my head up and turn around to see Roger, but Coop kept carrying me along.

"Well, tell him goodbye while you're getting into the car," said Coop.

"Bye, Roger," I yelled. "Nice seeing you."

"Nice to see you, too, Maggie. And I do mean that."

Coop shot him a hostile look.

When we took off, I asked, "Where are we going?" I was hoping to hear back to his house.

Coop disappointed me. "I have to go into headquarters and meet Roger. We have some things to go over. So, I'll take you home." He didn't look happy, and I didn't think it was because I got out of the car at the crime scene. He probably had too many oysters at Bouchon's and hadn't been able to work them out of his system.

I reached over and put my hand in his lap, starting to massage his manliness, as I like to think of it.

"Don't start something I can't finish," he said. Boy, he was a hard man. No pun intended.

He dropped me off and wouldn't even kiss me.

"I can't," he said. "It's too painful."

I watched him walk all of the way back to his car, get in, and drive away. I had the feeling our dates weren't working out well.

Chapter 25

I went into the house and wondered if a cold shower would help. Or did that only work for men? I decided to call Rick before my shower and fill him in on Ortega's murder.

"Rick here," he answered.

"Hi, Rick. Maggie here."

"What's up, Maggie? Don't you have anything better to do on a Saturday night?"

"Better than call you? I'm glad to see that I'm not interrupting anything, though."

"Who says you're not?"

"Too bad. Guess where I've been?" I teased.

"Starting another fight at La Tigra?"

"Nope, better. I just got back from the Red Rock Canyon area where police found Ernest Ortega's body."

"How do you stumble onto these stories?"

"I wasn't stumbling," I said. "I did have trouble walking in my hooker heels, but I wasn't stumbling. And, to answer your question, I find these stories by being a dedicated, dare I even say, dogged journalist."

"You're trying to bait me into asking why you were wearing hooker heels. You don't have a second job, do you?"

"No, I don't think I could support myself that way."

"What do you know about the murder?" Rick asked, apparently tiring of our witty repartee.

"My information comes from two guys I overheard talking. Ortega might have been out there since Monday. He took a shot to the back of the head and one in the back. They found tire tracks, but no gun and no money. When you talk to your Metro buddy," I told Rick, "be sure they check Ortega's cell phone to see if his wife called and left messages on Monday." I remembered that Judith said she had called her husband's cell when he didn't come home.

"Okay, I'll get on it."

"Also find out about the bullets and the tire tracks. Oh, I forgot he also had drugs in his pocket, but I don't know what kind. The most important bit of information though is what Ortega wrote in the dirt before he died."

"He wrote in the dirt?"

"Yep. He lived long enough to leave a clue. He wrote a capital *J* and small *a* in the dirt."

"Wow! I'd say that's bad news for Jaime Rodriquez. Any other *Ja* you can think of?"

"Not at the moment, but I'm going to look into it."

"It would be too much of a coincidence if the Garbarino and Ortega murders weren't related.

"I know. That's what I'm thinking," I agreed. "They must be related, but what's the connection? Drugs or the FBI investigation?"

"By the way, how did you find out about Ortega's body being found?"

"I was on a date."

He laughed. "You have great dates. I usually take women to dinner, maybe the theatre, back to my place for after-dinner drinks. Who's the guy who takes you on your exciting dates? It must be the ace FBI agent."

"Exactly."

"Did you close out the evening in the morgue?"

"No, and we weren't planning to close out our evening at Red Rock Canyon searching for clues to a murder."

"Really? How were you planning to close out the evening?"

"Do you have a prurient interest in my sex life or are you in on the office bets?" I asked.

"I'd have to say 'Yes' to both." At least, he was honest.

I suggested he might want to get his nose out of my sex life and into the story unfolding at the Ortega crime scene. He could probably get some information from Metro if he hurried.

"I'll wrap up a few things here and be on my way."

"Who are you wrapping up?" I asked. Now I was curious. "Is it anyone I know?"

"None of your business. And thanks for thinking about me so soon after getting home from your date."

"Don't flatter yourself. I'm just very professional." I didn't feel the need to explain that I was still horny.

After I hung up with Rick, I called into the night desk at the *Gazette*. I found a reporter and told him I had to change my column, which I'd already turned in for tomorrow. My column included only Ortega's disappearance. By tomorrow morning the news would be out about his murder, and my column would be behind the times. I didn't like to be behind. I told the guy that answered I would email my revision to him as soon as I wrote it.

"What's your name?" I asked.

"Stanley Morton," he explained. "I'm new here."

"Oh, well, I'm Maggie Hall, and I write *Crime after Crime*. The problem is that the column I turned in earlier today for tomorrow's paper is outdated. The guy in it was missing at the time, but now he's dead."

"I've heard about you, Maggie."

"What have you heard?" I hate it when my reputation precedes me. I suppose it could be good, but I thought that was unlikely.

"I heard you're a damn good columnist, a hard worker and dedicated journalist, the boss's niece, easy to look at, and a wacko."

"A wacko? What kind of a description is that for a journalist? You would think people who work with words could do better."

"Actually, Monroe said, and I am liberally summarizing, but I think I convey the gist of his comments, 'Maggie is fraught with sexual inconsistencies; her personality combines traits of Hedda Hopper, Scarlett O'Hara, and Typhoid Mary; her temperament is affected by uncontrolled volatility, and she is plagued with insecurity, at best.' I took that to mean 'wacko.' What do you think?"

"Hum." Creative and maybe interesting, I thought. Hardly wacko. "Tell Monroe that nobody uses the word 'fraught' anymore. And, I'd really like to talk to you longer, Stanley. This is such fun. But I'm emailing my new column in. Make sure it gets printed in tomorrow's paper, or you'll see my 'uncontrolled volatility' first hand."

"I'll have to call the boss."

"Call him. If he has a question, tell him to call me. Nice talking to you Stanley. I look forward to meeting you face to face."

"Yeah. Bye." I could tell Stanley was eager to meet me, too.

I typed my new column, but it wasn't easy thinking, having my anxiety heightened by my conversation with Stanley.

The Quick and the Dead

*If George Garbarino, strip club owner, was to be believed, County Commissioners Ernest Ortega and Joann Kirkoff and ex-County Commissioners Bruce Pritchard and Raymond Angelo were **quick** to take his money in trade for a favorable zoning vote.*

*Now, Ernest Ortega, once high up on the suspect list for murdering Garbarino, has been found **dead** near Red Rock Canyon, shot once in the back of the head and once in the back. The suspect becomes the victim.*

Who killed him? As yet, that remains unknown. Was his murder connected to George Garbarino's murder and the FBI G-sting investigation or to some other events?

What kind of a man was County Commissioner Ortega? When he should have been minding his P's and Q's as one of our commissioners, he was chasing the three B's—babes, booze, and bucks. None other than Garbarino supplied the babes, booze, and bucks for Ortega's vote. About to be exposed to the public that elected him—yes, Readers, that's you and me—he emptied out the bank account shared with his wife, took his clothes, and was trying to skip the light fantastic.

FBI copies of Ortega's bank statements, viewed by Yours Truly, show that over a three-year period of time he deposited well over $30,000 into the family's shared bank account. The FBI revealed that unidentified commissioners have smaller deposits into their accounts at the same time.

Yours Truly thinks Garbarino bought the votes at a bargain price. How much should a vote cost? It should be expensive; after all, the seller must relinquish pride, integrity, and duty owed the electorate. Maybe Ernest Ortega even had to sacrifice his life.

Garbarino paid more than he bargained for, too. He was soon-to-be indicted on charges of bribing public officials, he was talking freely to the FBI, and he was murdered. Rest assured, Dear Readers, with Ortega dead another suspect is on the horizon.

One more official in the saga of the G-sting operation to come under scrutiny is Assistant District Attorney John Barber. Poor John, now he might have more free time to watch the women bump and grind at La Tigra. You see, Readers, he's been suspended and accused of accepting favors from Garbarino also.

Yours Truly has one question, Readers. Are there no honest men and women left? Oh, except us.

I left the information about the *Ja* written in the dirt by Ortega out of my column because Coop said the police were holding that back.

After I emailed my new column to the *Gazette,* I lay in bed thinking about Ortega. Who would want him dead? And why? Maybe his womanizing finally got to Judith? He was such a scumbag of a husband, though not to hear her tell it. Maybe Kirkoff along with the canine duo was harboring a grudge for being dumped? After all, she could lie with a straight face, and Oodles and Toodles could be pretty snippy. Maybe Ortega and Jaime Rodriquez had a falling out over drugs? The initials *Ja* were near his body. I didn't know any other name beginning with *Ja* other than Jaime Rodriquez. Then, there were the drugs in Ortega's pocket. Maybe Ortega was going to talk as Ray said and the killer wanted him silenced? Maybe Ray or Pritchard, whom I hadn't reached yet, didn't want Georgy or Ortega talking to the FBI. Are the two murders connected? Why did my anonymous caller finger Rodriguez for Georgy's murder? The old *Keep It Simple, Stupid,* theory prevails most often. That meant that the murders of Ortega and Georgy were connected. Were they connected to Rodriquez or to one of the accused commissioners, though? I was normally a rather mulish columnist, but this time I had a personal stake in solving the crimes. The public and Mr. Garbarino were depending on me, and I couldn't let a friend down. This case, however, was taxing my skills. Still, I had no intention of abandoning it. I finally fell asleep, resolved to dig until I had more answers than questions. More importantly, I resolved to get Coop into bed somehow.

Chapter 26

I was lying on the couch the next morning reading the Sunday paper, especially enjoying my own column. Nothing like seeing your name in print, particularly if you're not the one being investigated or if you haven't been murdered. My cell phone rang. It was Rick.

"Hi. Did you hear about Rodriquez?" I could tell he was excited to have a secret to share.

"No," I said. "What's happening?"

"You mean I got to a story before you did? You're losing your touch, Maggie."

"It won't happen again."

"My guy at Metro just called to tell me they're bringing Rodriquez in for questioning. I guess they got to his condo early this morning with a search warrant. He lives in one of those high rises on the strip. Very posh. I bet his neighbors are enjoying this. Anyway, the cops have been tearing the place apart for some time now. Two detectives are bringing him in as we speak."

"Do they think he killed Georgy and Ortega?" I asked.

"The cops seem to be pretty interested. I guess *Ja* in the dirt sure points to him."

"If it's him, it could be something from their past or drugs. Have they found anything at Rodriquez's place yet?"

"Not that my guy has heard about. I'm headed over to Rodriquez's condo now. I'll see what else I can find out and get back to you."

After I got off the phone with Rick, I called Coop on his cell phone. "Hi," I said when I couldn't think of a clever conversation starter. "What are you doing?"

"I finally got home for awhile; took a short nap, showered, and dressed; and now I'm on my way back in to work. What are you doing? No, tell me what you're wearing? Tell me its something skimpy, lacy, and see-through. I need to be recharged."

If he wants to be recharged, I can oblige him. "Well, I'm lying here on my bed, and all I have on are my black lace panties. I'm lying on my back, thinking of you, and…"

Just then Kitty walked into the family room. "Oh, Mom, that's just disgusting." Then, she yelled near the phone. "She's fully clothed, sitting on the couch in the family room, reading the newspaper, and apparently talking dirty to some stranger on the phone. Just another Sunday." Then, Kitty headed for the kitchen.

"Way to break a spell," Coop lamented. "It's just as well. I'm here at headquarters now."

"Before you hang up," I said, "what do you know about Rodriquez being taken in for questioning?"

"I don't know much yet. Metro's handling Ortega's murder and the investigation. We're assisting since both murders might be connected with our investigation of Garbarino's payoffs to the commissioners. We have no clear evidence, at this time, to believe there is a connection, though. The only reason I'm telling you this much is in return for your putting me onto Rodriquez's drug business and the anonymous call. We passed the information on to Metro. Maybe it will help; maybe it won't."

"Will you tell me what goes on with Rodriquez?"

"That depends," he replied.

"Depends on what?"

"On what you give me in return."

"That's blackmail."

"No, that's really horny."

I was excited now. "Would you really trade information with me for sexual favors? Isn't that illegal?"

"Not when you're FBI. We do it all the time. Besides, I don't really have to trade information for sex with you. You're going to have sex with me no matter what."

"You're awfully sure of that."

"Yep! Gotta go. Bye."

I went into the kitchen. Kitty and Margaret were there. They were obviously waiting for Mom to come down and cook breakfast. I poured a cup of coffee for myself and sat down to wait with them.

"So," Kitty said, "you kind of like this Coop? I do hope that was Coop on the phone and not a wrong number."

"It was Coop. We've only been out twice; but, yeah, I kind of like him. He keeps getting called out of town, though. His job. I think the two of us might have trouble juggling a relationship, a personal life, and our jobs."

"He's certainly good looking," Kitty commented, and Margaret nodded enthusiastically in agreement.

"And he's got a real job," added Margaret. "You always go out with good looking men, but they're usually bums." Kitty nodded enthusiastically in agreement. "This one seems to have some brains, but I don't know. You don't let us talk to him very much. You scoot him out of here as fast as you can."

Mom walked in, dressed in a blue knit St. John's skirt with a matching short-sleeved blue and green top. She was wearing wonderful sandals with seashells on them. Kate Spade, I think. Funny, I hadn't seen them in her closet when I was snooping around before. I would have borrowed them.

You could tell Margaret, Kitty, and I reached the same conclusion all at once. We asked, "You won't be making breakfast?"

"No, you'll have to do without me. I'm meeting some friends for brunch at Lake Las Vegas. See you later." With that and not one other thought about us, Mom walked out the door to the garage.

We looked at one another. "Who's cooking?" I asked.

No one volunteered.

Finally, Kitty broke down, "I'll run out for Krispy Krèmes. What do you want?"

Didn't I raise a great daughter? I ordered two crème-filled, and Margaret wanted four glazed. Kitty saved the day.

While Kitty was off saving the day, I made more coffee. Margaret went to her room for a while, thereby contributing nothing except her appetite.

After stuffing myself with two chocolate crème-filled Krispy Krème doughnuts, I went upstairs to shower and get dressed. I put on an old pair of jeans and a glitzy DKNY t-shirt. I slipped on a worn pair of Ralph Lauren moccasins.

Having gotten dressed, I went downstairs to help Kitty cut out giant duck eggs with each student's name to be written on them later.

Before we started, though, Kitty turned to me and asked, "Are you ready to talk to me about moving in with Frederick?"

I put my scissors down and shook my head. "Not yet. Give me some more time. This is big." Then, to change the subject, I inquired, "What's with the eggs anyway?"

Kitty explained, "As the students progress throughout the year, they'll go from being eggs, to ducklings, to young ducks, to full grown ducks. Isn't that cute?"

"Yes," I agreed.

She elaborated, "I've developed a behavioral system to encourage my second graders to be good citizens and students. If they behave appropriately, they progress from egg, to duckling, to young duck, to mature duck, and to various levels of flight. The goal at the end of the year is to be a 'high flyer.' On the other hand, if they misbehave, they will move back one level: mature duck back to young duck, and so on. I read somewhere that a behavior system will keep them from killing me before the end of the year."

"I think some kind of a behavioral system for young children is great," I volunteered. "Shouldn't it reflect the real world, though?"

"What do you mean?"

"If students misbehave, they could get shot by a hunter hiding in a duck blind, eaten by a badger, grabbed in flight by the talons of an eagle, accidentally drown, or crash into a cliff while learning to fly."

Kitty looked at me in stunned silence. "I don't think you understand the fragile psyche of a second grader, Mom."

Just as I was about to begin cutting my share of the eggs, my cell phone rang again. It was Rick with more news.

"How are you doing?" he asked.

"Ducky," I said. I didn't think that required an explanation.

"Cops must have grilled Rodriquez all morning. They didn't find anything at his condo, though. So, all they have is the *Ja* written in the dirt, and Rodriquez's lawyer told the cops to check out the phone book to see how many Ja's there are in Vegas. The D.A. decided they don't have enough to hold him. They didn't even find drugs at his place and nothing to link him to either murder. They're talking to a lot of people about him, though. They'll get something soon enough."

"Did anything else turn up about Ortega?"

"Not much. No gun, no car, no money, yet. The tire tracks at the scene are consistent with tires that would have been on his car. Also, the bullets could have come from the gun missing from his house. The small amount of drugs was coke."

"So…" I was sort of thinking out loud "…someone took Ortega's car from the scene and maybe shot him with his own gun. That someone probably also has his money."

"That sounds about right," Rick agreed. "And, whoever it was is a good shot."

Just as I hung up, my phone rang again. It was Bruce Pritchard, my remaining commissioner. Rather ex-commissioner. Finally! He agreed to see me Monday. He said he was sorry he didn't get back to me sooner, but he had been out of town. He said we could meet Tuesday if Monday was not agreeable, but I replied that Monday was better, if it's okay with him. We agreed to meet at his house.

After talking to Pritchard, I called Judith Ortega with my condolences. She was pretty broken up. I asked if she had anyone to help her with the funeral arrangements.

She said, "No."

I gave her the phone number of a friend of mine who works at Palm Mortuary. I told Judith to mention my name. I was sure she would get a lot of help from my friend.

Judith thanked me. "You're so kind. And you don't even really know me."

Always the journalist, I asked if the police found the money or any trace of it.

"No," replied Judith, "but as I said, I have a little in savings, and Ernie's family, even though I've never been close to them, have offered financial help for the funeral. Then, down the road, I'll be able to use the life insurance money. It wasn't much, and I'll have to get a job. Maybe I'll move back home. Things are cheaper there."

"Let me know when the funeral is. I would like to attend."

"I will, and thanks, again," replied Judith.

I had an idea, but I needed backup. I called Rita. I decided on Rita because I was Kitty's mother, and my motherly instincts told me not to involve my own daughter who was safer sitting at home cutting out duck eggs. Fortunately, Rita was at home resting.

"It's great having a regular job. I know I've only been in it one half of a day, but I like not working at night. Now we can go out in the evenings sometime. I missed that," Rita said. "What's going on?"

I filled her in on my date with Coop and how the discovery of Ortega's body cut our time short. She was very sympathetic.

"I need you to come on an outing with me for moral support. Besides, I'm sure he won't try anything if there are two of us."

"Who's 'he'?" Rita asked.

"Rodriquez. He was just released by the police. They were questioning him all morning, and they searched his condo, thoroughly. I understand they found nothing associated with drugs or Ortega's murder. Anyway, I want to go talk to Rodriquez."

Surprisingly, she agreed. I could always depend on Rita to be up for almost anything.

I apologized to Kitty for having to run out on her. She seemed content, however, to just keep cutting away at the giant eggs without me. Secretly, I think she was happy. She seemed afraid I might offer more advice on running her classroom.

Chapter 27

Rita and I met in the parking lot of Panera's since it was easy to get to. I drove because this was all my idea.

Rodriquez lived in an exclusive high-rise condo on the strip. The place had to cost quite a bit. I'd have to ask Mom about it. The drug business must pay well because I was sure Georgy hadn't paid him enough to live here.

The lobby area was elegant. A red reception desk and leather couches stood out against a grey and black marble tiled floor. Large modern and colorful area rugs were spread throughout the lobby creating several sitting areas. The security guard at the reception desk rang up Rodriquez. He was home and told the guard to send us up.

Rodriquez met us at the door. He had on loose-fitting slacks and a lightweight silk sweater with the sleeves pushed up. He was barefooted, and still wearing way too many gold chains. He didn't look happy to see us despite the invitation to come up.

"Come right in, ladies. Rita, it's always so nice to see you."

I didn't think he meant it. He gestured that we should enter. I looked around. Hum! Nice. Lots of windows, leather, and chrome; manly modern, I think. The walls were stark white and devoid of any artwork. For a guy who decked himself out in excessive gold jewelry, he sure liked a minimalist living environment.

Either Jaime was a bad housekeeper, or the cops had not been kind. Drawers were pulled out and stuff was strewn everywhere. Jaime invited us to sit on a long black leather couch. He took the white leather oversized chair.

"Drinks?" he asked. Rodriquez already had a drink in his hand. We checked our watches. We looked at each other as if to say, "Why not?" Okay, we could have a glass of wine.

He went to the kitchen and came back with two glasses of white wine and another drink for himself.

"Thanks, for seeing us." I took my glass of wine.

"No problem. This works for me, too. I want to talk with you." He didn't sound as if he meant it in a friendly way.

"Oh, what about?" I asked.

"You first."

What a gentleman! "I understand that you and Ortega knew each other well?" I wasn't sure about the "well" part, but I thought it was possible. I was sure that they knew each other from Los Angeles. Rita, Judith, and Mr. Garbarino all indicated that Ortega and Rodriquez were friendly. I found out from Mr. Garbarino and Judith that they both came from L.A. The rest was phone calls and my stop at Judith's to pick up her husband's old high school yearbooks, which she told me he had saved.

"Not really."

Seeking clarification, I asked, "Didn't know each other well, or didn't know each other?"

"Let's just say we hardly knew each other. Ortega came into the club. That's all I know about him."

"Did you call him at his house?"

"Why would I do that when I hardly know him?"

I noticed that he hadn't answered my question. "Does that mean yes or no?" I asked.

"Well, it means no."

"I know you and Ernest went to the same school together in L.A. I also know that you phoned his house sometimes. I also know you two hung around together in the neighborhood when you were younger." I didn't know the last part for sure, but it sounded good.

"How do you know all that?" He sounded truly amazed.

I was glad I had done my homework. "Because the two of you are in your high school yearbook, because the school has records on both of you, and because the FBI showed me the phone records they have of your calls to Ortega." Again, the last part wasn't true, but it sounded good and didn't implicate Judith. Besides, I can make up facts when I want to get a source to talk. That's allowed in the newspaper business. "This is the age of technology, Jaime. I can even look up property records from years ago to see where you lived and where the Ortegas lived."

"Okay, Ernest and I knew each other. So what? We were pretty close growing up. Ernest had a real shit for a mother. So, he would stay with us a lot. He was pretty smart, though. After high school, he went to college. I think he had a scholarship or something. We kind of lost contact. I didn't go the college route. Then, all of a sudden he started dropping by here, and I heard he was a county commissioner."

"Why were you calling him?"

"For old time's sake. When Garbarino told me that he had bribed some of the county commissioners, that the FBI knew about it, and that he had to cooperate with them, I warned Ernest about the investigation. I told him he was about to be in real hot water with the FBI. I thought he deserved a chance to get out of it if he could."

That explains how Ortega found out about the investigation. "Did you have any reason to want him dead?" I asked.

"Ernie and I haven't always been on the best of terms. Like other old friends, we've had our ups and our downs. But, why would you ask that? I didn't have nothing against Ernie. Do you think I had something to do with his murder?"

"The letters *Ja were* drawn near Ortega's body. I wanted to know what you might know about his murder."

"I don't know nothing about his murder. If I did know something, the police would have found out during the three-hours they questioned me. But I don't know nothing. So, there was nothing to tell. That's why they released me. I didn't do it, and I don't know nothing about it."

He was adamant that he didn't know about the murder, but overall he appeared nonchalant and undisturbed that he had been suspected. Maybe, this happened to him often.

The English major in me wanted to point out Rodriquez's use of the double negative, but I decided not to do so. "Ortega was your friend. Surely, you have some idea about what might have happened."

"Ernie came into the club sometimes; when I saw him there, it was the first time I had seen him for years. He liked girls, and he liked booze. From what I read and what Georgy told me, I guess he liked Georgy's money, too. Because we had once been friends, I warned him about the FBI investigation. That's all I've done. I think I owed him that for old time's sake."

"What did you know about the FBI investigation?" I asked.

"Nothing. Well, only what George told me after he was already squealing on his friends."

"What did he tell you?"

"He told me that the FBI had proof that he had bribed some county commissioners for their vote on a zoning issue that affected La Tigra when it was being built. He told me who the commissioners were, and how he bribed them. And, he told me he was cooperating with the FBI to save his own skin."

"Why do you think Georgy told you all this?" I asked.

"He told me because I was the assistant manager of the club. I guess he wanted me to know the shit that was coming our way."

"You weren't involved with the bribery of the commissioners?"

"Nope. I wasn't even in town for most of the fun."

"What about drugs? Did Georgy know you were dealing drugs?"

I could see a dark expression pass over Rodriquez's face. "Dealing drugs? What makes you think I would deal drugs?"

"Well, that's one reason the police searched your place isn't it?" I explained.

"They searched my place because of Ernest's murder and *Ja* being written in the dirt."

"How do you account for the letters, by the way?"

"I don't know," Rodriquez explained. "Maybe somebody is trying to frame me."

I decided to go back to the drug connection. "Ortega was found with a small amount of coke in his pocket. Would you know about that?" I noticed that Rita was taking in all of the conversation. In her new job as an investigator for Petey, she could learn from my technique.

Rodriquez paused for a moment. He seemed to be thinking. I don't believe that's something Rodriquez does often. "You're the one, aren't you? You're the one who sicced the cops on me. And, what, your little friend, Rita, has been telling you tales about me? I don't take that kindly." Jaime stood up now, and he didn't look friendly.

Rita and I stood up and headed for the door.

"The cops tore my condo apart looking for drugs. They didn't find anything, but look at this place." He was gesturing wildly. "They pulled stuff out of drawers, they overturned furniture, and they emptied my closets. It's a mess. And, I take pride in this place."

"Speaking of this condo," I said, "how can you afford it?"

He started walking toward us with what I thought was a great deal of malice. I could tell he wasn't going to answer me.

I said hurriedly, "Well, thanks, Jaime, but we really need to be on our way."

"Wait a minute, Bitch. Do you think you can just do this and get away with it? I've been through hell. And I'll probably lose my job, if it isn't already lost. And I'll have the cops watching my every move. I'll have to lay low for a long time. In fact, my time here might be over, and I like Las Vegas."

Jaime caught up with me. He grabbed my arm, and I tried to pull away. I couldn't do it; he just kept gripping me tighter. Rita was ahead of me and almost at the door. She turned around and saw me struggling with Rodriquez, came back to where we were, and took action. She kicked him in his groin; knocked his hand away; and at the same time, kicked his foot out from under him. Boy, those Kickass classes were paying off. Rodriquez fell flat on his face.

We ran for the door and elevator as fast as we could without looking back. Luckily, the elevator was still on this floor. It opened; we scrambled in and hit the button for the lobby before Rodriquez reached us.

When we got to the lobby, we ran out the door with the security guard yelling after us. We got to my car and jumped in, locked the doors, and took off just as Rodriquez was coming out of the front door of the high rise. He didn't look happy, and from what I could see, he was limping. Rita wanted to go back and really do some damage. I didn't think it was a good idea. She liked getting a chance to use her Kickass moves. I so rarely got to see this mean side of Rita that I almost considered going back. I knew I liked having her around in a scrape.

"We didn't discover anything," said Rita.

I replied, "Oh, but we did. You have a lot to learn, Rita. Once you hone your investigative techniques, you'll see things as I do. You'll look beneath the surface. We learned he's more concerned with the cops nosing around him about drugs than he is with them thinking he murdered Ortega. We also learned it's a good idea to wear running shoes when interviewing a potentially violent suspect."

"Wow," Rita replied, with some insincerity. "I hope I can become as skillful and clever as you are."

"I hope you can too, but you're starting with a disadvantage."

"Yeah? What's that?"

"You're not me."

I said goodbye to Rita at her car.

"Just call me the next time," she said, "when you need some muscle. You know, you should consider taking the Kickass class at the gym with me. We have this shirtless, green dummy named Bill that we practice our kicks on. He's a human-like body bag with a fearsome expression, a flat nose as if it's been broken, and mean eyes. I show him no mercy. In your line of work, being able to defend yourself might come in handy."

"I'm not in a dangerous line of work," I replied.

"It is the way you do it."

I agreed.

"Remember," she said "when you did that story on somebody exploiting the homeless, and you were man-handled out on the street when you got in the middle of a fight between two old guys arguing over a whiskey bottle?"

"Yeah." I remembered it only too well. I had to duck and cover to save myself. They were going at it pretty strong, and I was caught between them on the ground. I kept getting jostled about and stepped on. I think I even caught a few punches. Lucky for me they were old and drunk. I finally got away, but I was pretty scraped up.

"That was a great column, though." It was called *The Bum's Rush.* I got an award for that one. Of course, I was also picking cinders out of my wounds for a week. "Maybe I will take a few classes. Let me know when you go."

"Well, I'll have to change to a night class now, but I'll text you with the info. Bye."

I went on home for the day.

Chapter 28

Judith phoned in the morning. "Ernie's funeral is Wednesday at 10 a.m., Maggie. I know you wanted me to tell you."

"Yes, I did, Judith. I'll be there. Is it at Palm?"

"Yes, and thanks for the support. You've been wonderful. Your friend, Pam at the mortuary was a great help, sugar."

"I'm glad. Have there been any new developments on the case? Have the police found out anything about your husband's murder?"

"No. Have you heard any new information?" I thought she was weeping quietly.

"I'm going to talk to Bruce Pritchard," I said. "He's the last commissioner I have to talk to. Maybe he can put some light on this. I talked to Jaime Rodriquez, the manager of La Tigra. The police took him in for questioning, but they released him. I didn't get anything from him either." I didn't add that he was a little touchy about a visit from Rita and me. I also didn't add that Rodriquez was an old friend of her husband and likely a drug dealer.

After talking to Judith, I drove to Pritchard's house. He lived in a modest neighborhood off Sandhill and Tropicana. Thirty years ago this was the only housing development out here. Pritchard's landscaping was well cared for, low maintenance, and drought tolerant. The front yard was brownish red rock with a riverbed running through it. Texas rangers and acacias surrounded two palo verde trees. Pritchard was obviously a conscientious desert-dweller. An older model dark-colored Ford was parked in the driveway. I rang the doorbell and waited.

An older man, I'd say about 50, opened the door. He could stand to lose a few pounds; and he was wearing a pale yellow shirt, brown pants, and a multi-colored scarf around his neck, like an ascot. A beret was on his head, and he had leather slippers on his feet. He reminded me of a Truman Capote wannabe.

Graciously, he said, "You must be Maggie Hall. I read your column all the time. I so enjoy it. Do come in, dear."

"Thank you," I replied, closing the door behind me. "I met you several years ago at one of the county commission meetings." I didn't remark on how different he looked now. At that time, Pritchard had worn a conservative suit, shirt, and tie; and, frankly, he wasn't so flamboyant then.

He said he remembered and invited me into his living room, which was decorated in mauves and creams. The room was equal to Pritchard's personal appearance. It too was flamboyant and a touch feminine. The carpet was the kind of shag I hadn't seen for years. It must require some upkeep.

I sat on a sofa that was much too soft. In fact, I was a little worried I wouldn't be able to get out of it without some help. I wiggled around a bit and stuffed some of the cushions behind me for support.

"Can I get you anything to drink?" he asked.

"Water or a diet drink would be nice," I responded.

"I have diet coke,"

"That's great."

When he brought back the drinks and sat down, I began. "If you read my column, you know that I've been reporting on the George Garbarino murder and the FBI investigation into political bribes. Garbarino told the FBI that he bribed certain county commissioners in trade for zoning help. You are one of those commissioners accused. I am also reporting on what was Ernest Ortega's disappearance and is now his murder. My questions will cover both of these areas."

"Yes, I read about Mr. Garbarino's murder and Ernest's death in the papers when I returned. Terrible. Terrible."

"Let's start with the bribery charges. What do you have to say about George Garbarino's accusations?"

"Well, I don't know exactly what his accusations were. Of course, I know what the FBI has chosen to tell me, and what I read in the papers. I cannot speak for the other commissioners that George accused, but I can speak for myself. I emphatically deny the charges."

"Garbarino did contribute to your political campaign, though, didn't he?"

"Yes," Pritchard replied, "he did. That was accounted for and reported accurately."

"Was money collected from donors for your campaign and, then, reimbursed by Garbarino?"

"Not that I know of."

"Did you take money from him to vote his way on zoning?"

"No, I did not."

"Why would George Garbarino have made these charges against you?"

"I don't know. What I do know about George, however, does not lead me to believe he was always an honest man. Don't you agree, dear?"

I had to agree with him on that one. "The FBI says they have taped conversations between you and Raymond Angelo. In those conversations, you are discussing the zoning vote and getting money in return for your vote."

"I have no idea what tapes you are talking about. I never took money for my vote. I certainly spoke to Raymond on many occasions about matters before the commission."

Okay, I could see he wasn't going to break on the bribery investigation. So, I decided to go on to the Ortega case. "How well did you know Ernest Ortega?"

"No better than I knew the other commissioners. I went to Ortega's home for a party once, a Luau. It was a lovely party. We had Mai Tais and pina coladas, roasted pig, sweet potatoes… ah, it was a lavish buffet. Mrs. Ortega planned down to the last detail. She was a gracious hostess, I might add. Other than that, I had lunch with him a few times to discuss commission business, went to some events with him, and saw him at commission meetings."

"Were you with him at La Tigra ever?"

"I went there with him once. It really wasn't my thing, though."

"Judith Ortega says you had a terrible argument with her husband on the phone once. Might I ask what that was about?" I asked but didn't necessarily expect him to tell me. Surprise! This is just another example of how people talk to me even when they shouldn't.

Pritchard struggled with his thoughts for a few minutes. "I might as well tell you. I'm sure it will all come out now that the FBI is investigating bribes and two murders. Frankly, dear, I'm happy it will. You see I've been living with a secret too long. I'm gay, and I have a boyfriend." He spoke rapidly, stopped, and paused as if in relief. "There! I've said it!" He stopped talking again for a moment and seemed to be assessing his health. Taking a deep breath, he continued, "My boyfriend will be moving in here soon. We've decided to be more open about our relationship, and I've decided to be more open about my sexual inclinations. Having this secret hang over my head all these years has been stressful. By hiding my lifestyle I left myself open for people to hurt me."

"What does this have to do with Ortega?" I asked.

"Don't you see? He's the one who found out about me. He used to tease me about women all the time. He repeatedly asked me to the club. Finally, I went with him just to shut him up. But as I said, it really wasn't my thing. I think he knew that right away. Anyway, some time later, he must have seen me coming out of a bar on Paradise with my partner, Bobby Lee. He started asking me about Bobby Lee, making sly suggestions, and poking fun at me. Ortega could be a very cruel man. Others overheard his innuendos, and I was embarrassed on numerous occasions."

"That must have really upset you?"

"It did. I called him on the phone at home and was livid, just livid. I yelled, screamed, and made an ass of myself; but it did no good. He yelled back, hurled unkind epithets at me, and laughed. He said, 'If you can't stand the time, don't do the crime.' After my phone call, his behavior towards me in public became worse. He called me 'faggot' and 'Loose Bruce' and other things I would just as soon forget."

"Were you mad enough to kill him?" I probed.

"Maybe, but I could never do that. Besides, I was out of town on vacation for a week. Bobby Lee and I just got back on Friday. We used our vacation to talk for a long time about what was happening. Bobby Lee has been open about his sexuality for most of his life. He saw how I was in pain and talked to me about being more comfortable with myself, more open. It has taken a long time, but I decided being honest was best. Bobby Lee and I took our first vacation together, staying in one room. That's the trip I just came back from. Bobby Lee had to be back to run his salon earlier. Then, he's moving in here next week."

Well, being out of town ruled out Pritchard. Besides, I didn't take him for a murderer. "Bobby Lee runs a salon?"

"Yes, a very lovely one on Maryland Parkway. It's called Shear Power. It's quite large; they do hair, nails, facials, massages, and permanent makeup. The works. They have all-day treatments and serve lunch and cocktails. Attached to the salon, is a gym. Clients can make a day of it—work out in the gym; relax with a massage; have lunch with champagne; and get their hair and nails done. A brilliant concept, really. Bobby Lee is quite the businessman. He brought the idea with him from Raleigh, North Carolina, where he used to have a salon."

Hum, I thought, Rita and I might have to try it. "Do you know why anyone would want to see Ortega or Garbarino dead?"

"Like I said, Ortega was not a very nice man, but I don't specifically know why anyone would want to see either one of them dead. I think Bobby Lee knows something, though. When I got back from vacation and read in the paper that George Garbarino had been killed and Ernest Ortega had been missing and then was found dead, Bobby Lee and I talked about the news. He said, 'Maybe the rumor at Shear Power is true.' I asked him what he meant by that; and he mysteriously said, 'Oh, it's not important. I don't talk trash about people. I hear a lot, but I don't like to share it.'"

"You have no idea what he meant?"

"None."

"Do you think Bobby Lee would talk to me about what he heard? It could be important."

"I would have to ask him. He's at his salon right now. Let me call and see."

Pritchard stepped into another room to call Bobby Lee. I walked around the room a bit, having struggled to get out of the couch. I tried not to make too many footprints in the shag carpet. They would show Pritchard that I had been nosing around. I had to hand it to Bruce; he had good taste in art. Original oil paintings and acrylics on canvas brought more color to the room. Mom would love some of his ceramic pieces.

I saw a tall sculpture that was mounted on a black base. I was busy starring at it and thinking that it looked remarkably like a giant penis when Bruce came back into the room.

"That's a terrific piece, isn't it," he said. "A friend of mine posed for it."

I was about to laugh when I looked at Bruce to see if he was joking. I could tell he wasn't. I thought his friend was well endowed and wondered if it could be Bobby Lee. If so, I could understand the basis of their friendship.

I admired the sculpture a few more seconds and thought of Coop. Then, I patted it and said, "Yep, pretty nice."

Bruce said that Bobby Lee would see me. He was just about to finish with one client and had an hour before his next appointment.

Chapter 29

Pritchard and I took separate cars and met in front of Bobby Lee's salon on Maryland Parkway. He was right. It was a lovely establishment. I had seen it often from the street and meant to pop in to have a look. Getting out of the car, I grabbed my cell phone and stuck it in my back pocket.

The salon was large, clean, and well decorated with tile and marble. The walls were covered with shiny black and pink wallpaper. The texture probably made the walls easy to clean. Each station along the wall was semi private. The middle of the salon was reserved for manicure stations. On one side of the back were the pedicure chairs and foot soak areas. A doorway on the right led to what I thought might be special treatment rooms for services such as massages. On the other side was the entrance to the gym.

A pleasant and happy hum of activity sounded throughout the salon. As we walked to the back where Bobby Lee serviced clients in his own room, several people called to Bruce and seemed pleased to see him. Bobby Lee's room contained its own hairdryers and sinks. A pink velvet couch was against one wall, and his client's chair was black leather. I stood in the corner. Bruce sat on the couch with his legs crossed while Bobby Lee finished with his client.

His client wore diamond rings, bracelets, and an expensive diamond and panther head Cartier watch. She gave a whole new meaning to "dripping in diamonds." Bobby Lee was giving her a very "youthful" hairstyle despite her years. Her age was difficult to tell, but she had that surprised look that comes with too much botox.

"There you are, my darling. Beautiful! Exquisite! As if I could add any charm to your already radiant appearance. Are you happy with the new look, dear?" Bobby Lee asked. Bobby Lee had a better bedside manner than Karen who did my facial.

"Oh, it's divine. You work wonders, Bobby Lee. As always." She stuck a wad of money in his pants pockets and walked out. It couldn't have been easy to get the money into the stylist's pants; they were very tight. The client's dyed blonde hair bounced gracefully as she walked away from us. It really was a great cut.

Bobby Lee turned to face us, waiting until his client was out of hearing range. "What a disaster! Her plastic surgeon is her closest friend. Some women just don't know how to age gracefully. She's on husband number three. The other two were loaded with money just like this one. She relieved them of some of the load, though. I don't think the new one is going to last long. I can tell she's already looking around. The signal is a new hairstyle. Every time she wants a completely new look, she ends up with a completely new husband, too." Bobby Lee gestured a lot with his hands when he talked. I wondered if that interfered with his cutting hair. Finally, he walked over and gave a peck on the cheek to Pritchard. Then, he stood there looking at me with his hands on his hips.

"What?" I finally said, feeling awkward being stared at so long.

"Oh, I read your column all the time, honey. But I didn't dream you were this lovely."

Bobby Lee had the kind of personality you warm up to quickly, especially when you're being flattered.

He walked over to where I stood and took hold of my face under the chin. He moved my face from side to side examining it. "What great hazel eyes, sensual lips, and high cheek bones. I'd love to work with your hair, though, make it a little wilder, a little sexier," he said, bouncing some of my hair in his hands. "What do you think? Should I have a go at it?" He looked eager to begin.

Bobby Lee sounded like my kind of guy. Anyone who was into wild and sexy could work on my hair.

"What are you thinking about?" I was suddenly conscious of my hair, but I was curious about his ideas.

"Well, so much depends on the cut. I'd use more layering so that your hair curled gracefully. Then, I'd cut it shorter around your face. Let that gorgeous face stand out more. Right now it's hidden behind too much hair. What do you think, honey?"

It was so tempting, but I was working on a column. I decided I'd have to come back, though. "Not today, Bobby Lee. I'm on the job, but how about if I make an appointment for next week or whenever you're available after next week?"

"Delightful." He clapped his hands together like an excited child. "Before you leave, see the receptionist at the desk. I can't wait to get started."

Finally, I thought, someone who appreciates my hidden beauty. Bobby Lee was tall and about seven or eight years younger than Pritchard, I would think. His tight black pants were topped off with a silky magenta shirt that was open to his belt. Judging by the bulge in his pants, he could have been the friend that posed for Bruce's sculpture. His hair was short, and mousse was used to create spikes all over his head. The color was brown, streaked with light blond. His complexion was fair, and he was clean-shaved and blue-eyed. On him it all worked.

Trying to get to the point of our visit at last, I stated, "Bruce said you know something about Ernest Ortega."

"Well, I'm pretty sure I do. I was thinking about calling the police, but it's all rumor."

"What can you tell me? I've been investigating George Garbarino's murder and Ortega's disappearance and murder." I didn't want to mention the FBI sting and bribery charges. I thought that might be a tender subject since he was Bruce's soul mate.

"Let's go outside in front. Some little café tables are out there for those of us who smoke. I'm in dire need of a cigarette; I've been working non-stop today."

"Sure," I said. Bruce and I followed Bobby Lee outside. I admired the salon owner's walk and wished I could swing my hips the way he did. I could have any man I wanted.

Once outside, Bobby Lee took a chair on one side of the table, and Bruce and I sat on the other side. I took my cell phone out of my jeans pocket and set it on the table. I was pleased that I had remembered to do that before I sat on it. One cell phone saved from extinction.

Bruce shook his head as if disgusted. "I've been trying to get him to stop smoking. It's so bad for his health. You know Bobby Lee, you can't smoke in the house after you move in."

I wouldn't dream of it, Bruce," taunted Bobby Lee, taking a long and exaggerated drag on his cigarette and blowing smoke our way. Bobby Lee was a ball breaker. I could learn a lot from him. "Bruce and I are moving in together," he smiled and winked at Bruce. I looked at Bruce who was blushing. I guess this out-of-the-closet routine was still pretty new for him.

I leaned in toward Bobby Lee so that I could hear him against the noise of passing traffic. I was about to start asking him my usual penetrating questions.

Just about then a car came speeding through the parking lot and abruptly stopped directly across from where we sat. I heard two loud bangs and car tires squealing as the vehicle sped out of the parking lot and down the street. It all happened so fast that I reacted without knowing it. My heart was beating fast when I threw myself on the ground. I must have accidentally taken the ashtray and table with me. I was brushing cigarette ashes off my pants and picking butts out of my hair. My cell phone was on the ground beside me, but it looked as if it had exploded. Before standing up, I picked up the pieces I could find and stuck them in my pocket. Bruce had dropped to the ground, too.

When the car was gone, Bruce and I stood up at about the same time, re-arranging our clothes and looking for Bobby Lee. Then, we saw him. He had fallen or jumped off his chair. I was sure he was just taking cover as we had, but I saw blood. Bruce rushed to him first.

"Bobby Lee," I heard him calling. He was holding his arm and moaning slightly. It looked as if he was wounded by one of the bullets. I would have been wailing loudly, but he was tougher than he looked. I asked Bruce for his cell phone. Absentmindedly, he handed it to me. I stood and moved a little to the side and called 911. Then, I went back over to where Bruce was sitting with Bobby Lee. He was cradling him in his arms and blood was everywhere.

Bobby Lee just kept saying, "I'm fine. I'm fine."

By this time people were gathering, and I could hear them talking, but everything sounded pretty muffled.

I used Bruce's cell phone again to call Rick at the *Gazette*. I gave him a watered-down version of what had happened and told him to come over for the story. Always the journalist. Then, I called Coop.

When he answered, I don't know what happened, but I just started talking rapidly.

He said, "Slow down. Slow down. Where are you?"

I told him where I was.

"What happened? Slowly."

I told him Bobby Lee was shot.

All he kept saying was "Are you all right?" When I didn't answer him, he just kept asking the same question over and over.

Finally, I said, "Yes, I'm fine, but Bobby Lee's not."

"Who's Bobby Lee?" Coop was a little confused.

I told him about my meeting with Pritchard and our coming to see Bobby Lee. "Can you come get me?" I asked. "I think I'm a little shook up."

"I'm already out the door and in my car. I'll be there shortly. Keep talking."

"I hear sirens. Police cars are pulling into the lot now."

"Are you sitting down?" Coop asked.

I had to check. "Yes, I'm sitting." I must have taken a seat and not known it.

"Good. Just stay there. Wait until the cops come up to you. They'll be asking you a lot of questions. They'll take your statement."

"I didn't see anything. I was too busy hiding. A car, dark and kind of beat up, I think, came into the lot and I heard two shots, I think two. That's all."

About this time, a paramedic unit and an ambulance pulled into the lot.

Just then, an officer came up to me. "I gotta go now, Coop. There's an officer here. Are you close?"

"I'm getting closer. I'm almost there. I'll see you in a minute." I disconnected and turned in my seat to face the officer.

I saw one officer pulling Pritchard away from Bobby Lee; other uniformed officers were moving people back out of the way. Bobbie Lee was being put on a stretcher and moved to the ambulance. He kept sitting up, though. The officer in front of me looked at me and asked, "Are you all right. Were you shot or hurt?" I remember thinking that he was very good-looking, though a little young for me.

"No," I said. "I'm fine. I wasn't shot. I think my cell phone was."

I took out the pieces, and he examined them. "Yep," he said, official-ly. "It looks as though it was shattered by a bullet. I don't think it would look that way otherwise." He was obviously a seasoned investigator despite his youthful appearance. Then, he handed the remains back to me.

He pulled up a chair that had fallen over and sat down beside me. I guess he could tell I wasn't moving. I was explaining what I knew to the policeman when Coop came through the crowd. He was holding his FBI credentials out for the cops to see and pushing people out of the way.

The officer looked at him and probably thought twice about challenging him. I'm sure most people thought twice about challenging Coop. Nonetheless, the officer said, "Could you wait until I'm through talking to this witness?"

"Sure," he stubbornly acquiesced, "but I'm waiting right here." And he pulled up another chair. The officer just shrugged, but didn't stop him.

I finished telling the officer everything I knew. He had me sign a statement. Then, Coop pointed at me. "Wait right here. I'll be back." He stepped aside with the officer, and they spoke for some time.

Coop came back and said, "Come on. I'll take you home."

"I've got my car," I explained.

"I know. One of the cops will drop it by your house later."

"Oh, that's nice. Let me say goodbye to Bruce first, and I have to talk to someone else over there."

I walked over to where Bruce was sitting on the curb beside a fe-male police officer. She was speaking very quietly to him. I sat down next to Bruce and hugged him. "I'm so sorry. So, so, sorry. I'm headed home now, but I'll talk to you later. Do you have someone to drive you to the hospital? I don't think you should drive." Bruce gave me a num-ber, and I called it. The guy said he would be right over.

Bruce told me goodbye, but he could hardly speak. I handed him his phone.

I saw Rick interviewing a police officer, and I went over to him. "Hi." My smile didn't have much zip behind it.

"Hi, yourself. Are you okay? Not hurt?" he asked.

"No, I'm just fine. A little shaken. I'll call later and fill you in on what I saw and didn't see. What have you found out?"

"So far, not much. The car hasn't been identified. The driver was wearing a hooded sweatshirt. The police say it could have been just a drive-by."

Was it? On the other hand, a bullet hit Bobby Lee and came close enough to me to destroy my phone. Who was the target? "Okay," I said. "I have to go now." I was feeling a little dizzy.

"Do you need a ride?"

"No. He's taking me home," I said, pointing in Coop's direction.

"Who's he?" Then, he saw Coop.

"You know, the FBI guy in the shadows at La Tigra."

"Hum. Okay. Talk to you later." Then, he went back to the officer, but he did turn around to look at Coop again. Rick nodded in Coop's direction. I had the impression that they knew each other. Coop was just leaning on his car with his arms crossed.

I walked over to where Coop was standing by his SUV.

"How did Steele get here so quickly?" he asked.

"I called him."

"Before or after you called me?"

Uh oh! "Before."

"Right," he said.

I could feel testosterone bubbling to the surface. If I hadn't been so dazed by nearly being killed, I might have enjoyed it. Right now enjoying a good macho rutting fight would be obscene.

"Do you know Rick, other than seeing him with me at La Tigra and with Rita?"

"We've bumped into each other."

"Where?"

"Around."

"Could you be more specific?" I asked.

"No," was all Coop said.

I didn't have the energy to pursue my line of questioning; so, I got in Coop's SUV, and we drove to Anthem.

On the way to the house, I said, "Maybe I should call home?"

"I don't think so," Coop replied. "We should tell them in person.

They'll take it better if they can see that you're okay."

"Okay." I was more compliant than usual.

"I told you to watch yourself," he scolded. "Two men are dead, now. Your life's not worth a story, is it?" His eyebrows were furrowed.

I didn't feel like being reprimanded right now. "It's not as if I knew I was in danger. I was going to a salon to see a hairdresser, for heaven's sake. We were in a public place with people around." I guess now was not a good time to tell him I went to see Rodriquez and was chased out of his condo. I'd save it for when he's in a better mood.

Chapter 30

We got to my house and went in through the front door. The whole gang was in the kitchen. Margaret, Frederick, and Kitty were sitting at the counter munching on crudités while Mom was stirring a pot on the stove and talking. I had the sense of mind to notice that Frederick was beginning to be a regular here.

Mom stopped stirring and turned around. "Oh, good, Maggie. You're just in time for dinner." She saw Coop. "How nice. You brought company."

Just then they all four looked at me. I was a little dirty and probably wasn't as well coifed as usual.

"Maggie, what happened?" Mom wiped her hands on her apron and raced over to me.

"Mom, are you all right?" said Kitty at about the same time, jumping up.

Frederick just stood with his eyes wide. He was beginning to realize that our family might not be normal. I wondered if he would rescind his offer to Kitty. He was definitely thinking that children were out of the question.

Margaret looked at me and said, "Your hair's a fright, dearie."

Coop and I both assured them I was all right, and I used my fingers to re-arrange my hair. I retold my story and heard a lot of "Oh, no's."

Coop said, "She shouldn't be working on this story anymore."

I gave him a steely stare that clearly said, "Mind your own business and shut up."

My look didn't have the desired effect on Coop, though, because he just kept talking.

"Two men are dead. Now, we've had another shooting. Maybe the deaths and shooting are related and maybe they aren't. Maybe one or both deaths and the shooting are connected to the Garbarino bribery case. The point is," and with this he glared in my direction, "we don't know. It's best to stay out of this mess and let the FBI and police do their job."

Mom and Kitty both agreed with Coop.

Margaret chimed in, "She's so stubborn. I doubt she'll pay you any heed. She always was one for stirring up trouble. Ever since she was a wee one." Margaret turned to Mom. "Remember in the old neighborhood when she convinced the other kids, except Rita who was no pushover, to eat mud pies? They all got sick, and you had their parents at your door. The kids ganged up on her, and she was a sight when she got home. She had mud all over her face, her clothes were torn, and she was crying like a banshee."

"I was not crying. It wasn't a fair fight. There were three of them and only one of me. I could have taken them one at a time," I explained, indignantly.

Frederick supported me. "I think she's brave."

Everyone gave him a look that said, "What do you know?"

"Thank you, Frederick," I responded, but he was quiet after that.

Mom was convinced I was okay for the time being. "Why don't you go upstairs, shower, and change clothes." Showering and changing clothes, along with a good hot meal, were her time-tested cures for all problems. "If you need anything call for me. And, when you are finished, come down for a nice drink and dinner." She turned to Coop. "And you, you're staying for dinner." It wasn't so much a question as a command.

"What are you having?" Coop asked.

"I'm trying out this Hungarian stew with a rich, thick sauce, lots of sour cream. A little sauerkraut's in it. Not everyone likes sauerkraut. How do you feel about it?" Mom lifted the lid so that Coop could peek into the pot.

"I love sauerkraut, and I can hardly refuse Hungarian stew," he said. "What can I do?"

"Nothing. Sit down with Margaret, Frederick, and Kitty. You've met them all before. No need for introductions. I put out some crudités to munch on." Frederick stood and got a stool for Coop.

He didn't look like a crudités man, but he wisely said nothing. His FBI training must be paying off.

With everything under control in the kitchen, I went upstairs, slowly. When I got into the shower, I started to wash my hair. I was reminded that Bobby Lee was looking forward to cutting and styling my hair. I just stood there crying. I slid down onto the shower floor and sat with my knees up, holding onto them.

I don't know how long I sat on the shower floor, but finally the door opened. It was Coop. He turned off the water and lifted me to my feet. He grabbed a towel and put it around me.

"I don't believe I'm wrapping you up in a towel," he said. "I like you much better naked, but this isn't the time or place."

"What are you doing up here?" I was trying to suck up my tears.

"Your Mom sent me to check on you. I don't think she thought you were still in the shower. If she did, she gets my vote for Mom of the Year." He was holding onto my shoulder and walking me into the bedroom.

I was pretty sure Mom wouldn't send Coop up if she thought I was in the shower.

"You've been up here a long time, and dinner's ready," he said. "What are you wearing? Come on I'll help you. This is pretty bizarre. I've been trying to get you out of your clothes and now I'm helping you get into them."

I could tell Coop was trying to be as cheerful as he could. I got out some tan slacks and a black t-shirt and sat with them on the bed.

"Come on," he urged, but he paused. "First, let me get another look." He took the towel off. "Yep, you are great to look at." His eyes lingered on me, and he twirled a pretend mustache like a villain in an old-time melodrama. That got a smile from me. "Okay, get dressed."

Coop grabbed my shirt and pulled it over my head but not without touching my breasts along the way. "Oops. That was an accident. Really."

I put on my slacks, and we went downstairs for dinner.

After dinner, Coop left, saying he was probably going out of town again. He'd call.

I went to my desk and called the *Gazette*. I talked to Uncle Dutch and told him what had happened and that I would write my column from home and email it within an hour. So, I wrote.

Murder, Mayhem, and Maybe

Yours Truly had a rough day yesterday. While continuing to investigate George Garbarino's murder and the bribery scandal that's rocking the county commission, I witnessed a drive-by. Bobby Lee was shot as we sat outside his successful salon, day spa, and gym, Shear Power, on Maryland Parkway. The other victims were my innocent cell phone and my nerves.

A yet-to-be identified old, dented, dark-colored car pulled up near where we sat, and the driver fired off, at least, two shots, wounding Bobby Lee, destroying a perfectly good cell phone, and sending Yours Truly ducking for cover.

Why Bobby Lee? Is his attempted murder connected to the George Garbarino and Ernest Ortega murders and the FBI bribery scandal? I admit, Readers, I don't know yet. But, I promise, I'm still on the trail. Yours Truly either can't be frightened off the job or is very stupid.

Bobby Lee is a friend of Bruce Pritchard, an ex-county commissioner accused by the late Garbarino, who owned several Las Vegas strip clubs, of taking a bribe in exchange for his vote on zoning and other considerations.

Yours Truly was meeting with Bobby Lee because he knew something that could shed light on one or more of these investigations. Pritchard gave me the tip and was at the same table when his friend was ruthlessly fired on. I still don't know what Bobby Lee wanted to reveal. Was he shot because of what he was about to tell me?

You remember Ernest Ortega, don't you, Readers? His body was found Saturday. He, too, was a county commissioner accused of accepting a bribe from Garbarino, and he is dead. What are you thinking? Are the two murders and recent shooting connected? Or, was Bobby Lee's shooting a random drive-by as the police suggest? Yours Truly does not believe in coincidence.

And here's a surprise. Accused commissioners are denying their involvement in any scandal, and unanswered questions about the bribes and two murders are running rampant.

I had already emailed my column when Rick called.

"Hi," I answered.

"You don't sound great. Are you okay?"

"Sure. Bobby Lee just seems like such a nice guy. And I've never seen anybody shot."

"What were you doing there?"

"I went over to see Bruce Pritchard. Like the others, he denied taking bribes from Georgy. He said, though, that his boyfriend Bobby Lee..."

"His boyfriend?"

"Yeah, Bruce is newly out of the proverbial closet. Anyway, Bobby Lee, who owns Shear Power, implied he knew something after he saw in the newspaper that Ortega and Garbarino were dead. So, we headed over to talk to Bobby Lee. He's a very knowledgeable man when it comes to style, fashion, and beauty. He admired my hair and other parts of me, by the way."

"What's not to admire," Rick said.

"We were sitting outside, and Bobby Lee was about to talk to me when this car comes up and bang, bang. My cell phone was blown to smithereens, too."

"What about Pritchard's argument with Ortega?"

"Oh, yeah, Pritchard told me about that. It was about his being gay. I guess Ortega was using an excessive amount of homophobic humor. With Pritchard being the butt of his jokes. No pun intended."

"Bad enough for Pritchard to kill him?"

"I don't think so. Pritchard was on vacation with Bobby Lee when both of the murders occurred. And, that should be easy enough to check."

"Maybe the two murders and this shooting aren't connected?"

"Maybe."

After we hung up, I was so tired I went to bed and fell right to sleep.

Chapter 31

In the morning, I called Coop to see if he found out anything new about the shooting.

He actually gave me some information. I think he was still feeling sorry for me. "The cops are exploring the idea that it was a random drive-by."

"Do they have any reason to support that idea?"

"Not that I know of. I guess they are latching onto that explanation in the wake of no other evidence."

"What do the forensics guys say about the idea of a drive-by?" I asked.

"I don't know. Their report will be ready soon, I guess. Remember, the police just tell me what they want me to know if it isn't related to our investigation of Garbarino and his shenanigans."

"Did they get a license number on the car?"

"No, everybody said the plates were dirty or the car was swerving too fast."

"What about a description of the car?"

"The only thing the witnesses could agree on was that it's old, dented, and dark-colored. They couldn't agree on a make, model, or year."

"What about the driver? Did anybody see the driver?"

"Nope. The windows were darkened. A couple of people said the driver had a hooded sweatshirt pulled up around his face."

"What about the bullets?"

"Like I said, the reports aren't out yet. I know slugs were recovered."

"Okay. Let me know about the case if telling me doesn't infringe on your highly developed sense of honor and obligation to the FBI."

"I want you off this case. You're going to get hurt."

"And I want to win the California lottery or Megabucks. There's not much chance either is going to happen. I am touched that you care so much about me, though."

"It's not that I care about you. It's just that it would be embarrassing if something happened to you. I mean, what with my being super FBI agent and tough guy. How would it look if I couldn't protect you?"

"I see your point. Though I would hate to cause you any embarrassment, I'm still on the story. I'm a crime columnist. I can't run and hide from the crimes I'm reporting. Not only do I like my job, but I owe Uncle Dutch the best I can do, and I promised Mr. Garbarino I would look into Georgy's murder. You don't want me to give less than I should, do you?"

"Yes, I do. I don't like it," Coop pushed.

"You don't have to like it. You just have to respect it."

Coop sure is stubborn. I think we ended our conversation by disagreeing to disagree.

After I talked to Coop, I decided to call Bruce Pritchard to see how Bobby Lee was doing.

Before I could reach Pritchard, though, Rita called, hysterical about the shooting.

"Are you crazy?" she yelled. I had the feeling it was more an accusation than a question. "You could have gotten yourself killed. What would I have done for a friend then? Who would go shopping with me for endless hours, who would go to the spa, and who would be as catty as I am about other women?"

I could see Rita had a point. I finally admitted how selfish and unconcerned about her feelings I had been. When I promised to do better, she hung up, satisfied. She didn't even give me a chance to ask about her new job.

Then, I called Bruce.

"Bobby Lee's family back in North Carolina are flying out here to make sure he is okay," he said. "Like I can't take care of him."

"When will he get out of the hospital?"

"Late Wednesday or early Thursday morning, the doctors say."

There was silence on Bruce's end of the line. Thinking that maybe he had hung up, I asked, "Bruce, are you still there?"

"Maggie," he eventually responded, "I lied to you, and I don't want to lie to you. I did take bribes from Garbarino. I knew that donations made by other people to my campaign actually came from him, but I wanted to get elected. He gave me money after I was elected too, but I felt guilty. So, I returned it. I did vote his way on the zoning matter, but I truly believed it was the right way to vote. You can put all this in your column. I'll be telling the truth to the FBI."

Of all people, I understood human frailty. After all, I had a few shortcomings under my belt, too. "Bruce, don't worry about that now. Why don't you wait; think about it. Whatever you do, talk to your lawyer first."

ℰℭ

On my way to the office, I stopped at Verizon. I think they were waiting for me. Dave and Paula looked happy to see me. I couldn't see the acne-faced kid. He was going to be sorry he missed this.

"We read about you in the newspaper and thought you'd be in. Are you okay?" Dave asked. He sounded genuinely concerned.

"How did you know about my cell phone, though?"

Dave responded, "It was just a guess. If you were involved in something dangerous, your phone was bound to be ruined."

I had to agree. Good point.

"You have the coolest job," Paula exclaimed. She looked at Dave and just shrugged. I guess working at Verizon was not cool. Trying to save her paycheck, though, Paula followed up with, "Oh, it's okay here, Dave. Relax."

"I'm gonna make your day." I pulled all of the phone parts out of my pocket and tossed them onto the counter. "I need a new one. This one was shot." I spoke matter-of-factly. After all, I was the one with the cool job.

"Wow!" Paula said. "That's a mess. I don't think I've seen one in this many pieces."

"I don't think I've ever seen a cell phone that's been shot. Has this happened to you before?" asked Dave.

"No, Dave, this is a new experience for me, too."

"Just think," Dave observed, "this could have been you."

"Nice of you to remind me, Dave. I had about forgotten."

"Sorry, Maggie."

A lady, waiting in the store for some time, was beginning to show signs of impatience. She was tapping her nicely manicured, candy cane red nails on the counter top. I could hear her sigh from where we were standing. Finally, in frustration, she asked, "Can anyone help me? I've been waiting here for some time. In fact, I was here before that lady." She was pointing at me.

In unison Dave and Paula said, "Not right now."

"How long will it be," she asked. She looked as if she didn't usually have to wait for service.

"I don't know," snapped Dave. "We're trying to solve a complicated technical problem here."

"Could I speak to the manager," she asked.

"You're speaking to him. Now be a little patient or leave."

Dave was showing a little spark of bravery. I was impressed by his attitude and lack of concern over losing a customer. I don't know if I liked being thought of as a complicated technical problem, though.

The lady left with a flourish, but Dave and Paula remained unconcerned.

They looked at my cell phone remains again. "How did it get shot?" Dave asked.

"Well, apparently, some people get really pissed when others talk on cell phones in public," I explained.

"You mean you were talking on your phone, and someone got pissed enough to shoot the phone?" Dave said.

"Wow," said Paula. "Were you holding the phone to your ear at the time? 'Cause that could've hurt."

"No, I was joking. I wasn't talking on the phone when it was shot, and somebody didn't get pissed when I used my phone in public. It was collateral damage in a shooting."

"In the shooting of the salon owner, huh?" said Dave.

"Yes."

"Who did it? You must know?"

"I'm not at liberty to divulge what I know at this time. The police are holding the information very close to their Kevlar vests."

They both nodded with understanding.

"Could I just have a new one?"

"What one will it be?" Dave asked.

"You pick it. I'm tired of thinking about cell phones."

They finally had their way with me and picked out the top-of-the-line iPhone with lots of features and gigs, whatever those were, that I didn't understand and wouldn't use. They did all their computer work, and I did all of the paper work. Finally, I walked out of the store with yet another phone, waiting for a catastrophe. I knew its life was limited, and I almost felt sorry for it.

Chapter 32

When I got to my office, I sat at my desk with my feet up. I had my arms crossed in front of me, and I was leaning back in my chair, thinking. Most of the time I struggled over what Bobby Lee could possibly have wanted to tell me. I'd talk to him about it when he got out of the hospital, but I didn't want to bother him again now. Every once in a while, I would come forward on my chair and grab a Snickers bar from my drawer, unwrap it, throw the wrapper on my messy desk, and lean back on two chair legs again.

I thought I would pursue the Jaime Rodriquez drug angle again. This time without talking to Rodriquez, though. I decided to interview Laurie about Rodriquez again.

I took my feet down and flew forward in my chair. I called Laurie, and she answered after about 10 rings. She sounded as if I had awakened her.

"What?" she said into the phone. She was a little short on phone courtesy.

"This is Maggie Hall. Remember me?"

"No. I ain't buying anything."

"No, no. I'm not a salesperson. I was over at your apartment the other day. I was looking for Jaime."

"Oh, yeah," she said. "I remember. Did you find him?"

"Jaime Rodriquez?" I asked.

"Uh, sure."

"Yes," I said. "I'd like to come over to talk to you again."

"Okay. I don't have anything else to do any more. The club's closed. I'll be home all day. I'll be out tonight though. I have to start looking for another job."

Hum. The club's closed again. I told her I'd be right over.

℘℃

I got to the apartment, and Laurie let me in. With her time off, she still hadn't used any of it to clean her apartment. If it was possible, it looked worse.

She offered me a drink. I refused. I was afraid she might put it in one of the dirty glasses lying about the room. They had already been used a number of times without being washed.

I started with questions about both murders. "You know Ernest Ortega's body was found don't you?"

"I do now," she answered. "I just saw it on TV." She looked a little disturbed by his death or my question.

"Do you know why anyone would want him dead?"

"A couple of people might want him dead," she said matter-of-factly. She had begun to pick away at her chipped fingernail polish.

"Like who?"

She thought for a moment. "Maybe Rodriquez. Maybe one of the commissioners. Maybe one of the girls at the club. Sometimes Ernest made people really mad."

"What about Georgy?" I asked. "Who would have wanted him dead along with Ortega?"

"Rodriquez might have a good reason. Georgy found out he was selling drugs. I think he was going to fire him."

"Okay, what about Ortega? Why would Rodriquez want him dead?"

"I don't know. Maybe it had something to do with drugs, too."

I looked closely at Laurie's pin again because she kept fingering it. "Did someone give you that pin, Laurie?" It didn't seem like something she could afford to buy for herself.

"Yes." She looked a little wary of where my questions were heading. "It was a gift." She wiped her nose with the back of her hand.

"Who gave it to you?"

Laurie touched the pin that was on her shirt. "It's lovely, isn't it?"

"Yes, yes, it is. But who gave it to you?"

"Well, it can't hurt now. George gave it to me."

That was unexpected! I thought for sure it would be someone like Ortega. "Georgy?"

"Yes," she replied.

Bombshell. I remembered, then, that Mr. Garbarino said Georgy wasn't the best husband. "You were having an affair with George?"

"Not so much an affair. George didn't have affairs. He had women. He made it clear that he would never leave his wife and that the fun would not go on forever. But he bought nice gifts in the meantime."

Wow! This really opened the field for suspects. Jealous lover, jealous wife, jealous husband. But, why would Ortega be killed too, assuming the killers are the same? I'd have to think about this.

"Other than Jaime Rodriquez, do the letters *Ja* for the beginning of a name mean anything to you?" I asked, taking a different line of questioning.

She thought for a minute and then said, "No,"

"Did Ortega use drugs?"

"I never saw him do drugs, but that doesn't mean he didn't."

"Who do you really think killed them?"

"I think Jaime Rodriquez killed George to keep his job. And Jaime is missing now. I've called him, and I even went over to his place. There was no answer and the security guard said he hadn't seen him for a while. He even went up to his condo and rang the bell for me. No answer. He's gone."

"You're the one who called me and told me that you thought Jaime killed Georgy, aren't you?"

"Yes," Laurie said.

"Why?"

"Well, the day before George was murdered, he found drugs here at my place. He was very angry with me, knocked me around a little. I guess I deserved it. Anyway, he was pretty mad. He asked me, and I told him I got them from Rodriquez. I knew then that he would fire him."

"But you don't know for sure why Rodriquez would kill Ortega? Did you know a man named Bobby Lee?" I asked.

"No," she said. "Never heard of him."

"How did you know that I worked at the *Gazette* when you called me to say that you suspected Rodriquez for the Garbarino murder?" I realized that I hadn't told Laurie I was a columnist when I visited her.

"I'm not as stupid as I seem. When I saw you in Jaime's office, I asked him later who you were."

I drove back to the office after talking to Laurie. I could see why Rodriquez would have a reason to kill Georgy, but where did Ortega and Bobby Lee fit in? Maybe they didn't fit in. Maybe the Bobby Lee incident was just a random drive-by shooting. What did he know about the whole mess though?

Chapter 33

I put in a full day at the *Gazette,* and finally went home. It was late evening. I scrounged around the kitchen and came up with some leftovers. I have to say, Mom's leftovers are better than most people's firsts. Eventually, Mom joined me in the kitchen.

She and I waited up for Kitty to get back from her date with Frederick, and I hadn't heard from Coop. He was probably off with some other woman. Heck, for all I knew he had a wife and eight children. The oldest is Coop, Jr. The kids are each a year apart. The boys look like him, and the girls look like her. His wife's blonde and petite with a great figure. I was getting mad at him just thinking about how he had betrayed his family and lied to me.

"Where's Margaret?" I asked.

"Oh, she went to bed early," Mom said. "She didn't like what I was having for dinner."

Kitty finally walked in. She knew we were waiting in the kitchen for the scoop. Whoever went out always had to fill in the rest of us about the evening. It was a house rule. Sometimes we had to live our lives vicariously through each other.

"Hi," she said, looking pretty happy. Mom and I eyed each other and smiled.

"How was your date?" I asked.

"Fun. We went out and had pizza and pasta at The Bootlegger." The Bootlegger is an old Las Vegas favorite. It began as the Fremont Pizzeria long before I could remember, moved to Eastern and Tropicana where it stayed for years as The Bootlegger, and is now in a new building on Las Vegas Boulevard. "Then," Kitty said, waiting dramatically for the effect, "Frederick took me to the library."

"The library?" Mom and I exclaimed together. "Wow!" We weren't sincere.

"Yes," Kitty smiled. "The library. He took me to one of the computers and showed me all kinds of websites that he had found. Websites that have lessons plans I can use with my kids, websites with artwork on ducks and Nevada wetlands, websites with science experiments dealing with aquatic animals. Just all kinds of useful things for me."

"That's pretty impressive," I said. "A sensitive guy. There aren't too many of those around."

Mom and I nodded, each having known our share of insensitive ones.

"He's really interested in what I do. He knows so much about computers and showed me how they can help me. Isn't that just too rad?"

Mom and I heartily agreed it was "rad." Kitty told us more about her evening.

"Rod was never like this, and he was a teacher, too. With Rod, his stuff always came first. Frederick is smart, creative, and attentive. And, he's patient when he explains computer things to me. By the way, I have Gram's opinion about moving in with Frederick. I'm still waiting to hear from you, Mom."

"I know. Stop pushing me. I just haven't had time to think about it with this case. Give me a few days."

"Okay," and with that she bounced off to bed, not upset that I hadn't given her an answer yet. I was more perturbed with myself for not finding time to talk to her about Frederick. But, in my usual Scarlett O'Hara style, I could think about that tomorrow.

After I had been upstairs for a while, my newly acquired cell phone rang. It was Coop.

"Hi," he said. "How are you feeling?"

"Okay. I've tried to keep busy so I won't think too much about Bobby Lee."

"Have you been staying away from the Garbarino, Ortega, and Bobby Lee cases?"

"Sure. Except I did talk to Laurie."

"Laurie who?"

"Laurie, the stripper from La Tigra. As I told you Rodriquez was selling her drugs. What you don't know is that she had a thing going with Georgy. I found out that she's my anonymous caller who told me she thought Rodriquez killed Georgy. She told me that Georgy found drugs at her house, and she told him that they came from Rodriquez. She's just sure that he was going to fire Jaime. She doesn't know why Rodriquez would kill Ortega or try to kill Bobby Lee."

"I couldn't persuade you to work on another story for your column could I?" he asked, sounding a little frustrated.

"Probably not. When do I get to see you?" I tried to change the subject.

"Maggie, Metro told me that Bobby Lee and Ernest Ortega were shot with the same weapon. You need to stay away from this case."

So, at least, those two cases were connected. We still don't know if they are connected to Georgy's murder, but it is likely they are. "I'll think about it. When can I see you? You're avoiding my question."

"And, you're avoiding my advice."

"I never was good at taking advice."

"Tomorrow night. I called to let you know that I'll be back in town tomorrow." Apparently, he had given up for the moment.

"Oh," I said, cheered already. "Do we have plans?"

"Yes, my plan is to see as much of you as I can. Well, I've seen you, and it was a great preview. But, I really need to see more for a longer period of time."

"Are we just going to have phone sex for the rest of our lives?" I asked. "Cause I could use some of the up close and personal kind."

"Hey, I'm in the mood for any kind. The dirtier the better."

"What about the wife and eight kids?" I asked.

"What?"

"You know the wife and eight kids. Coop, Jr. and the others."

"I have no wife, eight kids, and Coop, Jr."

"I knew that." Nonetheless, I was happy to hear him reassure me.

"By the way, is Jaime Rodriquez missing?" I asked.

He sighed. "The cops raided another place that Rodriquez had in town. He was stashing drugs there..."

"Is he missing?"

"I can tell you that the Garbarino clubs here in town are closed. We're getting ready for indictments."

"I already knew that. Laurie told me. You're not answering my question."

He sighed again and told me he'd call tomorrow when he got into town.

I called Rick with my news.

"What's up, Legs?"

"Are you going to stop calling me that?"

"Not until you get fat or have lots of varicose veins."

"Well, I've been working while you've obviously been sitting around obsessing on thoughts of me."

"Do you really think you should be calling someone else obsessive?"

"Oh, don't deny it. You think about me."

"Could you just get to your news?"

"Well, Laurie was my anonymous caller, and she and Georgy were having a thing. Not a thing. More like have body will sell for the right price. She suspects Rodriquez killed him because Georgy was going to fire Rodriquez for selling drugs.

"Hum," Rick said.

I could hear a pen dragging across paper. He was taking notes. I should keep better notes, I thought.

"Also, the cops found another place where Rodriquez was storing drugs. Now, I don't know where he is."

"How does this tie in with Bobby Lee and Ortega?"

"It doesn't. That's the problem, but I found out that Bobby Lee and Ortega were shot with the same gun. I can't get away from the fact that Bobby Lee knew something about something."

Rodriquez still seemed the likely suspect, but what did he have against Bobby Lee and Ortega?

Chapter 34

I went into the office early the next morning, hoping to see Rick. He might have some more information on the Bobby Lee shooting and Ortega murder. Rick wasn't in yet. I stayed around to explore some angles for my Friday column. So far I had more questions than answers.

I could feel someone standing over my desk, a big, obnoxious someone.

"How's it going, Maggie?"

"Fine," I said cautiously. I'm always suspicious when Monroe asks me anything.

He sat down in the chair in front of my desk and put his feet up. His shoes needed to be resoled, and gum was stuck to the bottom of one sole. Now I'd have to use Lysol on my desktop. He began moving things on my desk around, like my stapler and tape. I kept moving them back where they belonged.

"What do you want, Monroe? Other than to mess up my work environment."

"I just want to make sure you are okay after yesterday."

"That's nice of you." Uncharacteristically nice, I thought.

"I was just thinking that if you haven't had sex for at least two years, I might stand a chance soon. I'd hate to see you get yourself shot before then."

"You're all heart. But, you'll never have a chance with me. I have standards."

"Yeah, but they might be low," replied Monroe.

"Monroe, they'll never be that low."

He left, chortling all the way back to his desk. I never really knew what a "chortle" was until I heard Monroe.

℠℣

By the time I finished researching some leads, it was time for Ortega's funeral service. I wore black tailored pants and a crème-colored silk short-sleeved blouse to work today, knowing that I would be attending the funeral. I drove to Palm Mortuary on Eastern. The parking lot was significantly less than half full. When I walked in, I saw my friend Pam. She motioned to me and said that Judith Ortega wanted me to sit with her. So, Pam took me up front with Judith. I was introduced to a few of Ortega's relatives who had come to town. Either he had a small family or they didn't like him any better than anyone else did. Pretty soon I turned around to see who else was here. Ray Angelo and some county commissioners were in the crowd. The ex-mayor, Oscar Goodman, was here and a few other political faces I recognized. The pews weren't crowded, though. It was official; Ortega was not well liked. You could always tell a person's popularity by how many people attend his funeral

I noticed that Joann Kirkoff and Pritchard were missing from the funeral service. I really didn't expect to see them here.

Judith held up okay during the funeral. There were times when she had to remove that handkerchief from her sleeve. Sometimes she would hold onto my arm. I guess just touching someone helps. I couldn't avoid comparing this service to the one for Georgy. Georgy's was so much more personal, with friends of his getting up and telling funny stories. No one did that here. I wondered if no one really knew Ernest or if there were no funny stories about him. I didn't think it would be appropriate for me to stand up and talk about our fight at La Tigra.

After the service, Raymond Angelo and I were standing outside talking about classmates we knew and had just seen at Georgy's funeral.

I asked Ray, "Do you know of a Bobby Lee, a friend of Bruce Pritchard's?"

"A friend of Bruce's? Would this be a close friend?" He did the limp wrist thing.

"Ray, you're such a sensitive guy," I said, shaking my head. "It's no wonder you weren't re-elected."

"Is he the guy shot yesterday? What? Did he and Bruce have a lovers' quarrel? Maybe Bruce hired a hit on him."

Ray was getting to me. He took political incorrectness to new levels.

Judith walked up to us, and then my cell phone rang. It was Bruce Pritchard.

"Bobby Lee wants to talk with you again when he comes home today," he said.

I smiled sheepishly at Judith and Ray as if my smile made taking a call at a funeral acceptable. I moved a little away from them to be polite.

"I can't talk about it now. I'm running around making arrangements for Bobby Lee's homecoming. Can you come by my house later this afternoon?" Bruce asked.

"Sure, I'll come by later," I said. "About what time."

"Around 4 o'clock would be good."

"Okay, I'll see you at 4."

I returned to Ray and Judith. "Sorry, that was Pritchard. Bobby Lee is coming home today."

"I was so worried about you, sugar, when I heard. You could have been hurt, also."

Ray quipped, "Only the good die young." I wasn't certain what that said about Ortega, and I hoped Judith didn't read too much into it.

"Judith," I asked, "did you know the man who was shot, Bobby Lee?"

"I don't think I did, sugar. Why?"

"I'm just trying to figure out what could connect your husband and Bobby Lee."

"Maybe they're not connected," Ray suggested.

"That's possible," I agreed. I didn't reveal that they were both shot with the same weapon.

℀℁

After the funeral, I drove back to my office. I had a message to call Joann Kirkoff.

"Did you go to Ernest's funeral?"

"Yes, I did, Joann."

"Was it a nice funeral?"

How do you answer that? Nice for everyone but the dead guy? "Yes, Joann, it was a fitting service." As a journalist, I choose my words carefully.

Oodles or Toodles had a barking fit, and Joann put her hand over the phone and yelled, "Shut up. I'm on the phone. Can't you tell?" She was beginning to lose her patience with one of them.

"You're the only person I can talk to about Ernest," Joann explained. She spent some time telling me again how nice Ernest had been to her after her husband left. I heard her dogs continue to yap in the background. They probably knew I was on the phone.

Then, she asked, "Has anyone found out any more about his murder?"

"Not that I'm aware of. By the way, did you know a Bobby Lee who runs Shear Power?"

"Yes," she said. "I go to Bobby Lee to get my hair done. He's wonderful. Why?"

"Well, you're going to have to find a new hairdresser for a while. He was shot."

"Oh, dear, me. Is he okay? Will he still do my hair? I mean, he is such a nice man. I hate it that he was hurt."

"Did you know he was Bruce Pritchard's love interest?"

"Oh," she said, "that explains Bruce being in the salon. I saw him in the salon a couple of times visiting Bobby Lee."

"I'm going to see Bruce this afternoon."

"Tell Bruce to tell Bobby Lee to get well soon. He shouldn't let too much time pass before he gets back to his salon. It's a dog-eat-dog world." I hoped she wasn't referring to Oodles and Toodles. Though, I think if the circumstances were right, they would eat each other.

I tried Mr. Garbarino's cell phone but there was no answer. I left a message. Then, I called Rita at her new office.

"Rita, do you know where Mr. Garbarino is? I'm trying to reach him."

"Wait a minute." Then, she put her hand over the phone, but I could still hear. She yelled out, "Am I allowed to tell Maggie that Mr. Garbarino's here." I couldn't hear the answer. I don't know if Rita's going to be able to handle this confidentiality thing that lawyers are so picky about.

Eventually, she returned to me and said, "Mr. G.'s here. Do you want to talk with him?"

"Yes."

In her professional voice, Rita said, "Please hold. I'll transfer you."

I was wrong; she really was getting the hang of things.

"Hi, Maggie, what do you need?"

"Mr. Garbarino do you know a Bobby Lee?"

"Is that the guy who was shot, and you were right there?"

"That's the one."

"No, I don't know him. The clubs here in town have all been closed because of the bribery investigation and the indictments. It's a mess, but I think we'll get them open again soon. It sounds like it's getting dangerous out there for you, Maggie. I don't want you killed, too. Maybe you should stop."

"Well, Bobby Lee was a friend of Bruce Pritchard's."

"I figured that from the stories," he said.

"I'm going over to see Bobby Lee again today. I think he knows something about the case. I also wanted to give you a heads-up about Jaime Rodriquez. Just before Georgy was killed, he found out that Rodriquez was selling drugs. He was probably going to fire him."

"Well, I let him go anyway when the clubs closed. Heaven help him if he was connected with my son's murder. I know people. Bye, and, Maggie, thanks for keeping me informed. The police don't tell me much."

"That's what old friends do, Mr. Garbarino."

It was about 3:30 when I left the office, and I would have to hurry to get to Bruce's house on time.

Chapter 35

I was heading across the street to my car when I saw another car pull out from a parking space. It looked somewhat familiar. Then it dawned on me. This was the same car as the one at Shear Power. The car was speeding up now, and I was caught standing there in the middle of the street in shock. Whoever was in the car was coming at me fast. I finally snapped out of it and jumped between two parked cars just as it sped by. Actually, it was more like I fell between two parked cars. As I tumbled between the cars, I twisted my ankle and landed on my left leg. I heard a bullet ping on the trunk of the car near me as I rolled underneath the other car.

After the shooter drove off, people were on the street and coming over to me. I was rolling out from under the vehicle where I had taken cover.

A man was bending over me. "Are you all right?"

A woman near him had her phone out, and I think she called 911. I heard her say there had been a hit and run accident. She also gave the location. She said, "A woman might have been hit. At least, she's on the ground." Pause. "No, but I think she's injured."

The man kept talking to me, but I wasn't answering. Sounds and images were coming to me through a fog. I finally looked at him and said, "I think I'm okay." But, as he tried to help me up, I realized my left leg hurt. I couldn't stand.

"I think I hurt my leg," I told him.

"Help's on the way. You just stay there." Then, he started brushing some of the dirt off me. Nice man, I thought. I guess I had gotten dirty when I rolled under the car. I knew one thing, I was getting tired of this mystery car and dodging bullets.

Pretty soon I could hear sirens. Boy, I thought, I've heard this before. Police cars and paramedics raced into view.

The paramedics ran up to me first. A policeman was behind them, and I think other cops were talking to people in the crowd. I told the paramedics that I didn't think I could walk. They called for an ambulance.

About this time, Uncle Dutch pushed through the crowd. The sounds of the commotion on the street must have reached the *Gazette.* I could hear him yelling, "Let me through. That's my niece." He finally got over to me. "Maggie, are you all right?"

"I'm okay, Uncle Dutch. A little shaken. No, a lot shaken. And my leg hurts." I wanted to cry, just a little. I didn't, though, because Uncle Dutch never liked a whiner.

"Oh, your mother's going to kill me," he said, wiping his forehead. I could tell he was really worried but not about me.

"Uncle Dutch, this is not about you."

"Oh, you don't know. It is. It is. Angela will yell at me. She'll say it's my fault. That I don't watch out for you. Then, she'll call Ann. The two of them will gang up on me. My life's going to be hell." Now he was sweating, and I worried he might have a heart attack.

"I'm very sorry to be causing you so much trouble, Uncle Dutch," I said, sitting on the ground and rubbing my leg, which had begun to throb. "Not to change the subject, but what do you think about giving me a raise?"

"Why?" he asked.

"This is a dangerous job."

Though he didn't respond verbally, I could tell from his expression that the answer was, "No." Cheapskate.

"Hey," I said. "Get my purse and see if my cell phone is okay."

Uncle Dutch grabbed my purse, which was near the wheel of the car that had protected me. He looked inside and pulled out my cell phone. "It looks fine."

"Great," I said. "I can't take one more trip to Verizon."

Ⅎ℮ℛ

The ambulance drivers took me into the emergency room at Sunrise Hospital. Uncle Dutch followed them in his car and came into the emergency room. Two officers were there to get my statement.

My phone didn't stop ringing while they were interviewing me.

212

Mom called. Kitty called. Rita called. Uncle Gus called. Aunt Ann called. My brother Jack called from Laguna Beach. Except for Jack, they were all on their way over. Oh, boy, a party. Then, Coop called.

"How did you find out?" I asked.

"Your mom phoned me."

"How did she get your number?"

"I gave it to her when I was at your house the last time. That's beside the point," he said. "I just want to make sure you're okay."

"I'm sore, but I'm okay. My leg really hurts. The rest are cuts and scrapes. I'm a little unnerved. The last time, I wasn't the target. Or, at least, I didn't think I was. This time I am. That puts a whole new slant on things. I don't even know why I'm a target."

"I'm at the airport ready to get on the plane. I'll be at Sunrise in about one and one half hours. I gotta board now. See you in a bit."

Let's see, I thought. One and a half hours away. It will take him, at least, one half hour to get here from the airport. Some time to walk to his car, maybe get his luggage. He's close to Vegas. That means he is in Arizona, Southern California, Utah. I wasn't too hurt to try to figure out where Coop has been.

One of the two officers finally said, "Would you turn off the phone so that we can finish. The faster we find out what happened, the faster we can catch the guy who shot at you and almost ran you over."

"Okay." I was reluctant to turn off a phone that had been lucky so far.

He glanced down at his notes. "You looked up and saw a car pull out of a parking space. Then what?"

"Then, I noticed it was remarkably similar to the car involved in the shooting of Bobby Lee at Shear Power."

"And he shot at you?" asked the officer with the notes.

"Yes, but I was terribly busy trying to jump out of the way."

"Did you recognize the driver?"

"I couldn't even see the driver."

"Were you hit?"

"No, I hurt my leg when I jumped out of the way."

"Anything else?

"No, that's all. It happened so fast. I'm sorry."

The cop who had been silent to this point finally spoke. "Here's a blank statement form. Fill it out, sign it, and give it back to us. You can wait to fill it out, but don't wait too long. I've put a tracking number on it."

I filled it out while I waited for the hospital to attend to me.

By the time everyone arrived, I was in a little curtained off area in the emergency room, having come back from x-ray. I hadn't seen the doctor yet. Seven people were alongside my bed. Uncle Dutch, Aunt Ann, Uncle Gus, Mom, Kitty, Frederick, and Rita had come in at about the same time all talking at once. The effect was chaos, and Nurse Ratchet was having trouble handling it.

In exasperation, she said, "You have to leave. The doctor has to be able to get in here." She was trying to shoo them out, but they just sidestepped her arms.

Putting her thumb and forefinger in her mouth, the nurse let out an ear-splitting whistle. Everyone stood still. "Out," she shouted. "Now!"

Mom said, "I'm staying. So, he'll just have to work around me."

"I'm not leaving either," said Kitty. Boy, are they stubborn.

"I don't want to leave, but I'll wait outside," said Rita.

Frederick gave Kitty a consoling hug and walked out of the room.

Everyone else volunteered to stay in the waiting room also.

When the doctor came in, Mom was watching him closely. He was a nice looking man, about Mom's age. He was talking to her instead of to me when he put the x-rays on the light board on the wall.

"There are no breaks," he explained to Mom. "I think her leg and ankle are badly sprained, though. She'll have to wear a soft cast."

"Is that the dark blue kind with the Velcro straps that looks like a very unstylish après ski boot?" Mom asked.

"Yes." He grinned at Mom. "That's the one. She'll probably need to keep it on, at least, for a month."

"What about the pain?" Mom asked.

"I'll give her Percodan for that. The nurse will clean the cuts and scrapes and put something on them. Other than that, I think she'll be fine. You might consider taking her to her regular doctor in about a month."

"Thank you, doctor. Oh," Mom said, "In case you're ever in need of a house, I'm in real estate." She, then, handed him her business card. She was smooth. I should watch her techniques. Now he had her phone number. I'm pretty sure she noticed that he wasn't wearing a wedding ring. All I can say is I'm glad I could almost get killed so that Mom and the emergency room doctor could go on a date.

Kitty and I just looked at each other and shook our heads. The acorns didn't fall far from the oak tree, but Kitty and I lacked her sophisticated approach.

"You know, I was thinking of looking for a different house, something newer and bigger. I'll give you a call." With that, he put Mom's card into his pocket and gave it an extra little pat. That meant he'd be calling.

"Oh," he said. "If your daughter has any problems, here's my card. I'll write my home number on the back in case there's an emergency." He handed the card to Mom.

Just then, Coop came rushing in. The doctor turned to him and said, "There are too many people here. You'll have to leave."

Coop said, "FBI," and flashed his FBI credentials. They worked wonders. I needed some FBI credentials for my job. I wonder if you can find them at Target.

"What's going on?" Coop turned to Mom.

"Hello." I waved wildly. Enough is enough. "I'm over here. Ask me what's going on?"

"Okay. What's going on?"

"Well, Mom has a date with my emergency room doctor, and if that isn't enough, my leg and ankle are sprained."

"You look a little cut up and bruised, too. So, I'm going to ignore your generally surly attitude."

"How lucky can I get in one day?" I flung back with as much surly attitude as I could muster.

"Do you feel okay?" He sat on the bed next to me.

Finally, I thought, he was showing concern.

"I'm going to feel better when they give me Percodan."

I noticed Kitty was being very quiet. "What's wrong, honey?" I asked.

"Well, it's okay for all of you to be very light about all this, but I'm not all right." Then, she began to cry.

"I'm okay now," I assured her.

"I know, but somebody's out to kill you, and that bothers me a lot. I've grown rather accustomed to you."

"It bothers me, too, honey. But I'll be safe. I'll be okay." I held my arms open for a hug.

"You're just not careful," she sobbed, accepting my hug.

"I'll be more careful," I promised. "The cops will get this guy, whoever he is."

"We'll take care of her," Coop said, and he gave Kitty a little hug.

Nurse Ratchet returned and brought the soft leg cast and a Percodan. She put the cast on my leg. It had an attached boot-like thing on it, so Mom took my left shoe. The nurse gave me the Percodan and told me I couldn't drive or operate big machinery. That was too bad. I had planned to use the backhoe tonight. I assured her I wouldn't be driving or operating any big machinery. Plenty of people were here with cars.

The nurse insisted it was hospital policy that I go out in a wheel chair; so, I got a ride to the front of the emergency room area. Mom was waiting in the car, and Coop helped me in. Kitty got in the back seat. Coop said he would meet us at the house. Everyone else was coming to the house, too. I was right; it was going to be a party. By this time, I was getting a little woozy from the Percodan and was in the party mood.

Mom phoned ahead to Margaret and assured her I was okay and on my way home. Mom told Margaret to expect company, to get out cheese and crackers, to chill the wine and beer, and to put out some nuts and snacks. Mom is the perfect hostess, no matter what the occasion—reception, birthday party, near death experience, shoot-out.

Chapter 36

When we drove up to the house, Margaret was waiting in the driveway. She ran and opened the car door. She actually started crying and hugging me.

"What kind of trouble have you gotten yourself into now, dearie?" Margaret asked.

Coop was right behind us, and he got out of his car and walked over to help me out of Mom's car. He scooped me up into his arms and carried me inside. Margaret was giving him directions along the way. She had him set me on the couch in the family room. I was very relaxed now thanks to the medication. I think I may have even squeezed Coop's muscles in his arm and said, "Oh, what would the big strong man like to do now?" Everyone just looked at me, very understandingly, though.

Coop just laughed and said, "I'd like to put you on the couch."

I just put my head back on the pillow to rest. At least, my leg didn't hurt.

Coop, Kitty, Frederick, Mom, Margaret, Rita, Uncle Gus, Aunt Ann, and Uncle Dutch were all in the kitchen. I could hear laughter every now and again. Boy, I thought, they're having a great time.

Every so often, someone would come in and whisper, "Do you need anything, Maggie?"

I think I fell asleep, but I could still hear talking. So, it wasn't a deep sleep. It was one of those sleep/dream experiences.

I could hear Coop entertaining everyone with FBI stories.

"So, I handcuff this guy," I hear him say, "and as I'm standing beside him, he reaches down and bites me here on the top of my arm. Hard enough to draw blood. Then, he takes off running. I think I uttered a few expletives and then took out after him. He got his face shoved into the pavement, but I got this scar."

Mom must have been feeling his scar. "Oh, that left a big bump," she said.

"No," Coop replied. "That's my muscle."

My mother's a shameless flirt.

Kitty joined in. "When I was student teaching, a student bit me; but I don't have a scar." She sounded disappointed. Maybe next year.

"Frederick added, "Wow! Nothing like that happens in my computer lab. Sometimes we do have a raging virus attack."

They all laughed.

Mom assigned everyone in the kitchen a task. I think Coop was assigned to cut vegetables for the salad.

Somewhere in my drug-induced sleep, I heard Rick Steele come in. He was introduced to the people he didn't know, and they explained to him what had happened outside the *Gazette* offices.

I started waking up when I could smell dinner. I could also feel my leg again, and it didn't feel good. Everyone in the kitchen was still having a very good time. Someone would laugh now and again, and wine glasses were occasionally tinkling together.

"Hey, in there," I yelled. "Could I have a little attention? Remember, I'm the reason for the party; I'm the injured, nearly killed person."

They all came rushing in. Guilt, I think.

"Magpie, you're awake," Mom said. "Don't be so silly; we've been checking on you regularly."

Mom called me Magpie when I was little. It was strangely comforting now. I did the best lower lip pucker I could. "I know, but everyone out there is having such a good time, and I'm stuck in here. And, it's time for another happy pill."

"Do you feel like sitting up," Coop asked.

"I think so."

He carried me out to the kitchen where I took my pain killer and joined in the fun. What a guy! I sat on the stool and watched everyone working on dinner and drinking beer or wine. They wouldn't give me any alcohol because of the Percodan. Mom served poached salmon with fettuccini and a white sauce. We had broccoli and a salad along with it. We ate standing or sitting around the kitchen.

After dinner, we ended up on the terrace looking out over the pool and the lights of the city. I got the chaise lounge so that I could keep my leg up. Mom and Margaret served after dinner drinks, again to everyone but me. That's okay. I was having my own Percodan party.

"How's your job, Rita?" I asked.

"It's great," she replied. "I helped solve a case already, but I can't talk about it. The work we do is confidential. Anyway, this lady was divorcing her husband who was found *in flagrante delicto*, and needless to say, I photographed him about as *in flagrante* as he could get. Oops! Is that violating confidentiality?" She laughed and looked around for consensus.

We all told her we didn't think so since she wasn't very specific. Coop said she might be walking a thin line.

"Maggie, maybe you should lay off this story for a while. Let the cops and FBI do their work." said Uncle Dutch.

Everyone who knew Uncle Dutch well was in stunned silence.

"It must be the Percodan, Uncle Dutch, but did you tell me not to get a story. Are you trying to protect me?"

He shrugged. "I almost had a heart attack today. The paramedics had to take my blood pressure. They told me to cut down on stress in my life. I'm just looking out for my interests. Besides, if something happens to you, your Aunt Ann will divorce me and your mother will sue me."

Aunt Ann and Mom raised glasses and said, "Here. Here."

"Do you want Rick to stop work on the story, too?" I asked.

"No. Nobody's shooting at him yet."

I didn't respond, but I think everyone knew I would continue pursuing the story. I raised my water glass and proposed another toast. "To almost getting killed and one hell of a party." They all looked at me as if I were crazy and refused to toast. No sense of humor.

After drinks, everyone except Coop left. Margaret just looked at me and started crying again.

"I could stay down here if you need me, dearie," Margaret said.

"No, you've been wonderful, and I'll see you in the morning."

Margaret left, promising to be her old self tomorrow and to give me a scolding on being shot at and nearly run over. As if it were my fault. I was really looking forward to getting the old Margaret back. I could understand her better. I didn't know who this woman was.

Mom asked Coop to carry me upstairs. Kitty came along to help me with my pajamas and to get settled in. Coop set me on the bed and gave me a very nice, almost sisterly kiss good night. Getting shot at, my leg cast, and my daughter in the room put a damper on my fun tonight.

"I had different plans for us this evening," Coop explained.

"So did I."

Kitty just stood there smiling. "Sorry." She sounded gleeful. "But, I'm not leaving. So, you'll just have to carry out your plans some other time."

When did I raise such a bossy daughter? Coop spent some time being genuinely angry with me for pursuing my story at such a cost. The Percodan let me listen to him rant without taking him too seriously. I just kept smiling and nodding in agreement. Finally, he gave up and left. Kitty helped me into bed and my pajamas.

"Was Rick here earlier?" I asked Kitty.

"He sure was. He was very worried about you. I guess he talked to the police and got all he needed for his story and, then, rushed over here to find out about you."

"How did Coop and Rick get along?"

"Just fine."

"Hum," I was a little disappointed. "Nobody threw down a glove and fought a duel over me."

"Maybe tomorrow, Mom." Kitty kissed me goodnight and turned off the light.

I tried to think about who would want Georgy, Ortega, Bobby Lee, and me dead. Was Rodriquez missing because of the drugs or was he on a murderous rampage? But why Ortega, Bobby Lee and me? The Percodan wasn't going to let me think for long. I fell asleep quickly.

Chapter 37

The next morning, I gingerly swung my legs over the side of the bed, stood up, and got ready without any help. Showering was a feat appropriate for a gymnast. I balanced on one leg while trying to clean myself as thoroughly as possible. I dressed with a considerable amount of trouble, putting on what I thought would be the easiest outfit. A peasant skirt and short top would have to do. I could only wear one sandal because of my leg cast.

Somewhere in one of my drug induced dreams, I had resolved to talk to Kitty as soon as possible. After all, life could be short. So, I went to her bedroom before I left. I knocked on her door. She was awake.

"Okay, I'm ready to talk about this Frederick guy?"

She was still lying in bed; so, I sat down on the edge as I had done so many times before.

"Just plain Frederick, Mom."

"Okay. Just plain Frederick."

I started with the same direct approach that I used in interviews. "Why do you want to move in with him?"

"Well, he asked me to marry him, but I want to see how we work out living together first. I want to see if I am as comfortable living with him as I am with you and Gram. And, I want to make sure that we're right for each other."

"Nobody's asked you the big question, Kitty. Do you love him?"

"Yes, yes, I do, Mom." She didn't even hesitate. That was a good sign.

"Does he love you?

"I believe he does."

"Is he a good man?"

"Yes, he's a good man." She smiled and again answered with no hesitation.

"Well, then, I'm ready to tell you what I think. I think I'll be lonely without seeing you every morning when I awake and every night before I go to bed. I think I've been dependent upon you for so long, Kitty. But, really, I don't think…"

Kitty interrupted. "Sure, you might be a little lonely, Mom. But, you've never been dependent upon me or anyone. You've been the strong one. I've depended on you my whole life. You were always there. You worked hard so that I could have things. You hardly ever dated. Most of the time when you and Rita went out, you dragged me along. You took me any place I wanted to go—Disneyland, the petting zoo, birthday parties, movies. You played every stupid card and board game late into the night. No other single mother I knew was like that. You moved us in here with Gram so that I would have extra supervision when I was in my teens and so that someone was at home everyday when I got out of school. When I was hurt, I came to you; when I was scared, I came to you; when I was wondering what to do with my life, I came to you. And, now that I want to know whether to take this next big step, I'm coming to you. Sure, we live with Gram, but you are the most independent person I know. You'll be fine without my being here all the time, but it's time for me to be the person you raised me to be. And, it's time for you to have a life of your own outside of me."

It was my turn to interrupt. "I don't regret that you were my life or that I didn't date much, Kitty."

"I know you don't, Mom. That's what makes you great."

"Kitty, you didn't let me finish what I was saying. I was about to say that I don't think you want my consent so much as my approval. You've already made your decision, and I want you to know that I approve of it. I approve of your moving in with Frederick and starting a life of your own."

"How did you know I'd already decided to move in with Frederick?"

"I'm super mom, remember? Besides, I raised you to think for yourself. And, I'm proud of how you turned out."

We hugged, and finally, I asked the big question when we let go of each other, "When are you moving out?"

Kitty was smiling. "Not immediately but before school starts. I want to get settled in before I start teaching."

Tears started to roll down Kitty's face. I wiped them away as I had always done. "What's wrong now? I thought you would be happy that I approve."

"I am. It's just that I'll miss you."

"That's not possible. I won't give you a chance, Kitty. I'm just down the street, and Frederick is about to see more of me than he thinks." Now I had tears, too. Growing up was hard, but I guess it was time I started. We talked some more, and I left Kitty's bedroom, letting her think I was going back to my room.

Instead, I wrote a note and set it on the kitchen counter. I explained that I had gone into the office. Then, I sneaked down to Mom's car. I had to use her car, because Coop had not gotten mine home from the *Gazette* yet.

It was a good thing that my left leg was the injured one because I had enough trouble operating the car as it was. I didn't take any Percodan this morning because I knew I would be driving; so, my leg and ankle were hurting.

I thought I might find Pritchard at home this morning. I had to try. I turned off my cell phone and left it in the car because Mom and Kitty would just be calling me when they found out I was gone. The ringing would make me feel very guilty.

When I walked up to Pritchard's door, I could hear loud noises coming from inside. I rang the bell. I didn't think anyone could hear it, so I walked in. The door was unlocked. People were shoulder-to-shoulder all throughout the house.

The crowd inside looked like the band from *Star Wars.* They were every shape, sex, and dress. Some looked like stand-ins for Legends in Concert; some wore brightly colored clothes and the tightest pants I'd ever seen; and some were dressed professionally in very nice suits or dress slacks. The women were well coifed; I guessed they were clients at the salon. Pritchard was rushing about with drinks and snacks. I could see him moving from group to group. All in all, it looked like a really great welcome home party for Bobby Lee.

Bruce spotted me and rushed over. He hugged me. "I'm so happy you're here. We're having a homecoming brunch. Look at all these people. Bobby Lee has so many friends. They just stopped by to cheer us up." He shook his head in disbelief.

I had to agree as I looked around the room. Bobby Lee had many friends, and most of them were characters.

Just then, Pritchard saw my leg. "What's that?" he asked pointing to my cast.

"I had an accident yesterday."

"Does it have anything to do with your not meeting us then?"

"Yes, and it's a long story," I explained. "Let's just say someone doesn't want me to keep looking into the Garbarino and Ortega murders."

"You must learn to be more careful, dear," Bruce said.

"Have you been talking to my mother," I joked. "Anyway, I was on my way over to meet with you when this happened."

"Speaking of that," he said. "Come with me, dear. Someone wants to talk with you."

We pushed our way through the crowd of people, hearing bits of conversation and stories about Bobby Lee. Most of the partygoers were laughing. Occasionally a guest patted Bruce on the shoulder or hugged him as we maneuvered through everyone. Pritchard took me into the study. There was Bobby Lee holding court from the settee. He looked like the male imitation of Camille. He was leaning back on the settee, his shoulder was bandaged, his feet were up and crossed at the ankles, and I think I saw him touching his forehead with a dramatic expression on his face. Woe is him.

"Maggie," he yelled from his position. "Come here, love. Shoo, shoo, everyone. I have to talk to this lovely lady." He patted the settee near his feet. There was just enough room for me to sit.

When everyone but Pritchard had left the room, Bobby Lee told me the gossip at the salon, ending with, "I never like to repeat what I hear, but I thought this might be important. What do you think?"

"Hum," I said. "I think you might be right.

Bruce sat in a chair across the room, waiting patiently while we finished.

I thought I knew who might have killed Georgy and Ortega, who shot at Bobby Lee, and who tried to run me down. More importantly, I thought I knew some of the why. I was starting to piece the puzzle together, and I remembered what had bothered me.

A little absentmindedly because I was still connecting some dots, I asked Bobby Lee how he was feeling.

"Great! But, I won't be at work for a while. What I need is a great substitute. Someone like me."

"Oh, there is no one like you, Bobby Lee," Bruce said sincerely.

"I have a friend, Gary. Anyway, Gary's out of work for a while. He worked at one of Garbarino's places. I remember that he used to be a hair stylist. I don't know if he has any interest in returning to that line of work, but if you're interested, I could give him a call. He'd bring customers in. Everyone who meets him likes him. We'll talk about it later, Bobby Lee. Give me a call if you're interested."

"Thanks, Maggie. I will call you."

Bruce walked me back through the crowd and to the front door. I was careful to avoid getting my foot stepped on.

"What are you going to do now?" Bruce asked.

"Oh, I have a stop to make."

"You'll be careful?" he warned.

"Of course. I'm genetically programmed to be careful."

Chapter 38

I turned on my cell phone to call Rick.

He answered right away.

I asked, half begging and half demanding, "I need help. Please, help me? It will make a great story."

"I'm afraid to ask. What do you have in mind?"

I explained where I was going and why.

"I'll be right there. Wait in the car until I get there. Will you do that?"

"Of course, I'll do that. That's why I called you. I'm not stupid."

"No, you're not stupid. You're irresistibly drawn to disaster."

"Thanks for the confidence."

"Oh, I have confidence in you," Rick said. "I'm confident you'll manage to get yourself hurt before I get there."

"Be quiet and drive fast." I hit the disconnect button and remembered to turn the phone off again.

I drove to the house and sat at the curb, giving myself a little pep talk. I thought we could handle this okay, and we needed answers. This could be a great column. What a scoop! I could see a new award on my wall. I looked at my watch and figured it would take Rick, at least, a half hour, maybe forty-five minutes to drive here. In the meantime, I cranked up the radio and was doing some serious singing along with the music to take my mind off my leg. Then, I did a little dancing in the seat, bobbing to the rhythm of the tunes.

I jumped when there was a knock on my window. I rolled it down.

"Well, Maggie, hello. I wasn't expecting you, sugar."

I turned down the radio. "Hi, Judith." I smiled as if I was genuinely happy to see her at my car window. "How are you?"

"Well, I'm just fine for someone who's just buried her husband. How are y'all?"

"I can't say I'm in great shape."

"Having problems?"

"Oh, nothing I can't handle."

"Let's cut to the chase. Why are y'all here?"

"Oh, nothing important. I just had a few questions. Tying up loose ends. You know."

"Of course." That slow Southern charm of hers was working overtime. "Get out of the car, and come on in."

"Let's talk out here," I said. "It's such a nice day."

"We can't do that," Judith pulled a gun from behind her back and pointed it at me.

Why had I rolled my car window down? Why didn't I just drive off when I saw her beside my car? Why didn't I park down the block?

"Come inside now." I could tell she was going to be quite insistent.

Well, this didn't work out very well, I thought. If I get myself killed, Mom, Kitty, Coop, and Rick are going to be very upset with me. I didn't see what choice I had at the moment. I had to go inside with Judith.

I opened the car door as Judith stepped back. I started to reach for my cell phone.

"Just leave it where it is," she ordered.

Judith walked behind me up the walkway and into the house. The entire time she kept looking around. So did I, but I didn't see anyone to help me.

Judith had me open the front door and walk into the house. When we got inside, she told me to sit on the couch. She sat in a chair.

"Ask your questions. That's what you came for." She still pointed the gun at me.

I had to admit, I had other things on my mind at the moment, like escaping with my life, but the journalist finally got the better of me. And, I did need to stall until Rick arrived.

"You were having an affair with George Garbarino, weren't you?" I asked.

"Yes, how did you know?"

"I realized that you and Laurie, a stripper at Georgy's club, both have the same pin. Georgy was having an affair with her and gave her that pin. He gave you the same piece of jewelry because the two of you were having an affair."

She seemed a bit indignant about Georgy's giving both of them the same gift. In fact, I thought she might rip it from her blouse, but she just took a deep breath and kept the gun pointed at me.

"So, Georgy was cheating on me with a stripper. I suppose it's to be expected. No loyalty."

I'd have to think about that one. Her ethics were mind-boggling. "I'm just not sure why you killed him. Did you kill him because he was seeing other women or did you kill him because of the FBI investigation?"

"I did it for Ernest and me. I met George through Ernest. George could be very persuasive and appealing. We started seeing each other right away. George had a way of making me feel special, and Ernie was usually so drunk that he didn't pay attention to my time away from home. Also, by seeing George I made sure that the extra money kept coming. Ernie and I had a lot of expenses. George made sure we had what we needed."

"The phone calls to the house from George were for you not your husband. Right?"

"Most of them. George didn't call Ernest very often."

"So, how did you find out that George was cooperating with the FBI and was about to ruin your cozy set-up? Did he let you know?"

"No, George didn't have the guts to tell me. Ernest came home Sunday night all liquored up, smelling of cigarettes and women, and looking as if he'd been in a fight. He said that George was telling the FBI about the bribes he gave. Ernie thought he would be indicted for accepting bribes and, if convicted, go to jail. I couldn't let that happen. We had a reputation to maintain. So, I went to the club. The alley was deserted and I parked there. I went in the backdoor to George's office. I often used that door for our rendezvous. No one was there but him. I wanted to convince George not to talk to the FBI. We argued, but he told me I was too late. He was already talking."

She paused. "Then, he laughed at me, telling me I would have to live within my means and find someone else to comfort me instead of my drunk, philandering husband. Feeling defeated and cheapened, I got George to escort me back to my car. After he closed my car door, I calmly rolled the window down, took the gun from my seat, and shot him as he walked back into the club. It was nice and tidy. How dare he involve us in his mess and then point the finger at us. Like we're the criminals."

Judith really did have an interesting moral code. I explored it some more. "Why your husband?" The longer I kept her talking, the longer I stayed alive.

"When he got up Monday morning with his usual hangover, he got a call from Raymond Angelo. Ernest told him that George was cooperating in an FBI investigation that could send them all to jail. When he got off the phone, I told him what I had done. I thought he would be happy that George's indiscretions were no longer hanging over our heads."

"But your husband wasn't happy?" I queried.

"No, the bastard. All he could think about was himself. He said I was crazy. Me. The only one with any balls to take action. He said he would be a suspect in George's murder, but I told him there was nothing to connect him to George's death. That didn't seem to help. He was irate. He said terrible things to me. The nerve of that man! After all I did for him."

Judith was right. The nerve of some men! You commit adultery and you commit murder for them and they just get upset.

She began to reminisce. I met Ernest in Los Angeles, and we married. The ceremony was not so grand, but I was so devoted to Ernest. I ran a wonderful household and made a most gracious hostess for all his political events. In fact, he never would have made anything of himself if it weren't for me. I was the showpiece he could take to his dinners and gala events. I talked to his constituents; I socialized with his politician friends and their spouses. I kept up on the issues and told him how to vote."

"And, then?"

"And then he started cheating on me. Joann Kirkoff wasn't his only indiscretion. He began going to that La Tigra. He made friends with Ray Angelo and George Garbarino. I begged him to see what he was doing to his reputation, to his career, and to me. He didn't care. I could smell the women all over him when he would come home. He started drinking too much, and he was always gone. When I found George, I decided that two could play the game."

"What happened on that Monday?" I asked. I was hoping Judith would relax her guard, but she kept steadily pointing the gun at me while she talked. I had to keep her talking, though. It was my only chance to find a way out.

"On Monday I went to get my nails done as I said. When I got home, Ernest had packed and was going to leave me. He said he wasn't going to take the fall for me. He had the money from our account and was headed out the door. I couldn't let that happen."

I asked her, "So, you killed him?"

"I got out the pistol again and made him get into the car. The money and his bags were already in the car. We drove out into the desert, we got out of the car, and I shot him. I think that really surprised him. He really was a fool."

I'm sure getting shot by his own wife did surprise him. I know that getting shot at always surprises me.

"I didn't think he was still alive," she continued, "after I shot him the first time. I'm a good marksman. Daddy taught me to shoot when I was little. And, I certainly didn't think the body would be found so quickly."

"Why would he draw *Ja* in the dirt?"

"He didn't. He drew *Ju*. That's when I shot him again before he could finish 'Judith.' Then, I thought I could use what he had done. I just drew an arc at the top of the *u* and made it into an *a*. Clever, huh?"

I probably should have considered something like that. "What happened to your husband's car?" I had the feeling Judith was enjoying telling me all this.

"I brought it back, rented a storage unit in another name, and dropped off the bags and money. I parked the car on the street in that area behind the Stratosphere, what they call The Naked City. Since I left the keys in it, I was sure it would be taken to some chop shop and spread throughout Nevada almost immediately. I called his cell phone a few times and left frantic messages. I thought that looked good. It made me seem concerned, you know, sugar?"

"Where's that old beat up car you used?"

"Oh, that's a clunker I bought for cash. After I would use it, I would park it in the Sun Coast's lot and then get into my car. It's really quite easy. I just moved the old car around occasionally. I wore an old sweat-shirt and kept the hood pulled up around me. The windows were tinted dark on the car. I didn't think I was taking too much of a chance."

"Why did you shoot Bobby Lee?"

"I was a regular at Bobby Lee's salon. I followed you sometimes. Just to see what you were up to. I tracked you from Bruce's house to the salon. I didn't like your talking to Bobby Lee. Those salons are dins of gossip. Old biddies. They have nothing else to do but talk, talk, talk. And, you! You are a busybody, nosey bitch. You couldn't leave every-thing alone. Then, as luck would have it, the three of you came outside. I shot at you but missed. I was in a hurry. I thought maybe Bobby Lee told you something about me, but at Ernest's funeral, you didn't seem to act any differently towards me and your column didn't indicate that you knew what was going on. Then, I heard you make an appointment to meet at Pritchard's at 4 o'clock. That sounded like bad news to me."

I was puzzled. "How did you get from Ernest's funeral service to the *Gazette* yesterday where you nearly killed me?"

"It was a tight squeeze, but I made it. After the funeral service, I went to the gravesite immediately. Nobody hung around very long. It's not as if Ernie was a very popular, well loved guy. I hurried home, went to the Sun Coast to exchange cars, and raced over to find your car still at the *Gazette*. Then, I just waited until you came out." She stopped talking and waved the gun at me. "Now, stand up."

"Wait a minute," I said. "I still have some questions."

"Too bad. No more questions. Stand up." This wasn't the same Southern lady I'd had tea with last week. She stood up and motioned for me to get up, too. We walked around to where I was behind the couch.

Just then there was a loud knock on the door. At first, I thought it might be Rick, but, then, I heard, "Police! Open up!"

Judith was startled and looked around toward the door. I lost my balance when I stepped onto my left leg to move out of the way. I fell over the back of the couch and rolled onto the floor where I was wedged between the couch and the coffee table with my skirt over my head.

My mother was right. Always wear clean underwear. You never

know what might happen. My fall wasn't graceful, but it worked. Judith fired one shot at me, but missed as I went tumbling over the couch. She ran out toward what I assumed was the garage.

The police had now broken down the front door and were on their way in. I was happy to see so many of them.

I had the sense to yell, "She's in the garage."

Coop was behind the first wave of police. He came over to where I was still on the floor. When he saw I was okay, he just sat on the couch with his elbows on his knees and his head in his hands.

I waited for a while. Finally, I said, "Hi."

"Hi, yourself."

"Do you think you could help me up?" I asked. My left leg was dangling over the edge of the coffee table, and I was smoothing my skirt down around me.

"I don't know if I want to. I might just knock you down again," he said.

"Oh, come on. I've been through a lot. I need some sympathy."

"No! No! You need to have your head examined. What were you thinking?" he yelled.

"Well, right now I'm thinking it's not a good idea to wear a skirt when a crazed woman is gunning for you and your leg is in a cast."

"You are crazy. You could have been killed." Now he was yelling loudly. In fact, he had the attention of all the police in the room. I'm sure they thought this was no way to treat a victim, but nobody stepped forward to stop him. Law enforcement people stick together.

"It's no wonder," he said, "no man has married you."

"What do you mean? I've had offers. My mother says I'm just picky."

"You shouldn't be so picky. You're way too much trouble to be picky."

Judith came into the room, being roughly escorted by two officers. She didn't look like the calm, Southern lady I had known. Her hair was a mess, and her clothes were askew. I guess she had put up quite a fight. I hoped somebody had to slug her.

She just kept pointing at me and yelling," You bitch! You bitch!"

If I could have gotten up, I would have slapped her. Lucky for her I couldn't get up.

The police led her outside, and Coop finally decided to help me up.

When he did, he took me in his arms and held me quietly for some time. Finally, he said, "I don't know whether to kiss you or hit you. I'm so mad."

"Well, if I have any say so in the matter, I vote for kissing me." And he did just that.

By this time, the knowledge of what happened was beginning to sink in because I started to shake a little.

"How did all of you get here?" I asked. I fell back onto the couch since my legs were shaky.

"The cops and FBI had Judith's place under surveillance. Roger was suspicious of all the phone calls Garbarino made to the house. We knew that Ortega was at La Tigra Sunday night, but Garbarino called the house and stayed on the line for some time. We involved Metro and told them what we suspected from the phone records. By this time, we were sure that Jaime Rodriquez was not involved with Ortega's murder. We've had him in custody, and he knows more about the bribes given to the commissioners than he first led us to believe. He's talking. When some of my buddies on stakeout saw you come to the house, they called me. I think what they said was, 'That crazy girlfriend of yours is about to get herself killed.' Then, we immediately got enough officers and agents together to raid the house. Rick showed up and was about to come barging in, but we stopped him. Oh, and I got a phone call from your mother telling me that you were out somewhere, not at your office, and likely to get into trouble."

"Girlfriend?" I asked.

"What?" Coop looked perplexed. I hate it when a man can't follow a conversation.

"You said one of your buddies said, 'That crazy girlfriend of yours.'"

"Is that all you heard?"

"I have a knack for going right to the core of an issue. That's why I'm a good columnist."

Coop shook his head sadly and changed the subject. "How did you know about Mrs. Ortega?" he asked.

I explained why she had killed Garbarino and her own husband. I told Coop that she admitted to trying to kill Bobby Lee and me."

"I can't believe you came in here alone?" he said. I could tell he was getting angry just thinking about it.

"I hadn't planned to. I called Rick for backup, but Judith showed up at my car."

"You called Rick?"

Oops. "Well, I couldn't call you. You're with the FBI. It isn't as if you would accompany me to Judith's so I could get a story."

"Damn straight."

"Are you jealous I called Rick?"

"You must be kidding. The best thing that could happen to me would be for Rick to take you away."

"Oh, you don't mean that. I can tell."

I think he said, "Humph" very quietly.

I would have been smiling more, but by now my leg was hurting pretty badly. Coop said he was taking me home. He would arrange for me to give my statement to the police tomorrow.

"What about Mom's car?" I asked.

"Don't worry. I'll have someone drive it home later. I'm using up all my favors just getting people to drive your cars home."

I saw Rick talking to some officer as I left. He saw me, nodded, and smiled. His lips moved, and I could tell that he was asking if I was okay. I waved and mouthed that I was fine. His attention immediately went back to his story. That's a reporter!

୫୬

Coop took me up to my front door, but said he had to go. A lot was going on with the bribery investigation and with the Judith Ortega case. He gave me a gentle kiss and opened the front door.

"Are you in town for a while?" I asked.

"Yep, all tonight and tomorrow."

"Aren't you going to ask me out?" I didn't approve of pleading, but it seemed necessary in this case.

"I don't know. I'm still angry."

"Anything I can do to change that?" I toyed with the buttons on his shirt.

"Okay. Pick you up at 8 o'clock tomorrow night. I don't think you're going to feel like going out tonight. We'll go to dinner tomorrow and then see how your leg feels."

He's such a pushover, but I love that in a man.

I squared my shoulders and went inside to face Mom, Kitty, and Margaret. They were waiting for me, and they didn't look happy. I played on their sympathy, though, and it worked. They didn't yell too much.

Before I took my Percodan and a nap, I called Pritchard and Bobby Lee to fill them in, I called Rick with all I knew about Judith, and I called Mr. Garbarino satisfied that I fulfilled my promise. I, then, called Uncle Dutch and told him I was emailing another column. Finally, I sat down to write it.

Dalliance, Desire, and Dirty Deeds

Yours Truly was invited into the home of a Southern lady yesterday—at gunpoint. Judith Ortega, widow of Ernest Ortega, admitted to Yours Truly, as she held a Smith and Wesson in my face, that she killed George Garbarino and her husband. As discerning readers, I know you are asking, "Why?"

This crime spree started with a dalliance. Not the romantic under-the-moonlight kind of dalliance but the sleazy wham-bam-thank-you-ma'am kind. Judith Ortega had an affair with George Garbarino.

Then, the desire for money was another motive. Garbarino was not only a loveable guy, but he was paying her husband money for his vote also. That's a twofer.

Judith Ortega's dirty deeds didn't end here. She killed Garbarino because he was selling her hubby out to the FBI. It didn't help that his payoffs had stopped coming her way, too.

She killed hubby because he didn't like the idea that she killed Garbarino. Mostly, he didn't like that he might have to go to jail for her.

As if all that's not enough, she went after Yours Truly and Bobby Lee. She tried to kill Bobby Lee, owner of Shear Power, because hair salons are a hotbed of gossip. Apparently, she and

George Garbarino were the talk of the hairdryer. If you doubt the information you can find out at a hair salon, just ask my mother.

Judith Ortega tried to run me down yesterday with her car and before that she tried to shoot me. I know, Dear Readers, you are breathing a sigh of relief because she failed in both attempts

Now, Readers, the crimes are solved. Judith Ortega is in custody. Though murdered, George Garbarino's indiscretions live after him. His clubs in town have been closed. Indictments are coming for Ray Angelo, Bruce Pritchard, and Joanne Kirkoff.

What do I always tell you, Readers? All together now: "Crime does not pay."

After I finished my column and emailed it to Uncle Dutch, I took my Percodan and put my leg up on pillows. Debts were paid. I slept through the night without waking for dinner.

Chapter 39

Coop took me to Spago's at the Forum in Caesar's Palace. Because it's one of my favorite restaurants, it was my suggestion. We sat in the cafe along the railing where we could watch the shoppers go by and observe the ceiling change from night to day and back again. I had my usual, the meatloaf with garlic mashed potatoes. We split a bottle of Chianti. Coop hadn't eaten at Spago's before, so I introduced him to the meatloaf. He thought it was terrific.

He told me he had been working undercover in Los Angeles those days he was out of town. It would seem that Mr. Garbarino's problems weren't over. Georgy bribed city officials in L.A. also. There he bribed them for their votes to repeal the "no touch" laws at strip clubs. Poor Georgy. At least, he wasn't a murderer.

Coop also filled me in more on Rodriquez who had been found in his old neighborhood in L. A. He made a deal with the FBI to tell them about the bribery of the commissioners in Las Vegas and the bribes George paid out in L.A. Apparently, he knew more than he originally told the FBI.

When I heard this development, I excused myself to go to the little girls' room, hobbled over to where Coop couldn't see me, and phoned Rick to give him a heads-up on Rodriquez's information on the L.A. sting. Monroe answered Rick's phone, though.

"Yeah," he said. I recognized his voice right away.

"Where's Rick?" I asked.

"He's takin' a leak. What do you want?"

"I need to tell Rick something."

"Tell me," Monroe said.

"No, put Rick on the phone," I demanded.

"Are you having your period?" he asked. "cause you sound awfully cranky."

"Cranky, Monroe? I've nearly been run over, shot at, and held at gunpoint. I've reached the end of my line. Now, put Rick on, or the next time I see you I'll kick your ass!"

"All right. No reason to get touchy."

When Rick got on the phone, I told him about Rodriquez getting picked up in L.A. and about the new developments.

After I returned to the table and sat down, Coop said, "So, what did Rick think about the new information?"

Oops! Busted!

Coop asked if I had learned my lesson. "Of course, I've learned my lesson. I've learned that my life has been predictable for so long, but things change. Old friends die. Daughters leave home."

"That wasn't the lesson I meant. I meant have you learned to leave dangerous cases alone?"

"I'll never learn how to do that. I have a job to do. Even though other things in my life have changed, I still have my column."

"And don't forget about me. I'm a big change in your life. You know what they say 'one door opens and another closes.'"

"That's 'one door closes and another opens.'"

"Same thing. The point is I'm here now. I'm an open door. All you have to do is walk in."

"Yes, you are here." I took Coop's hand. I wanted him to be part of this new life I was going to live.

As Coop and I were leaving the restaurant and walking through Caesar's casino, he stopped and said, "Wait right here; I've got an idea. I'll be gone for a minute."

He then walked away, leaving me sitting on a nearby chair with my leg propped up. I was enjoying thinking about how he was going to be an important part of my new life, my life without Kitty as the center of it.

When he returned, he was smiling and waving a plastic room entry card.

"I'm not waiting any longer," he said. "I booked us a room here."

"But I don't have a nightie or anything."

"I didn't plan on having you wear one anyway."

Oh, I liked that.

We walked quickly through the casino, into the elevator, and up to the room. Coop had to help me along.

When we got into the room, he began to kiss me. Passionately.

I said, "Stop."

"What?" He seemed surprised, even shocked.

I started to pat him down. I don't think he minded that so much, especially since I paused a long time at his crotch.

He said, "Is that what you're looking for?"

"No, but it's nice."

"Nice. I'm offended. It's better than nice."

"Okay, really great and big and hard." I admit, I was momentarily distracted. "But it's not what I'm looking for right now. I'll get back to it later."

"Promise?"

"I promise." With that, I hurried on with my pat down search. Finally, I pulled his cell phone out of the inside pocket of his sports coat. I turned my back to him and told him to close his eyes. He did, and I walked away from the door and into the room.

When I returned, he said, "You didn't destroy FBI property did you. Cause that's a federal offense and I'd have to arrest you."

"Hell, no. I'm not crazy," I said, handing him his phone. "I just hid the battery."

"Where is it?"

"I'm not telling, and you won't be able to find it."

"You'll have to submit you to an FBI interrogation. And I have to tell you, its one of my strengths. I'm a trained professional in interrogation techniques."

"Start the interrogation," I said, "cause I'm not telling." Things were looking up. I had never been interrogated by a trained FBI agent. I was warm all over just thinking about it.

He kissed my neck and, putting his hands on me gently, began to open my blouse slowly. "Will you tell me now?" He was smiling his best interrogator's smile.

"No."

He took my blouse off, gradually lowering it over my arms. He moved down from my neck and began kissing the top of my breasts. "Now?"

"No," I said softly.

He touched my breast and began caressing it. Using both hands to unclasp my bra, he asked, "How about now?" He slipped the bra straps off my shoulders.

I was having a little trouble breathing, but I gasped, "No. I'm really tough. You're going to have to work a lot harder."

"I've got all night." He removed my bra and unbutton his shirt. Reaching his hands under my skirt, he pulled my panties down. Then, he lifted my skirt up to my waist while he continued to interrogate me. "And I took the day off tomorrow."

"Hum, nice." I knew I was weakening. I wondered who was going to win the office bet.

-30-